# Little Cottage by the Cornish Sea

# The Little Cottage by the Cornish Sea

## NANCY BARONE

HEAD of ZEUS

*An Aria Book*

First published in the UK in 2025 by Head of Zeus,
part of Bloomsbury Publishing Plc

9 7 5 3 1 2 4 6 8

A catalogue record for this book is available from the British Library.

ISBN (PB): 9781035911547
ISBN (E): 9781035911554

Cover design: Gemma Gorton
Typeset by Siliconchips Services Ltd UK

Printed and bound in Great Britain by
CPI Group (UK) Ltd, Croydon CR0 4YY

Bloomsbury Publishing Plc
50 Bedford Square, London, WC1B 3DP, UK
Bloomsbury Publishing Ireland Limited,
29 Earlsfort Terrace, Dublin 2, D02 AY28, Ireland

HEAD OF ZEUS LTD
5–8 Hardwick Street
London EC1R 4RG

To find out more about our authors and books
visit www.headofzeus.com
For product safety related questions contact productsafety@bloomsbury.com

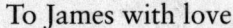

To James with love

# 1

## London, April 1st, Morning

I woke up in a bright pool of sunlight. I had fallen asleep in an armchair in my boyfriend Will's luxurious Victorian home in Belgravia, waiting for him to come back from his work dinner so I could put an end to our relationship.

Over the five years we'd been together, Will had so slowly become domineering and controlling that only recently had I realised that I had Boiling Frog Syndrome, whereby if you put a frog in a pot of boiling water, it'll jump right out. But if you put it in a room-temperature pot and gradually heat the water until it boils, it'll stay, adapting to the slowly rising temperature, until it dies.

That was a perfect portrait of our relationship. In the beginning, he'd been so charming and caring and attentive. But lately, it had become so bad that he would ridicule my thoughts and words and even put me down in public. So this frog was now ready to jump.

Only he'd beat me to it, because it was 7 a.m. and *no* work dinner lasted that long. He had obviously spent the night elsewhere, just as I'd suspected for weeks now as he'd kept finding excuses to not spend any time outside the office together. And even when he asked me to bring him this or that brief at work, he was distant to say the least. I had suspected something was afoot, and now I knew exactly why.

An expensive female perfume still hung heavily in the air, and dresses were draped around every stick of furniture as if *she* had lived here forever and only popped out for a pint of milk. Because it was obvious she had moved in and made herself at home, whereas I hadn't been invited over for months.

Realising my presence here was completely unnecessary, with a mixed sense of relief and sorrow, I lifted my handbag from the Berber rug as my mobile pinged with a new message. It was Tamsin, my best friend and co-worker at the law firm Wise & Templemann where Will was a junior partner and where our relationship had begun.

Kate, where the hell r u? Confidential files on some of our biggest clients who were being blackmailed are missing and Will has accused you! The police have found them in your flat. Please go in and tell them you didn't do it and that he put them there, the scumbag!

I stared at the screen in disbelief. Will was blackmailing some of our best clients and blaming me? And now the police were at my flat looking for me...

There was no way that my word would prevail over the word of junior partner Will Compton. He was a real shark and had made the firm loads of money. He was practically a deity at Wise & Templemann. The police would never believe me, not in a million years.

And even if they did, Will would surely use his influence to blacklist me from every law firm in London. I was in between a rock and a hard place and my only option was to immediately disappear off the face of the earth, where no one could find me. And as quickly as possible.

I couldn't go back to my own flat to get any clothes as the police were waiting for me, so I ducked into the massive dressing room, ransacked the chest of drawers for something to wear over the next few days, hardly able to see through my panic as I threw some of *her* jeans, trousers and jumpers onto the made bed. She had more than enough to spare. Will had never allowed me to leave so much as a toothbrush. How blind had I been to the obvious?

I found a make-up bag and some silk pyjamas, along with a pair of boots. A rainbow of fancy cocktail dresses swayed as I brushed past them: they must have cost thousands. The top drawer contained a passport. There she was, Sophie Graham. Not in the flesh, but real all the same. If you squinted, and removed the tons of make-up on her face and stripped her of every extravaganza that money could buy, her honey-coloured hair was very similar to mine even in length, and her eyes were green like mine. Even our build was similarly petite. If she needed to, she could pass as me. Not that anyone would want to be me when they could be Sophie Graham. But maybe, just maybe, I could pass off as her. Just until I got far away enough to clear my name.

I crawled under the bed where I knew Will kept his empty travel luggage and reached for one of his backpacks. I turned it upside down to get rid of any of his residual belongings and a waterfall of documents poured out onto the rug, all marked with a big, red *CONFIDENTIAL* stamp.

I rifled through them, recognising the names of some of our most esteemed clients. There was top-secret information about a couple of MPs, famous business magnates and even a couple of mayors. This was where he kept the bulk of the stolen stash. This was proof of his crime, a crime he was trying to pin on me. If only there was another witness who could verify my discovery. But I was alone and apparently, only Tamsin believed in my innocence.

The sound of a car door shutting in the quiet street made me jump. The police? Did they know I was here? I ran to the staircase and peered over the banister as the front door opened. A woman took off her coat and donned an apron. Only the cleaning lady, thank God! I hefted the backpack onto my back and whirled around, searching for an escape, but there was none. The woman downstairs was now humming to herself, still moving around in the entrance hall, the only obstacle between me and the front door. There was only one other exit. I quietly eased open the door to the balcony and looked at the garden two floors down. Jesus Christ almighty.

The humming became louder as she made a start up the stairs, moving closer and closer to my hiding place. A few feet away from the balcony was a huge magnolia tree just about to bloom. It was certainly sturdy enough, but was I? I had no choice. Cursing myself and all the bad decisions I'd made, I pinpointed the strongest-looking branch within my reach and lunged for it, feeling the greedy pull of the void beneath me.

There was no time to think about getting caught. There was no time to think about anything but my own escape. I climbed down as fast as I could, wincing as the surrounding branches scratched my face and hands. Powered by adrenaline, I sprinted down the back garden, vaulting clear over the low brick wall and into the street. After all, I was good at that. Running.

I grabbed the keys to my car from my pocket and whizzed around the corner where it was parked and I did the only thing I could think to do. I ran away.

# 2

I ran and I cried. Why would he do that to me? Wasn't it enough, the way I had let him treat me all these years? If he'd wanted to end it, why not just tell me, like I had thought to, rather than accuse me of a crime and potentially ruin my life forever?

I cried so hard, I could barely see the road before me as I fled my life, my job and my home with all its memories. Never again would I walk through my front door and sit in my living room, surrounded by all my books, family photographs and records. Never again would I sleep in my own bed, drink from my favourite mug, soak in my own tub. Never again would I do anything that was me. And never again would I see my best friend Tamsin and her family. The simple life of simple Kate Miller, now accused of corporate blackmail, was no longer. I supposed I'd better add burglary and identity theft to my list of crimes, too, what with Sophie Graham's clothes and ID staring at me from the passenger seat.

My heart ached for everything that I'd lost in one

moment. I had severed all ties to anything that was me, the real me. In the space of a few minutes, my life had been thrown upside down.

But how do you leave yourself behind, just like that? Even if all my memories would follow me, I'd have to try and find space for new ones. And my persona? Would I have to smother it, like those people in witness-protection programmes? Yes, the less I gave away about myself to anyone, the longer I'd stay safe. Survival and freedom were the only things that mattered now.

My only regret was leaving Tamsin and her family. Her husband Mike was going through chemo, and now I'd no longer be there to hold her hand or babysit little Jake while Tamsin spent hours on end by Mike's side. It broke my heart to have to do this, but better to not think about it right now and keep busy with the practicalities that would save me from going to prison.

My first stop was at an ATM machine where I took as much cash as I could from my accounts, which was not a lot. It would have to last me as long as possible. There was of course a queue, and every minute I fought not to scream out, *Please hurry!* to the people in front of me. I lifted my collar against the wind and slipped on a pair of oversized shades, trying to look as calm and indifferent as possible, even bored, while on the inside I was screaming.

After that, I ducked into a Co-op and bought a few bottles of water, a sandwich and a jumbo packet of Hobnobs. There was no telling how long I was going to be on the road. No telling where I would end up. I kept envisaging someone tapping me on the shoulder and sussing me out. *Keep your shades on and your head low.* Anything to look inconspicuous, and hide the panic that threatened to spill over at any moment.

And that was when I received a message from Mr Templemann, the senior associate of the law firm:

Kate, bring back the documents and we won't prosecute. You have my word.

As if. Mr Templemann had been like a grandfather to me, but there was no way I could trust him now. Not until I could figure out how to prove my innocence. Business was business, and the fifty-year reputation of his firm came before any personal feelings he held toward me.

My next stop was to buy a new phone. It used a significant chunk of my already meagre cash supply, but I needed a number that Will didn't know. I took screenshots of some of our text conversations and transferred them over, just in case. Then I took my old phone apart and ditched the pieces into different rubbish bins along my way. The bridge to the past was gone.

My first call on my new phone was to Tamsin but I withheld my new number from her. She had enough problems without having to deal with mine. I gulped down a lump of tears. When her answering machine kicked in, I almost breathed a sigh of relief because the last thing I wanted to do was face her knowing that I wouldn't be able to see her for a while. I took a deep breath and gathered all my nonchalance.

'Tams, I didn't do it! But no one will believe me so I'm going away for a bit. I'll call you when I can.' Realising it sounded a bit too dramatic, I fake chuckled. 'It's too late to talk me out of it, you have no idea where I am.' Which was true. *I* didn't even know where I was going. And before I burst into tears, I swallowed and cried, 'Love you!'

The dread of what lay ahead, total uncertainty, nearly choked me.

How had I let this happen? How had I let Will squash my dreams and very willpower like this, turning me someone so fearful? So easy to get rid of? My father would be heartbroken if he'd seen what I'd become. He'd be absolutely outraged. And he'd be right.

An uncertain life full of questions and doubts stretched out before me. Just where did I think I was going? How was I going to survive on a limited wad of cash? And without a job? In any case, I had to get away from Will's sphere of influence. He'd already convinced everyone I had stolen those documents. If Mr Templemann believed him, I had to take my hat off to Will's superb powers of persuasion.

So now things were going to change. I had suddenly changed. *Sophie Graham's strong perfume must be going to my head*, I cackled to myself, just to give myself a boost of courage. I was fully aware that there was absolutely nothing to laugh about.

I had to find a way to get my sanity back. In a safe place, where I could start a new life. Reboot, and all that, with decent people around.

When I hit the M25 and was practically ensconced in the facelessness of humanity, I began to panic again. Now what? Where could I go? It wasn't like I'd been planning The Great Escape and had figured everything out. Any direction was just as good as the other.

*Think, think fast!* Or maybe it was best not to think and just follow my instincts.

I took the first exit and found myself crying with relief as I hit the M4 leaving London. If I could escape Will, I still had a shot at a semblance of a life. Secretive, fugitive, but at least not behind bars. It was the price I'd have to pay.

Without even thinking twice about it, I punched in my destination. I now knew exactly where I was going. Or returning to. Cornwall. More specifically, the place of my childhood holidays which Will had never even bothered to ask about. The barely known seaside hamlet of Starry Cove.

# 3

'I'm sorry there's not much furniture left in the cottage, Miss, er, pardon me, I've forgotten your name…?'

I looked at the elderly woman in her gingham dress and then around at the four damp-stained walls, the stiff-with-dirt curtains and the sagging, green settee. A perhaps once-loved but now forgotten, chipped, gate-leg table crouched against the far end of the wall where a dusty hearth dominated the room that hadn't been cleaned, much less used, for what seemed to be a lifetime.

It was the best place I could find. At such short notice, I was lucky to find anything at all. With nary a flower in sight, Tulip Cottage was far from any image its name may have conjured. It was abandoned and derelict, very much like myself, but I almost cried out for joy. I had made it to Starry Cove. I was safe.

Despite its condition, the cottage was perfect because it backed onto the woods, an essential escape route should Will, or the police, ever find me.

'My name is Sophie,' I replied, realising she was waiting

for an answer. 'Sophie Graham.' It still sounded so alien, and yet, for a while, it would have to do. If I could take her stuff, I could take her name too.

'Sophie Graham,' she said, as if trying the name out for herself to see if it convinced her. If it did, I was home free. Because my future now depended on her gullibility. I hated lying, but trying to gather the courage to leave it all behind me, I'd finally run out of options.

'I'm so sorry to interfere or be nosey, but are you okay, dear?' she whispered, nodding to the scratches on my face left by the magnolia tree. 'Do you need... help?'

I opened my mouth to speak, to make up yet another excuse, but I'd used them all up. I shrugged, almost apologetically, but then straightened. 'I fell into some bushes,' I offered. It wasn't far from the truth.

The woman studied me at length, shrewdly, until the silence became almost unbearable. I had eluded the police and was terrified it wouldn't last long. *No. Chin up.* I'd got this far, hadn't I? Now was the beginning of something good. It had to be, because, from where I was standing, the only way left was up. I couldn't envisage sinking any lower than this. I couldn't imagine a better time to do what I'd just done.

'I understand, love. My, that's a beautiful ring on your finger.'

My thumb automatically went to the back of Will's promise ring. A ring I'd have to get rid of ASAP. 'Thank you.'

'Will your husband be joining you here in Starry Cove, then?'

A shiver shot up my aching spine. 'No, no husband. It's just me.' All I needed was to be left *alone*.

'I didn't think that anyone would answer my advertisement,' she said apologetically as she looked around the room. 'My grandson wants me to sell up but I can't bring myself to do it. I thought that maybe if I had a tenant who could fix up Tulip Cottage, become a kind of caretaker, he would change his mind.'

I wondered what made her grandson feel so entitled to making decisions like that for her. It seemed that wherever I went, there was no running away from men making decisions for women.

'Tell you what,' she finally said. 'If you don't mind waiting a couple weeks, I can get the basics straightened out. New carpeting, a lick of paint—'

A couple of weeks? And go where in the meantime? I couldn't risk going to a hotel. Only a private home would suit me. I cleared my throat. 'No need, I'll take it as it is.'

She nodded. 'I understand, pet.' The kindness had spread to her eyes as she leaned forward, perhaps to pat my hand. But I was quicker, moving out of the reach of her sympathy. I didn't need it. I couldn't afford to depend on it. From now on, I was completely on my own and needed to toughen up. Maybe one day, I'd make some friends. But for now, I could only count on myself.

'I have the first and last months' rent here,' I said as I pulled some pound notes out of my pocket in the hope I'd convince her if she was still on the fence.

She looked at my outstretched hand and chuckled. 'Oh, my grandson deals with that stuff. I'll have him come round with the contract tomorrow morning and you can talk to him; how does that sound?'

'Tomorrow morning sounds good,' I replied, disappointed

that I couldn't tick my first hurdle off the list completely and get the tricky legalities over with, but at the same time relieved to be able to just close the door on the world and finally sleep, knowing I was safe.

'Right then, I'd best be off,' she said and gripped the edge of the table to haul her tiny frame up. 'Goodnight, then.'

'Thank you, goodnight,' I replied as she took forever to get to the door, poor dear. My desperation to be alone now was like waiting for a starting gun to go off.

And then she turned and planted her eyes on me once more. 'Just one thing, Miss Graham. This is a tiny village in the middle of nowhere where nothing ever happens. Newcomers are always the centre of interest.'

Ah. Here it was: the runaway/dubious/shifty/loose woman/single girl advice.

'Mrs Nankivell, I can assure you that I am going to stay out of the village spotlight. I conduct a very simple lifestyle and intend to keep very much to myself.' Which reminded me. I'd have to cut my hair and change the way I looked somehow.

'I didn't mean it that way, pet,' she replied swiftly. 'All I meant was that if you're hiding, he'll be unlikely to find you here in Starry Cove. We look out for each other.'

A cold shiver swept up my legs and nestled into the pit of my stomach. If an elderly lady could see through me, surely everyone else in the village would, too. If Will and the police turned up, they could single me out in no time.

The better part of a day had passed since I'd fled. He would have certainly called my mobile. *Good luck with that.*

'Okay, then,' she said as I was looking for an appropriate

answer, her papery hand clutching the chain of her glasses. 'I'll be off. You have my number if you need anything.'

'Thank you, Mrs Nankivell. I'll be okay.'

'Now you take care of yourself. And welcome to Starry Cove.'

'Thank you,' I said as I followed her to the door and waited until she passed the cottage across the way. For good measure, I checked the row of terraced houses as she gingerly tottered down the hill. The one next door to mine seemed empty, and so did a couple of other ones. Excellent. Fewer neighbours, fewer questions.

And now there was no turning back. To my boss and the police, I was a criminal. But I had done nothing wrong. Yes, I had stolen Sophie Graham's ID and clothes. But only because I hadn't had the time to run home and get my own before disappearing.

Suddenly, all the adrenaline drained from my body and the weight of the day came crashing down on me. But at least now I had a roof over my head. I let out my breath slowly, trying not to fall apart. This was a fresh start. A new life. There was just one thing I had to do.

# 4

Three minutes is a long time when you're waiting for a home pregnancy test.

Will had no idea of my suspicions, and it was just as well.

'When we become a family,' he'd promised me once, 'everything will be different. I'll be less stressed. We'll start to enjoy ourselves more. I'll spend more time with you. And together, we can start our own dynasty. The Compton dynasty!'

That had been years ago. Four, to be exact. In the following years, everything had changed. Will was no longer nice or even indifferent. He had become impossible to be with. He was always angry; sometimes more than angry. So instead of challenging him, I stayed out of his way. But then he'd charge into my office and start berating me for something I'd done or hadn't done, it didn't matter to him. He took any chance he had to put me down. And now the ultimate betrayal. How could he do this to me, accuse me of theft and blackmail? Had he *ever* truly cared about me?

The three minutes were up.

I took a deep, deep breath and closed my eyes tight. I could handle this. I could handle whatever came my way. When I'd gone to his house to break up with him, I knew there was a chance I could be pregnant. But even for a child's sake, I couldn't let Will stay in my life. And now I had no choice but to keep my big-girl trousers on, just like I had done all my life.

With my heart hammering against my aching ribs, I forced myself to open my eyes and stared at the stick. *Pregnant.* I knew it. I was going to have a baby. Bloody Will's baby.

So finally, at the end of the worst day of my entire life, I let go and cried again. I cried in anguish for this baby who was one day going to ask me where Daddy was. What could I possibly say? I cried for all the years I'd stayed in the hope that things would get better. I cried because I'd been so weak, as if paralysed by the fear of loneliness and the dread of change. I cried because it had been the first time in my life that I'd ever been afraid of anything. I was afraid of letting my baby down, of not being brave and smart enough to give it the best I could. But I'd give it my all.

With unsteady arms, I braced myself against the sink and looked at my reflection. My normally bright-green eyes were now spent, and my once glossy hair looked matted and dull. But what completed the dismal ensemble were the scratches on my face. I was a mess and Mrs Nankivell had been right to doubt me.

*Too late to cry over spilled milk. Just bloody get on with it now.* There was only one thing I could do. Soldier on. Make the best of what I had and try to create a new life for myself here in Cornwall.

Shrugging off my worst thoughts, I nipped back to the

kitchen to take stock of the place. Old but solid, with a butcher's block in the centre, all it needed was a good cleaning and a couple of personal touches. Who cared if it was old?

Obviously, no one had lived here in ages, and judging by the contents of the drawers, they had left in a hurry too. There was a set of brass cutlery, a ceramic cooking pot, an old pewter jug, an old baster – though the plastic bubble on the end had seen better days – alongside a rusty runner bean stringer, a metal colander, an old set of scales missing the weights, and a bent whisk. A tea strainer completed the forlorn ensemble. Yes, I would definitely have to nip out to get some basics tomorrow.

Had I been clever, I'd have seen all this coming. I'd have secretly packed an emergency bag or two with some survival essentials while I found my feet elsewhere. But I had never thought that it would get this bad. I had been an absolute idiot to believe that things would one day get better. That all I had to do was have faith.

But now, in this old, terraced cottage, I could start from scratch. It would be just me and these thick walls, the low, beamed ceilings and the huge hearth that took up half of the tiny sitting room. It had very good bones and loads of character, with a tiny window seat, sash windows and flagstone floors. A decorator's dream. Now if I only had a decorator's budget to fix it up. I couldn't let a baby come into the world and live here in this state. Hopefully, by the time it was born, I would have made it much more welcoming and homely.

In the kitchen, just a few feet away from the tiny sitting room, I leaned over the ceramic sink and pushed out the window to breathe in the chilly night air. I couldn't see a single thing of the garden in the dark, but I remembered from the photos on the website that it was a good-sized one. Even if it needed some work, I could make it perfect. I envisaged borders in full bloom and hanging my washing in the sun while singing to the baby, who sat in the shade, perfectly content to gurgle and laugh at her mummy's silly antics.

Interrupting my musings, I closed the kitchen window and climbed up the narrow staircase to where, thank you, God, a tiny bathroom was squeezed in between two bedrooms. And it even had a tub! Probably not big enough for an adult, but I was tiny myself. For now.

The smaller bedroom was completely bare, as if no one had ever occupied it except for the dust mites. The larger bedroom, as musty and drab as the rest of the house, featured a massive brass bed that had turned black with time and neglect. There were no personal belongings anywhere except for an old, battered sea chest in the corner. And that was it.

Not that I was expecting much, but this place had absolutely nothing.

I went back downstairs, grabbed a pen and notebook from my bag and leaned against the butcher's block to make a list that made me consider how much my freedom and a new life were going to end up costing me. I had very little savings, but if I was careful and spend-thrift, I could at least get the bare necessities: cups, plates, glasses, bleach (lots of it), some washing up liquid and some cleanser of sorts. A couple of tea towels, milk, tea and oh, more Hobnobs. Perhaps I should start being sensible and get some fresh fruit and vegetables as well. I also needed to get bath towels and sheets. The rest would come slowly, slowly, after I found myself a job somewhere.

I looked through the window at the magnolia tree under which I'd parked the car. It was very similar to the one I'd crawled down only hours ago. I hoped that it was a good omen for me and my freedom.

The only luxury I had with me was my coat: a memory from my mum. At the thought of her beautiful smile and sing-song voice, my throat constricted. And I realised that, for different reasons, she had run away too.

I went and grabbed Will's backpack from the car; it contained my new life, along with another bottle of water and the packet of Hobnobs that would have to be both dinner and breakfast.

Tomorrow, I'd go out and get a few essentials. New life, new start, one little thing at a time. But I'd have to make do with the contents of Sophie's make-up bag. I peered inside. There were some travel-sized luxury shampoo bottles, a new toothbrush, thank God, and some toothpaste too. And a new, still-wrapped bar of soap. It was pathetic how happy it made me. The thought of having a bar of soap that wouldn't be touching Will's skin made me want to cackle with bliss.

It annoyed me tremendously when he came to my home and left the dirty suds to dry on the bar instead of rinsing it off. I knew it sounded anal, but what was the point of leaving dirt on the soap for the next person? It was because, just like everything else he did, he didn't *care*. There was no consideration whatsoever for anyone else but himself.

I dug the pyjamas out of the bag I'd thrown together,

praying that the water in this cottage worked, even if it was cold. A decent wash would help to rid me of the adrenaline still pumping through my system, keeping me in a constant state of stress.

I turned the taps, and breathed a sigh of relief as I heard the pipes gurgle to life in the walls. Only… no water was coming out. Or, there was, but only the faintest of a trickle, and it *was* cold. I couldn't help but be disappointed. I fiddled around with the taps to eke out a decent flow but to no avail. And now, tired and fed up, I couldn't even turn the tap off. The trickle had become constant. I couldn't go to bed as manky as I felt, even if the old bed was worse off than me. I remembered seeing a bucket under the kitchen sink so I ran downstairs and fetched it, careful not to slip.

I ran back upstairs and placed the bucket under the tap, and when it was enough, I washed my face and hands and brushed my teeth. I'd have to ask Mrs Nankivell to call someone sooner rather than later.

Exhausted and finally coming off the adrenaline high, I plunked myself onto the brass bed which sank and slightly bounced, but not quite back into place. It was like when a dog burrows a dip to keep cool. Without any bed linen but the damp, green coverlet, I opened the airing cupboard and found an old, wool blanket. I had nothing else. So, still shivering from the shock of today's events and the cold, I wrapped up like a sausage roll to ward off the dampness hanging in the air. Tomorrow, I would take care of everything, but now, I was too exhausted by all the miles, all the hills and dales seen through a haze of terror.

But that was all behind me now, hopefully. Yes, granted, there was always a chance Will would find me, but a frisson of excitement passed through me. The baby and I would wake up here every morning to a new, wonderful Cornish life, and hopefully, she would know nothing about my past. I would never let Will come near me – or my baby – again.

I lay on my side in Sophie's flimsy silk pyjamas covered by one of her thickest jumpers, another one rolled up under my head as a pillow. Tomorrow, I would face everything. All I needed to know was that, for tonight, I was safe.

Only I couldn't sleep. Or maybe I did for a few minutes, but I woke up feeling even more exhausted as I tossed and turned like the fugitive that I now was. It would have been unfair to blame the bare, lumpy mattress. All I could think of was my future. In the quiet of this very dark night, I tried to start making a plan and then changed it as soon as it went awry.

From here, unless Will or the police found me, there was no going back. Kate Miller was gone, her place taken by Sophie Graham, a complete stranger who would have to build a new life from scratch. I had been stripped of anything I owed, loved and missed. There was nothing left of me but my essential core, and the baby now inside me.

# 5

I must have fallen asleep eventually, as a loud repetition of croaks woke me and I sat bolt upright, surprised by the blinding light coming through the threadbare curtains. Morning already? And *what* was that awful *ribbit* sound? Surely there wasn't a frog in the room?

When I eventually managed to unravel myself from the bedding and reach the creaky staircase, the sound became more metallic, like two rusty pipes scraping against each other. And then I got it: it was the bloody doorbell!

For a brief, panicked moment, the harrowing suspicion. *Did* Will know where I was? Yes, he was controlling and overbearing, but to have someone follow me? And yet, the more I thought about it, the more sense it made.

'Miss Graham?' came a voice from beyond the front door. 'Miss Graham? It's Robert Armitage.'

*Who?* I slinked closer to the door, brandishing an old brass reading lamp shaped like a rooster. It wouldn't kill anyone but it would certainly make them think twice before coming close to me.

'Mrs Nankivell's grandson? She asked me to pop by this morning?'

*Oh!* I raked back my hair that was practically standing on end from the fright and cautiously opened the door a cinch. Standing back from the door was a tall man hefting a large box. He was wearing a wool coat and a checked flat cap, the kind that country gentlemen wear. The look on his face was undecipherable.

'Hello,' he said. 'I'm so sorry to have woken you.'

'Oh, no worries,' I answered politely. *You simply scared ten years of life out of me is all.* 'I was expecting you. Please come in.'

A wry grin split his face as if to say, *I wonder what you'd look like if you* hadn't *been expecting me.* I looked down at myself only to see that my – er, Sophie's – pyjamas had rolled their way up to my chest and that they had been buttoned up wrong. Good first impression, no doubt.

He followed me to the old gate-leg table where he put down the box. 'I'm terribly sorry, Miss Graham, but there's been a mistake…'

I frowned. 'A mistake?'

'Yes. You see, my grandmother… I don't even know how she got onto the internet in the first place, but she doesn't understand that the house is in a state and not fit for renting, so I'm going to have to ask you to find somewhere else, at least until the due renos are completed. I'm sorry…'

*No, no, no!*

'But it's fine, honestly,' I assured him past the huge ball forming in my throat. I had already seen myself living there. My first dream in this house was of dancing in a ray of sunlight streaming through the kitchen French doors with my baby. I couldn't leave now! 'I already assured Mrs Nankivell that I didn't mind this place being a fixer-upper.'

'Well, I'm afraid that it's really not fine at all, Miss Graham. The piping is temperamental. It takes forever to get hot water. The electrics are prehistoric and there must be several holes in the roof. And the rain...'

'I'll use *buckets*,' I urged him. 'All that really doesn't matter to me, honestly Mr, er, Armitage...'

'Robert.'

'Sophie,' I whispered, really trying hard not to blub for the third time in twenty-four hours. He couldn't do this! He couldn't take away my own safe place from me! 'I don't mind a bit of work,' I said. 'I'm handy.'

'You are?' he said.

'Don't look so surprised. I painted my parents' home all the time and fixed things here and there.'

He grinned. I swore that if he was going to laugh at me, I'd clock him. 'That's good. Fixed things like what?'

I shrugged. 'Everything that needed fixing. Hinges, windows, doors, skirting boards.'

'But not plumbing or electrics, am I right?'

'Well, actually, when I worked for my father's building company back in London—' I started before clamping my mouth shut. The less this man knew about my past, the better. 'I can manage all right until you can send someone round to fix those.'

'I'm sorry, the place is a liability and needs an entire overhaul,' he said.

*No...*

'But,' he said, jerking his head toward the box. 'My grandmother has sent you some bits as a peace offering.'

Unless there was a fold-up home in there, nothing would cut it now. I'd spent all night coming up with ideas to make this house a home for my baby and me, and he wanted to kick us out of our new little paradise just like that?

'Here,' he said, dragging two rickety chairs to the gate-leg table where he pulled some bags out of the box. 'There's some nice coffee and some melt-in-your-mouth croissants.'

I ignored the soft rumble in my stomach and folded my arms in front of my chest. 'You're kicking me out and you think you can make it up to me by giving me breakfast?'

'I can help you find somewhere else in the village. It'll only be temporary.'

'Mr Armitage,' I huffed, bringing us back from a first-name basis to a more formal, serious situation. 'I drove all day yesterday to come right here, to this very cottage, after having spoken to your grandmother. Now, I understand that it needs a little TLC, but that's okay. I'm not a demanding person.'

He chuckled as he handed me a croissant. 'I'm sure you aren't, Miss Graham.'

'Nor am I asking for anything but to stay. I won't be any trouble to anyone, I promise.'

He took a bite of his own croissant, eyeing me pensively as his grandmother had done the night before. He said nothing about my scratches, thankfully.

'I'll tell you what,' he finally said. Her same expression. 'You eat up and get dressed, and then we'll have a solid look around the house. How does that sound?'

'Promising, for a start,' I admitted.

Robert Armitage nodded. 'Good. I'll go get some tools from my car.'

Ah. So there was room for some wiggle there. I'd badger the bloke all the way until my due date. Chain myself to the log burner in the hearth if I had to. Or maybe not, as that would certainly stir the curiosity of the local rag and goodbye anonymity. I needed to stay here. I *wanted* to stay here. And not just because, having seen Starry Cove from the top of the hill while driving in, I had fallen in love with its fairy lights and nativity scene looks all over again; not just because I could envision turning this rundown cottage into a real home. But also because it was the farthest I could get from where I had been, and I didn't mean geographically. Cornwall was not just a separate county for me, but a different state of mind. A state of sheer, unadulterated, happy, childhood memories.

'So?' I asked the soles of Mr Armitage's boots as he stood at the top of a ladder round the back of the cottage.

'Actually, it's not as bad as I thought. Just a few slates need to be replaced, but otherwise, it's looking pretty solid up here.'

*Thank you, God!*

His long legs came into view as he hopped down the ladder and stopped to study me again. He had a rather nice face under that flat cap. Kind, piercing blue eyes.

And then I realised that he wasn't studying me, but my scratches. X-raying me, practically.

'I'll tell you what,' he said again.

'Is that all you ever say?'

'I beg your pardon?'

'*I'll tell you what…*'

'Oh.' He shrugged. 'I like to meet people halfway, is all.'

'Right. So what's the deal?' I prompted. 'Are you going to let me stay or not?'

He took a long, deep breath. 'I'll have someone come round and look at the plumbing and the electrics. If it's easily fixable, I'll let you stay.'

'Thank you!' I almost cried. Never mind that – I almost hugged the bloke.

'On two conditions.'

There you go. I knew there was something. More money, of course. I'd have to do some figures when he left. 'Which are?'

'One, that you stay at the local inn while the work is being done.'

I mentally ran the sums. I couldn't really afford to do that.

'My treat,' he added.

'Absolutely not!' I countered. 'Thank you, but no.'

'I have to. It's only right. There is a contract.'

'But you haven't signed it yet,' I pointed out.

He dipped his head. 'I haven't, but my grandmother gave you the go-ahead over the phone, which in my mind is binding. Where is one supposed to go at such short notice?'

*Indeed*. 'And the other condition?'

'That you swing by my office and let me check you out.'

'I beg your pardon?'

'Easy. I meant for a check-up.'

'You're a doctor?'

'You've got some nasty scratches.'

'I fell into a rosebush.' Again, it wasn't technically a lie.

'When was the last time you visited a doctor?'

'Uhm,' I wavered, looking for the right lie. I hadn't been to a doctor in years.

'I'm not asking for the world, am I? Just come in for a check-up and… you can stay in the house. Okay?'

I eyed him. I knew he wasn't going to make me a better offer; I could see it in his eyes. And I really didn't want to go anywhere else now. Plus I needed to be healthy for Baby.

'Have we got a deal?' He stuck out his big hand and I shook it. It was very warm. Enveloping.

'Okay,' I agreed. 'Thank you.' Go figure how, but despite all that had happened to me and my promise to myself to be wary of everyone from now on, I somehow trusted him.

'Your hands are frozen,' he said, opening the front door for me. 'Let's go in and get the fire started. And maybe you can get the kettle on? I'm a coffee addict, just so you know.'

'Uhm, I'm afraid I don't have a kettle yet,' I said.

'Yes, you do,' he said as he cleaned out the log burner. 'It's in the box on the table.'

I peered inside. There was a toaster, a loaf of bread, coffee, tea, some butter, cheese, chutney, fruit, and a jar of peanut butter.

'Peanut butter! My favourite. But wait, what is all this?' I asked as I painfully slowly filled the kettle with water from the screeching tap. *I'm no charity case*, I wanted to say, but the thought of a nice cup of tea did appeal to me, especially after having spent all that time out in the cold.

He chuckled as he looked up the chimney. 'Nana has a sixth sense about these things sometimes. It's her idea of a welcome wagon. Welcome to the neighbourhood, Sophie. If you're in with the old dear, you're in with the entire village.'

The entire village was what I was hoping to stay *away*

from out here in the sticks. All I needed was one nosey person and bang went my cover.

A loud crack filled the air and I started, realising that Dr Armitage already had a nice fire going. Instinctively, I stretched my hands out to defrost my fingers. The silence was tangible. I knew he had a million questions as to why a young woman would beg to live in a place like this. Questions that I didn't want to answer.

After he left with the promise of sending someone over to check out the cottage, I marched upstairs and, with a pair of rusty scissors I found in the cabinet under the sink, hacked a good ten inches off my long, beautiful hair, leaving me with a boyish look. If Demelza had passed herself off as a boy by wearing her brother's clothes, short hair would completely change my looks, too.

That evening, disguised with my new look, I went for a short stroll. Tulip Cottage was the last one on the edge of the village, with what looked like vast woods to my left. It was beautiful, with ancient trees and birds chirping to salute the end of the day.

Lifting my collar against the chilly air, I had only taken a few steps when, out of the blue, I was met by the funniest-looking dog I'd ever seen in my life. It was a million colours, like a kaleidoscope of creams and russets and greys and browns, with upright ears and big, dark eyes. It looked like a Photoshop of many different dogs rolled into one with a hacksaw fur-cut. This huge, motley jumble of dogs looked fearsome, but it came up to me, wagging its crooked tail and sniffing my outstretched hand. There was not one normal thing about this mutt.

'Hello, and who are you?' I cooed. 'Did you get caught in the spin cycle? You're cute, aren't you?'

And at that moment, I felt a strange sensation of being watched. I stood erect, ears and eyes alert. It wasn't my imagination. Someone was watching me. I was pretty sure of it by the way my hair pricked at the back of my now bare neck.

'Wolf!' came an ominous rumble and the mutt's ears pricked as it froze to listen. 'Come!'

At that, Wolf dropped me like a hot potato and bounded back from where he came. I stood for a moment, trying to gather my wits about me, when his voice startled me again.

'You! This is private property. Piss off!'

'Oh! I—I'm sorry!' I called into the trees.

And that was all I needed to make a run back to the safety of my own cottage. Breathless, I closed the door and locked it, peeping through the curtains. But he didn't follow me. Obviously, he wanted to be left alone as much as I did. I could understand that. What I couldn't understand was his rudeness. I was only saying hello to his dog.

# 6

I spent the entire morning cleaning the cottage as best I could, including the windows that, on closer inspection, were barely held together by layers and layers of chipped paint. But it did now finally afford a view of the rectangle of weeds that had once been the garden.

But I could see dots of colour under the grey brambles. It was April, after all, and some flowers were trying to reach the sun. Oh, those poor, poor blooms! I went around to the potting shed in the back and found a tiny hoe. It looked like it must have belonged to a child, but it was all I had, so I began to whack away and pull out everything that was dry and grey.

By the time I'd cleared most of the bramble, scratching my hands and face even more, I discovered that there was indeed a splendid garden desperate to live again. Daffodils, tulips, black-eyed Susans, bluebells, dahlias, agapanthus, forget-me-nots, all at various stages of blooming, and even fruit trees in bud! There was a pear tree, an apple tree, a cherry tree and even green tufts of rhubarb. If all this was out already in April, I couldn't wait to see what the summer would bring.

Wiping my forehead from the ghastly work, I filled at least three heavy-duty compost bags I'd found in the shed and sat on the stoop of the open French doors leading into the kitchen. From there, I'd be able to see all this beauty. How lucky had I been to find this place after all? My garden would be my sanctuary. I couldn't wait!

After I got my stamina back, I found the hose, hoping it was connected to the mains and not to the mystery that was the household water mess, and yes! Victory! Water flowed freely, so I gave everything alive a good soaking. It was too bad there was hardly any water inside the house as now I needed a major wash from head to toe and it was too cold to wash outside. So I lugged a few buckets inside which I poured into the kitchen sink, too tired as I was to haul water up to the tub upstairs.

Then I cleaned out and disinfected the chest of drawers in my new bedroom and put Sophie's clothes away. I wondered how Will would justify a burglary in their home where none of the jewellery had been taken. Surely Sophie would be suspicious.

By now, furious that I hadn't unwittingly walked into work only to be nabbed by Scotland Yard, he would have contacted Tamsin, who could honestly say that she had no idea where I'd gone. But that would not have stopped Will. He would have fed the police more stories about me. As if depicting me as a criminal wasn't enough.

*A criminal.* That was what I officially was now.

I didn't think Will would go so far as to splash my picture online in his search for me; he wasn't very hip to social media. I, on the other hand, was obsessed with it at one time. My Instagram channel, *Where Are They Now?* would only confirm my interest in the lives of celebrities, nailing my coffin shut once and for all. Because the firm did have a few celebrities as clients. They probably thought I'd cottoned onto some famous person's darkest secrets via the confidential files of my workplace and that I'd used the information to blackmail them. Funny, though, how I had become the one to seek privacy and anonymity. Perhaps it served me right for not letting sleeping dogs lie.

In my defence, my channel was always very respectful of the celebrities and I never made any assumptions on where they were physically today. I simply reviewed their career with old footage that was available on the internet, stirring the nostalgic fans' memories of how great those days were. I had never searched for nor divulged their whereabouts.

But lately, I had tired of it all. It had only been a hobby, something to do when I wasn't at my job, and lately, it hadn't been giving me any pleasure. And now, more than ever, I understood the value of privacy. Why dig into the past of these people who now just wanted to be left alone?

Of course now, the irony of it all did not escape my notice; after digging these people up from oblivion, karma came back to bite me on the arse. Now I was the one to want to hide, and Will and the police would do everything in their power to find me. I had already cut my hair. I'd wear hats and shades and avoid getting too up close and personal with anyone.

So I needed to find a job quickly to put me in a stronger position and to allow me to stay hidden for as long as possible. Anything that would allow me to pay my bills.

After a delicious lunch of bread, cheese and chutney washed down by a nice hot cup of tea, I brushed my short hair and put on my hat, shades and coat to reacquaint myself with Starry Cove and see if I could find any *Hiring* signs.

I threw open my front door like Julie Andrews in *The Sound Of Music* and breathed in the air with gusto. Practically skipping down Meadow Lane with its beautiful Georgian cottages, I admired the pretty little windows looking out onto miniature front gardens with daffodils and flowers of all kinds already shooting up proudly to meet the cobalt sky. You wouldn't think, looking at me, that I was a fugitive.

Halfway down the lane, I came to a wide brook crossed by an old stone arched bridge. A few yards in, I stopped to look down into the swirling waters and imagined children playing pooh sticks, or tiny rabbits hopping along the banks. It was like a Beatrix Potter story and if I stopped and looked just a little harder, I might have encountered Mrs Tiggy-Winkle or Jemima Puddleduck. What a gem this place was!

On the other side of the bridge, Meadow Lane melted into School Lane which led straight to the centre of the village and then to the seaside that held many dear memories for me. And it was so apt that my new life had started where my happy one had been interrupted by, well, life. But hopefully, my new life had begun!

'Good day!' I greeted an elderly man on my way. So much for keeping my head down. He was holding the back of his grandson's bicycle as he was just learning to ride. The little boy's face was happy but determined, his eyes focused ahead and his chin jutting out. It was such a lovely picture of happiness and security. This child was obviously much loved.

The man looked up and smiled at me. 'It certainly is now that the sun's come out, ma'am!' he called back.

I almost stopped in my tracks at the unexpected kindness. *Ma'am?* When had anyone ever called me that? Where I came from, all people said to each other in the street was, *Sorry* when about to collide with one another. The city way. Ah, but here, we couldn't be any further from a city. No, Starry Cove, as per my childhood memories, was just as idyllic as ever.

I wondered whether the ice-cream kiosk on the seafront still existed. Or the beauty salon my mum used to go to. And the toy shop where Dad used to buy me something every summer as a souvenir of our holidays. I would spend most of our days on the beach building sandcastles with my father while my mother ran her errands, which included visits to the local beautician, fashion shops and what have you, so she'd look properly dressed for dinner, as she'd always say.

Dad and I would snicker as we ate with our hands and plunged our feet into the soft sand and built our castles full of dreams. And then he'd lift me onto his shoulders and we'd walk along endless beaches, and I'd close my eyes in sheer happiness against the caressing sea breeze, happy to be alive, wishing September would never come. Those summer days were suspended in my mind and heart like the snapshots that we used to take of each other making funny faces in the camera.

My father would never haul me up onto his shoulders or

swim with me again. I would never feel his reassuring hand around mine, never hear his gravelly voice or his bellowing laugh. All I could do now was strive to make the same lovely memories for my own child and make sure that she would never feel neglected or sad. She would never know her father, God willing, but it would be okay, because I'd be both.

On my way toward the centre of the village, I walked past quaint little shops with colourful signs and original names, like Bend Or Bump, which seemed to sell everything from safety pins to sailboats, no kidding. There was a sign that read, *For sailboats ask Jago*. What a typical Cornish name!

I decided I had a good chance of finding pretty much most of what I needed in this little emporium and I was not disappointed. Household furnishings, kitchen items and bath accessories were neatly stacked in separate sectional areas so that it was very easy to locate everything and within ten minutes, I had filled out my list. In the next room was nursery furniture, but I avoided going in there lest I attracted attention from the other pregnant ladies in there ooh-ing and ah-ing over this cot and that changing table. There was time for that later.

Feeling a great sense of accomplishment nevertheless, I hoarded my purchases over to the counter where a carbuncular boy in his early twenties tallied everything up for me. He didn't say much except for the total cost, but then again, I was too excited to leave and be on my way. I wondered if he was Jago and how many sailboats he actually had for sale.

As I lugged my essentials along the High Street, I got the

strange sensation of being followed. The possibility of Will somehow discovering my whereabouts loomed at the back of my mind, and I wondered how long it would take me to stop looking over my shoulder at every turn. After all those hours of driving, all the miles between us, shouldn't I feel at least somewhat safe?

I ducked into a bakery/café called The Rolling Scones. *Scones? Don't mind if I do.* I rubbed my hands in anticipation and went inside, the fragrance of baked goods just out of the oven immediately filling my nostrils, along with the smell of freshly ground coffee.

At the very back, next to the window, was an old pub piano. I hadn't been in the same room with a piano for years. I didn't even know if I could play anymore.

I sat at a tiny table away from the windows, shoving my bags under my chair as an elderly man whom I assumed was the owner smiled at me and brought me a menu.

'Mornin', Miss,' he chimed. 'What does your sweet tooth require this morning? Can I tempt you with a nice big wedge of carrot cake?'

'Ooh, yes please,' I answered, despite myself. I knew I shouldn't have been spending my money so carelessly, but it was difficult not to swoon. The entire glass counter was full of a huge assortment of everything, and maybe cake and a cuppa would calm my frazzled nerves. 'Your shop is beautiful, as is Starry Cove.'

He nodded. 'Thank you. We like it too. It's one of Cornwall's best-kept secrets. We want it to change as little as possible.'

'I agree. It's such a warm and welcoming place. The people are so friendly!'

At that, he laughed. 'Well, most of us are.'

'I came here as a little girl and it's still such a beautiful little village, just as I'd remembered it, with the breakwater and even the small island off the coast. What is it, Squally Isle, I seem to remember?'

'Ah, some people now call it Tempest Island, but I think it's dreadful. Why change a good thing?'

'Who would want to change such a quaint name?' I mused. 'It sounds so removed from the real world.'

'It does. But everyone knows it's become the place to run and hide.'

I snapped my head up, panic licking its way up my insides. 'I'm sorry, w-what?'

'A lot of celebrities call this place home. The scriptwriter Nina Conte, and the journalist Natalie Amore and her sister Yolanda Amore.'

'The celebrity chef?'

'Yes. And then the architect Henry Turner and the interior designer Faith Hudson. And so many more. They all live along the coast.'

'Oh, my word, what has this place *become*?'

'A well-kept secret. I hope you will respect that.'

'Oh, of course,' I promised. No one craved anonymity as much as I did. Everyone had a right to be left in peace, to not have to inform anyone of their whereabouts. Even if their very future didn't depend on it. They could always open shop somewhere else, what with their millions, but where was I going to go?

'Here, I always give newcomers free muffins in the hope they'll come back for more,' he said with a chuckle as he put four muffins in a bag and set it on my table. 'For those long, dark nights in front of the telly,' he said with a wink.

'Thank you, but you don't have to do that. Let me pay you for them.'

'Nonsense! Just come back for that slice of carrot cake another time.'

I promised I would, though with my limited budget I didn't know when that would be. I had to save up for Baby, and I didn't have a telly or a laptop, for that matter. That would require some serious saving, and anyway, I wanted to put it off for as long as I could just in case Will tried to track me. I didn't even know if that was possible, but if it was, Will would know someone who could do it. He knew a lot of people who owed him favours.

The rest of my afternoon was spent exploring an old-fashioned candy shop, an antique shop, a miniature boat model shop, a basket-weaver and even a gallery full of glass art made of glass that had washed up on the beach. It was comforting to know that there were still people working with their hands, making beautiful things that people appreciated and would pay good money for, although beauty in my mind was priceless.

As I ambled past the harbour, every now and then throwing a cautious glance behind me until I convinced myself it had all been my imagination and that no one was following me, I caught sight of the breakwater from which Dad and I used to jump into the sea, shrieking with delight as we hit the water, never letting go of each other's hand. Then we'd slowly float back to the surface and burst into laughter for the sheer joy of being alive. Together, we'd swim back to the shore and have lunch, after which a chocolate lolly for me and a vanilla cone for him. I understood only now what it was all about. Happiness. I hadn't had that in a long time. But my best memories were here, in Cornwall, and that was why I'd come here: to try and recapture it.

The crisp wind made my eyes water and I swiped at my cheeks.

At the very end of the quay, just before the next cove, I stopped in sheer, newfound delight at the sight of a barge covered with fairy lights. There was a sign reading:

Books On The Barge. Come in and have some cake, a cuppa and a read! No need to buy.

Books? More cake? Had I died and found my very own personal Nirvana? I wished I had come here sooner. I wished I had left Will years ago, and returned to Starry Cove to settle into a quiet life, and not in faceless London where, had it not been for Tamsin and her family, I would have been completely alone.

'Hi! Fancy a wander?' came a soft voice from the door. It belonged to a pretty girl with beautiful eyes and a kind face.

'Oh! Yes, thank you, I—'

'Come in, come in!' she beckoned and I found myself inside the barge, surrounded by walls covered in books. There were armchairs sided by lamps everywhere. Warm and cosy, it looked like many lovely living rooms in one. In the warm air hung the fragrance of freshly brewed coffee.

'Sit, sit, you look frozen! Can I offer you a nice hot drink? I have these amazing scones that Ralph from the bakery made an hour ago.'

'Oh, you mean the bloke from The Rolling Scones? He just gave me some muffins…'

'Save those for later! I'm Emmie,' she said, holding out her hand. 'And this,' she said, turning to a crib in the corner, 'is Felicity.'

I jumped out of my seat to take a peek at the little face under the tiny, pink bonnet. I'd never really been a baby person, or even known a baby except for little Jake, Tamsin's baby, i.e., my godson.

'Oh my God, she is so *beautiful*,' I swooned despite my promising myself that I'd never be one of those women who lost it over a baby. But here I was, close to tears because of the beauty of such a little miracle. It must have been my hormones wreaking havoc on my brain. I'd read about it, but I never thought it would happen to me. And right there and then, it hit me in all its reality. Soon, I too would have a baby in my arms. From a man who'd happily fed me to the police.

Emmie's face dropped when she saw my tears. 'Oh, I'm so sorry, I didn't mean to trigger anything…!'

'I'm sorry, I'm all right,' I said, swiping at my eyes with my little finger and bending down to Felicity, who continued to sleep without a care in the world. What the hell was wrong with me? I never cried, and yet, the moment I'd left London, it was like a dam of pent-up tears had broken. Better get a hold of myself. 'I'm Sophie, by the way.'

'Pleased to meet you! I'm glad for the company. My husband is at his own shop and I miss him when he's not around.'

Now *that* was a feeling that I had been estranged to for quite a while.

'Aw, that's so sweet.'

'Oh, yes. Now that we have the baby, he's extra attentive. He always jumps up in worry, "What's wrong, honey, are you okay, can I get you anything?" Talk about being smothered with love, you know?'

I smiled and nodded, wishing I really did know what she was talking about. Memories of Will slamming doors behind him were all I had.

'Coffee or tea?' Emmie asked.

'Tea, please.'

Baby Felicity suddenly woke up and began to cry.

'There, there, sweetheart,' Emmie soothed. 'She does that every once in a while. I just rock her a bit and then she's okay. Would you like to rock her crib?'

I bit my lip. People were so weird and afraid for their babies nowadays, but Emmie seemed perfectly normal. I wondered whether I was even able. How was I ever going to manage with my own baby?

'She likes it when I rock her. Here, have a go,' she said with a wink.

I reached out a hand and gently pulled the crib to and fro, softly humming some indistinct lullaby I remembered snippets of. She immediately stopped crying.

'Well done,' Emmie whispered. 'You're a natural.'

'She is a little miracle,' I couldn't help but murmur over a tight throat.

Emmie chuckled. 'She is, when she's sleeping. Awake, she's gurgly and burpy and never stops moving. I love her to pieces.'

'You're a good mum,' I blurted out before I could stop myself. What right did I have to judge her? What did I know about mothers? My own had seemed like the best. And yet, she'd left.

'I try. Of course it's not easy, but Jago is always there for us.'

'Did you say Jago? Does he own the Bend Or Bump, by any chance, or is it another Jago?'

She laughed. 'That's him, the one and only Jago in the village. I don't know what I'd do without him. Raising a kid is no easy feat. I'd be in real trouble if he wasn't around.'

I nodded absently. This was something I was going to have to do on my own. I didn't have a Jago.

'Sophie? Are you okay?'

'Huh? Yes, yes, sorry. I was just… nothing. I got, uhm, some stuff for the cottage at your husband's. Tulip Cottage, if you know it?' Emmie nodded in recognition. 'The place is… completely derelict.' As was I. The cottage was not the only one needing some TLC.

'Why don't I go get those scones and the tea?' she said gently. I had the feeling she knew I needed a minute to recompose myself.

'That would be great, thanks, Emmie.'

She smiled and turned to the counter, where a kettle sat under an owl-shaped tea-cosy next to a glass bell full of scones. I looked down at Felicity, who slept in utter peace, her pink mouth slightly upturned as if she were smiling in her sleep. She was a beautiful, happy baby. She was also obviously well-loved.

My baby would be just as loved. I would love her with all my heart and more. She would never suffer for anything, and the lack of a father was never going to be a problem. Because I would be Mummy *and* Daddy to her, just like my father had been to me. I'd do my very damned best to make sure she felt loved every single day of her beautiful life.

'She positively loves you,' Emmie whispered as she put a steaming cup on the low table before me, well away from Felicity. Next to it, she put a plate heaped with scones, and two pots: one with jam and one with cream.

'You think?' I whispered back.

'Absolutely. She never settles so quickly. You must have some magic secret.'

I grinned. 'Hardly.'

'Are you planning on having children? Sorry, is that too forward? My friends say I'm too nosey. Well, not all of them. Rosie is just like me. We're the softies of the group.'

'Group?'

'People call us The Coastal Girls. It's all very funny. How long are you staying? Oh, you have to meet them.'

I debated. The more I laid low, the better. I'd come here to disappear, not to make friends. Yet, besides Tamsin, I had no friends, and I couldn't risk calling her again so soon, no matter how much I longed to tell her all about the baby, and the new life I was about to create for myself.

'I'm... not sure yet.'

'But you're staying at Tulip Cottage for now?'

I sighed. 'I am. The owner wants to do some renovation work to make it more comfortable. It is a little derelict, but I don't mind.'

'Hm, sounds like Mrs Nankivell is at it again.'

'Yes, that's right, it's a Mrs Nankivell; how did you know?'

Emmie giggled. 'The poor woman, she has a heart as big as Cornwall, but she glosses over the practicalities sometimes. Her grandson is the local GP. Why don't you talk to him?'

'I have. He's the one who offered to do the work.'

'That's Robert, all right. He's an absolute sweetheart.'

That was not how I'd have described him exactly, but I could see that he had a good heart.

'Okay, Little Miss Moon, let Sophie drink her tea now…'

I smiled. 'I like that: Little Miss Moon…'

'Let's hope she likes it too. It's her surname. Tomorrow, I'll take you to meet my friends, yes?'

This was not how it was supposed to go. I needed to lie low, not make friends left, right and centre. If everyone was so polite and kind, how was I supposed to hide away?

'Can I let you know tomorrow? I've got some stuff to do.'

'Of course. I'll be heading over anyway, so be here at midday if you want to come. Now drink up!'

We spent another hour together and I had to admit that I enjoyed her company immensely. She was happy and considerate. If I didn't have to keep myself to myself, I could see us becoming close. Such a shame. But that was the price I had to pay in order to keep Baby and myself safe.

On my way back to Tulip Cottage, I decided to take the long way home.

I chose a country lane that split a huge, green field in half. It was delightful, bordered by pine trees and bushes that dotted the gently rolling hills. It was like the illustrations that you see in children's storybooks. It was a dip into happiness.

A loud roar from behind me made me jump to the side of the muddy path as an oncoming car honked for me to get out of the way, splashing me from head to toe in mud. I didn't see the driver, but I did recognise Wolf, that motley, patchwork dog, sitting in the back seat with his head out the window and his tongue hanging out a mile with what I could almost swear was a smile. *Rude Bloke strikes again...*

Once inside the cottage, I dropped my bags and darted up the stairs to change out of my muddy clothes and rinse the streaks of mud from my skin with one of my newly purchased towels. If I ever came face to face with that piece of work, I'd tell him a thing or two, I would. I knew he'd seen me – did he think to even slow down? Or, realising he'd soaked me from head to toe, had he stopped to apologise? Not even remotely. Really, what shameful behaviour.

Now warm and dry, I rushed back down the stairs, eager to splay out the rest of my brand-new purchases. Like a little girl with a new set of dolls, I divided everything based on the rooms they needed to go to and dashed back up the stairs with my towels, loo paper and sheets. The blue towels looked pretty against the glass towel railings and hooks. Maybe I could get a few beachy items in, like some driftwood or a bottle filled with sand and maybe some shells? Will had said it was too cheesy when I'd bought some beach-themed items at my home. But now, I didn't need his approval.

With my new sheets, I made my bed and plumped up the pillows. I'd need a new mattress but for now, it would have to do. I was so pleased with the day's progress in my new home that I did a little victory lap to admire my work.

Slowly, slowly, the little bird builds its nest.

# 7

The next day, I woke to the sound of birdsong, which was a huge improvement on the rusty frogs, i.e., the doorbell. I opened my eyes and peered out the window where a little red robin was scrounging around the windowsill for something to eat. I surreptitiously stretched out a hand for the packet of Hobnobs I'd brought up with me last night and eased out of bed ever so slowly, but the minute my feet touched the floor, it flew away.

I looked at my watch and realised it was time to get ready to meet up with Emmie again. I'd decided that as long as I kept my mouth shut about where I'd been before Starry Cove, there shouldn't be any harm in spending a bit more time with her. How nice it was to make my own plans for the day without having to ask for anyone else's approval!

I slipped into my coat, thinking how strange this was. A few days ago I had no hope whatsoever of a better life, and here I was now, going to see a very sweet girl and her delightful baby. I picked my way down School Lane and soon reached the quay where Emmie's barge was moored.

She was already at the door, a huge smile on her face. To think that she was so pleased to see me gave me hope and I blinked away some silly moisture gathering at the base of my lashes.

'Hello, you!' she chimed, throwing the door wide open for me.

'Hi,' I said shyly. 'Thank you for inviting me again.'

'Of course! The kettle's just boiled, come and warm up by the log burner!'

'Thank you,' I said, rubbing my hands together.

'I've got some more amazing goodies from The Rolling Scones today! Look, carrot cake, éclairs, chocolate fudge cake, apple pie and even baked Alaska!'

I found myself charmed by her enthusiasm for the small pleasures in life, wishing I could be more like her. 'Are you trying to turn me into a glutton, Emmie?'

She smiled cheekily as she poured me a nice hot cup of coffee. 'Is it working?'

I reached forward to receive it, literally gagging for my daily dose of caffeine. 'Absolutely!'

She raised her cup in a toast. 'To new friendships, then!'

I swallowed. I *so* wanted to have real friends here, truly I did. But I was somewhat still afraid of attracting too much attention to my presence here in Starry Cove and getting too close. But Emmie had been so welcoming, I couldn't refuse her kindness. Besides, it would be weird if I avoided people, wouldn't it? Perhaps I was exaggerating. This was a tiny, peaceful village at the end of the day. What harm could come to me here?

After our coffee, we threw on our coats, got little Felicity up from her nap and I followed her as she pushed her pram down through the villages of Wyllow Cove, Perrancombe, Penworth Ford to Little Kettering where The Old Bell Inn sat on the edge of a cliff facing the sea.

To say it looked like a scene out of a Rosamund Pilcher book was an understatement. It was a beautifully preserved building backing onto fairytale woodlands where robins flitted from branch to branch like you see in cartoons.

It was all so beautiful and storybook-like.

'So what are we doing here?' I asked.

'Meeting a friend!'

I was hesitant to meet other people. People I'd have to lie to and live in the same community with. This made me very uneasy. I wanted friendships, eventually, of course, but based on honesty. I didn't want to start anything dishonest. So I'd have to be very careful and not get attached to anyone. Just casual acquaintances.

'Come,' Emmie said and we plunged into the olde-worlde atmosphere of the old inn. Every end table was covered with Easter egg nests and paper birds of every colour and real chocolate eggs just for the taking. *Note to self: don't be a glutton.*

'Hi Laura, is Penny around?' Emmie asked of a young woman at the Reception desk. 'Sophie, this is Laura, Head of Reception. Laura, this is my new friend Sophie.'

'Hi!' she chimed enthusiastically, and I couldn't help but smile at her.

'Emmie!' called another young woman with long, red hair and a striking face. She was absolutely gorgeous and had a no-nonsense air about her. 'Where have you been hiding? You know I need to see Little Miss Moon every day or I get sad!' And to the baby: 'Hi, little princess!'

Felicity gurgled and stretched her arms toward her, begging to be lifted. The red-head obliged, turning to smile at me.

'Sophie, this is Penny. She is manager of the place. Penny, this is Sophie, DFL.'

'Hi, Sophie, DFL!' she greeted me cheerfully. 'Welcome to our little paradise.'

'Thank you. What's DFL?' I asked.

'That's Down From London.'

My eyes widened. There went my plan not to reveal anything about my past. 'But I never said—'

Emmie grinned. 'Your accent is a dead giveaway.'

'We mean it in a good way, for you,' Penny hastened to explain. 'And for the hotel business, of course.'

'Ah, I get it,' I said. 'It's becoming a problem here, isn't it, all these Londoners flocking to Cornwall?'

Penny dipped her head. 'I'm not complaining. But for the buying market, yes. The locals are being priced out of their own turf.'

'Well, I won't be buying.'

'She's renting Tulip Cottage,' Emmie informed her, and I couldn't help but feel a tiny stab of apprehension. I shouldn't have come here today to meet these people. I was digging my own grave, not to mention deceiving these people by withholding my real identity and purpose.

'Oh, you're a bit out of the way. Safe from all the village hustle and bustle, good for you,' Penny assured me, in more ways than she could understand. 'We're a bit out of the way here too. You have to have a real reason to come here.'

At that, both Penny and Emmie turned to me expectantly. I had never mentioned to Emmie just why I had come here. Not even in the shape of a lie.

'Well, I used to come here as a child on vacation with my family,' I volunteered. Beyond that, I would say no more.

'How amazing is that?' Emmie said. 'So technically, you're more native than we are! I'm a DFL and Penny's dad is Irish. So, have things here changed much since you were a little girl, Sophie?'

'Uhm, no, not that much, actually. That's what makes it so special, I think.'

'You got that right,' Penny chimed as she rocked Felicity, her eyes never leaving my face; I wondered if I'd managed to cover up my scratches well enough. I could tell she was a sharp one, although she was slightly younger than me and Emmie. And yet, she commanded the room which she surveyed with eagle eyes. This was her workplace and from what I could see, she ran it like a tight ship. It was spotless and staff were busy going about their business quickly and quietly, almost invisibly.

'Would you like the tour?' Penny asked, taking me off the spot. 'It's a small hotel but we've even got horses. My little brother Danny likes to help after school.'

'I'd love that,' I said.

Emmie took Felicity off Penny, who showed us the lobby, the restaurant and the dining room. It was indeed small, but so lovely and warm, it actually looked like a large home.

'It's so beautiful,' I commented.

'Thank you. Faith did the décor.'

'You'll meet her later,' Emmie promised me. 'She's an amazing interior designer.'

*More people to deceive. Just great...*

Penny took us to the grounds out to the side and front where the paddocks and stable were. Now, I was no expert, but the horses were stunningly beautiful and obviously well cared for.

'Danny does most of the grooming,' Penny said. 'Can you stay for lunch?'

Lunch? At a hotel? That would cost me quite a few bob.

'It's on the house,' Penny assured me. 'I'm so happy to have non-hotel company, if you know what I mean.'

'Thank you,' I said. 'If Emmie has the time…'

'You bet I do! We make a point to see one another as often as possible.'

And so we stayed for lunch, sitting at a table by the window overlooking the sea. We were close to the edge of the cliffs and I could clearly see the waves cresting and breaking on the rocks down in the coves of the bay. This was a truly breathtaking place, and I couldn't see anyone, let alone myself, tiring of the wildly beautiful seascapes.

A couple of hours later, Felicity began to fuss and on that note, we took our leave.

'She's been as good as gold,' Emmie said as we stood up, 'but it's time to go home.'

I turned to Penny. 'Well, thank you so much for such a lovely lunch. It was great meeting you and seeing your beautiful hotel.'

And then, Penny surprised me by hugging me. 'Come back any time, please,' she said. 'I get bored with all these bureaucrats behind the desk.'

'I will, thank you. And maybe you could both come round Tulip Cottage for a meal, although it won't be as good as today's.'

Eek, what had I just said? I was in absolutely no condition to host a meal, let alone have even one person over for coffee. I had nothing to offer! Plus, I was supposed to stay low.

'That would be great!' Penny said, squeezing my shoulder lightly.

What was this place, *Instant Friendshipville*? I had definitely played my cards wrong if I'd meant to keep to myself.

'Uh, great,' I managed, trying not to look worried. But I needed to get out of here. I needed to get back to the cottage to light a fire for the night and tell myself it would be okay. Even in my head, that had sounded almost primeval, like a Neanderthal woman, stripped down to the basics. Warmth, Protection, Food. Slowly, slowly. One step at a time.

We said our goodbyes and made our way along the coastal path through other tiny villages that were attached to Starry Cove. Emmie did not seem to notice or comment on my discomfort, quietly humming to Felicity, who slept most of the way home.

Once back at her barge, Emmie turned and hugged me.

'Be good, and don't hesitate to call for whatever you need around the house. Jago is handy.'

'Thank you, I'll keep that in mind.'

'See you tomorrow?' she said.

'Right,' I said and then made my way back to Tulip Cottage. I wanted to see Emmie again and meet her friend Faith the decorator, for instance, but if I kept on like this, I'd meet the entire village by the end of the week. I had met so many people already and only been here for a couple of days. So much for remaining anonymous. And yet, I couldn't resist the warmth and generosity of her offer. Back in London, apart from Tamsin, no one had ever treated me like family after just having met me. But this? This was a whole new world. I swallowed back a sense of gratitude.

*Get a grip*, I told myself. *The more you act weird, the more you'll attract people's attention. Just be normal. Act like you're a single girl looking for a change of scenery. Nothing more.*

And yet, I had to give myself a pat on the back for even leaving London and my old life and, I had to admit, I was already feeling much better. I was not one to make drastic changes. In anything. I always ate the same foods, chose the same ice-cream flavour and the same clothes. So for me, this was a huge deal. But in all fairness, I hadn't had a choice.

I hadn't been able to bring myself to action, like a prehistoric body stuck in a prehistoric bog. Inert, helpless and hapless. So I'd retired into my own silence. Will always thought it was because I liked being left alone a lot. Imagine being with someone who lacked the basic understanding of, well, *you*, and how you felt. Solitude seemed to be the only cure at the time, but lately, I'd come to realise that forced solitude and inaction were only plasters that wouldn't stick long enough to cure and repair all the damage that had been done under the surface, like cigarette ash kicked under the carpet.

But most importantly, and what made me crazy, was that I'd never understand how I let him get away with it all, from the fits of jealousy to organising my every single decision. And I'd let him, just to avoid another entire evening of yelling and arguing, then finally falling asleep from exhaustion (and not, say, holding hands in the dark and talking away into the night the way I pictured other couples did) on the nights that he was with me, having told his new girlfriend, I now realise, a bunch of fibs.

Not to mention the bitter morning aftertaste, almost like a hangover, which cast a shadow on the next few days. Not to mention the sense of heartbreak and the queasiness from lack of sleep. Until the queasiness had become constant, taking its place next to a new sense of fear. I thought it was just a new thing that had settled in along with the other novelties.

Follow your dreams, they say. Do what makes you happy. But Happy was a big word for me.

The next day, I was back at Books On The Barge, helping Emmie put some tomes back in order. I needed to work. Financially, I was stuck and only a steady income could get me back on top of my finances. But I couldn't tap anyone, let alone Emmie, for a job, could I? I mean, I had only been here a few days. How desperate would I look? Also, as far as I could see, there were no Hiring signs anywhere.

'I think I'd like to look for a job,' I blurted out of nowhere, feeling the blush creeping up my neck. It wasn't the shame of needing work, but of why I was so desperate for one. I did my best not to let my desperation show.

Emmie looked at me, her face lighting up. 'So you really are minded to stay?'

I grinned. 'I think so.'

'Oh my gosh, that's fantastic, and there's so much you could do! Robert's secretary is almost always off sick, Nina's baby-sitter is going to be away and—or did you mean a different kind of job?'

'Anything that will pay my bills,' I assured her, more comfortable now that she had made it sound so easy.

'Okay, I'll see what we can find for you! I'm so happy, Sophie!'

'Me too,' I said. I truly was happy here. This had to be the beginning of a good thing. I just knew it. A new life and a baby on the way. And speaking of, tomorrow I'd swing by Dr Armitage's office and see if he could squeeze me in for a quick check-up. This new life I'd started, I wanted to do it properly, and this time my own way.

# 8

'So how long has it been since your last visit?' Dr Armitage wanted to know as he warmed up his stethoscope.

'Uhm…'

'Sophie. You know it's not good to avoid visiting the doctors.'

'I'm fine.'

'Nothing new you want to share with me, then? Nothing worrying you?'

He had a point. If I was going to be the best mother I could be, I had to tell him. 'Well, yes. I am expecting a baby…'

He sat back, studying me as he did. 'Congratulations, Sophie. And, if I'm not too forward, how are you feeling about that?'

'Over the moon. And… a little freaked out. I've never done this before…'

'You'll be fine. You're young and strong. May I ask… is the father on the scene? I'm only asking so I can gauge your total wellbeing. You can depend on me as your doctor to give you all the support you need. Plus I'll put you in touch with the best gyno in Cornwall.'

'Thank you. No, it's just me. Please don't tell anyone.'

'You can trust me, Sophie. As your physician, I'll always put your wellbeing first. Can you take a big deep breath for me now, please?' he said. 'Okay, it all sounds pretty good here. Now we'll check your blood pressure. Give me your arm.'

When done, he looked up at me, his eyes narrowing.

*Uh-oh.* 'Is it too high?'

'Just a tad. You need to decompress. Relax,' he replied, releasing my arm from the blood-pressure cuff. 'Whatever is troubling you needs to stop now. Please step onto the scales.'

'Oh. Okay. Are you going to listen to my lungs?' Anything to get off this subject.

'Why, are you a smoker?'

'No.'

'Are you having trouble breathing?'

'No.'

'Then you're okay for now.'

'Are you sure?'

He sighed. 'The last thing you want to be is paranoid about your pregnancy. Just eat healthily, take your vitamins and go for walks in the fresh air. You'll be fine. In the meantime, you contact Dr Chenoweth and get checked regularly, hear?'

'Thank you,' I said and that was the end of that. I knew I'd be in good hands.

The next day, I was having a closer inspection of the house and making plans on how to make it more homely. After I found a job, I would be able to afford maybe a rug and perhaps a pair of curtains. They didn't have to be new. I loved vintage and pre-loved things. If there was anything I couldn't stand, it was feeding landfill sites. As soon as I could afford to, I'd return to Bend Or Bump to get a tiny table and two chairs for the garden to enjoy the summer and all the following seasons round again and again. Slowly, slowly, I'd make it my home. Mine and Baby's. There would be no Will to tell me what we were having for dinner, or what flowers to pick or even what coverlet to use.

I closed my eyes and envisaged the way I wanted it to look, eventually, and how to decorate the nursery. Was I having a boy or a girl? I'd been referring to the baby as 'she', but really I had no instinct at all about what they would be. And then the obvious dawned on me. I could choose my own child's name! Will would have absolutely no say in how I brought it up, where it went to school (Note to self: remember to check out local Northwood Academy for the future). It would be just us. Yes, Tulip Cottage was perfect and I couldn't wait to share it with Baby.

A knock at the door made me jump. I was still in my pyjamas, nursing a hot cup of decaf tea and bingeing on chocolate Hobnobs. I stood at the foot of the stairs, debating. Who could it be? I had to stop being afraid. Will didn't know I was here.

'Hello? Anybody home? Dr Armitage sent me. I'm Noah, the handyman!'

*Oh!* I hurried to unlatch the door and stepped back to see a bloke who would've been better placed on a California beach: tall, tanned and with longish, blond hair, he had a contagious smile and an easy-going manner. He was the exact opposite of Will, which was perhaps why I liked him immediately. And the fact that he was carrying a toolbox.

'Hello!' he said in an Australian drawl. 'You the new tenant in need of a fixing up?'

He looked for all the world like your typical playboy and nothing like a handyman, if you didn't count the toolbox. Well, okay, maybe he looked like those blokes in jeans and a fitted T-shirt girls dreamed about. But not me. I was here for some peace and quiet, and to raise a baby. No time for any shenanigans. But he did seem genuinely friendly, or maybe it was the accent drawing me in.

'Can I come in, or are you going to leave me on the threshold?' he said with a friendly grin.

I stepped aside to let him in.

'Wow, is this place tiny or what? Talk about bijou,' he said.

I bristled. 'It suits me just fine.'

He shrugged. 'If you're happy. You live here alone, then?' he asked. 'I'm not asking in a stalker-y way, mind you,' he reassured me. 'On the contrary, if you need anything, anything at all, don't hesitate to ask.'

Three seconds in and Surfer Dude was already grating on my nerves. But I should be happy he had come.

'Thank you, Noah.'

'Care to show me around?' he asked.

'Of course. This is the living room and the kitchen is through there.'

He laughed. 'I was joking! You could hardly get lost in here, could you? Now, let's check the electrics first,' he said, opening his toolbox to retrieve a screwdriver.

Not knowing whether to stay or go as he removed the socket plate by the front door, I sauntered into the kitchen to busy myself with the kettle. Which reminded me. I hadn't yet sent Mrs Nankivell a thank-you note for all the goodies she'd sent. Perhaps I could bake her a cake. I hadn't checked if the oven worked.

I flipped the switch but nothing happened. The kettle was as dead as a doornail. 'Uhm, Noah?' I called over the six feet separating us. 'There's no power.'

'Of course not, do you want me to get electrocuted while I work?' he called back. Good point. For being a builder's daughter, I was a bit rusty.

And then he began to whistle. I hauled myself up onto the kitchen counter and listened. The last person I'd heard whistling was my father. He used to literally whistle while he worked. How I missed him! How I missed the sense of security his presence gave me! When he was alive, nothing could go wrong. If only he were here now. My best friend always.

'The system here is antiquated as hell. Needs a complete overhaul,' Noah called. 'Dr A said that might be the case.'

*Dr A. Cute.* 'How long will that take?' I asked.

'Oh, about a week,' Noah answered.

'That's okay. The important thing is the plumbing, which is a nightmare.'

'There's no hot water?' he asked.

'There's no water, period. At least, not upstairs. I have been filling a bucket from a trickle but it takes forever. If I had water, at least I could boil it for a bath.' Although the idea of lugging buckets of hot water up the steep staircase was not appealing to me in the least.

'Aw, geez, that's bad. That changes everything. Now I reckon it'll all take about three weeks.'

'Three weeks?' I almost wailed.

'At least, and that's before I even paint the place. What's the matter: can't wait to get rid of me already? And there was me thinking I might have found a new friend. I'm new here and don't know anyone yet.'

*Aw.* 'I'm sorry. I didn't mean to be rude,' I assured him. I knew a little about loneliness myself. 'You're Australian, I'm guessing.'

'You got it,' he said, flashing me a brilliant-toothed smile. 'Got here two weeks ago. I'm hoping my girlfriend will join me one day.'

'Oh, that's nice. And you did well to find a job so quickly, good on you.'

'Actually, I was a surfing instructor back home. There are a few places in Newquay I checked, but no one's hiring at the mo.'

'Right.' That was not good news for me.

'And you?' he asked as he motioned to the kitchen tap which he needed to check so I jumped off the counter. 'What do you do for a living?'

'I'm... sort of in between jobs at the moment.'

'Ah,' he said as the hot water tap screeched like a banshee.

Still nothing came out. 'What kind of work did you do in London?'

'London? Who said I was from London?'

He pulled out a wrench from his side pocket and without looking at me, shrugged. 'I just assumed, judging by your posh accent.'

'I don't have a posh accent.' I was anything but posh. *Will* was, granted, but I never had been and that was one of his biggest problems with me. Well, not anymore.

'So what kind of work will you be looking for, assuming you're not a trust-fund child which, judging by the state of this place you're renting out, you are not.'

'You certainly know how to win a girl's heart,' I said distractedly, really fancying a cup of tea just now that the power was off.

'So I've been told time and again,' he said with a wink.

It was all I could do to not roll my eyes.

'If you're making a cuppa later, I'll have tea with two sugars and milk, thanks.'

'Do you think that maybe you might take a look at the oven for me?' I asked. 'I want to make a cake.'

'Anything for cake, darl,' he said with a twinkle in his eye. He said it like an American would say doll.

After Noah had switched the power back on, I busied myself with the teas and reached up into the cupboard for the biscuit tin Mrs Nankivell had so generously supplied. I saw myself from the outside. Anyone watching would think they saw a young couple going about their morning breakfast routine. Little would they know that she (I) had a baby on the way, and that this young and handsome man had absolutely nothing to do with it. Because I was completely on my own. But that didn't mean I couldn't thank the people that were nice to me. So I sat down to write Mrs Nankivell a thank-you note.

Dear Mrs Nankivell,

I hope you are well. I would like to thank you for letting me stay in your lovely cottage. Also, I'd like to thank you for the welcome gifts that you sent me with Dr Armitage.

She was such a nice old lady. Very sweet. I missed my own grandmother very much. Before I could stop myself, I added:

When and if convenient, I would like for you to join me for a cup of tea here at Tulip Cottage.

Yours truly,
Sophie

Surely there was no harm in befriending a sweet, elderly woman, was there? She looked like she understood more than she let on, with her batty ways and all, but her eyes were keen and kind. God knew I needed someone who might understand the predicament I was in, even if I couldn't divulge the finer details.

'Right,' Noah said just as I finished my note. 'I've got a good idea of which tools I need. I'll be back tomorrow morning to make a start. Does nine o'clock sound okay?'

'Nine is perfect, thank you.'

After he left, I lay down on the old settee and called the number of the gyno that Dr A had given me: Dr Gwyneth Chenoweth. I managed to make an appointment for the next day.

Dr Chenoweth was very kind and welcoming, giving me a complete check-up. I was roughly five weeks pregnant, which meant my due date would be around December. A Christmas baby, what a gift! She assured me I was in excellent health. She gave me good tips on exercise and diet and mindfulness.

On my way back home, I stopped at the general shop in Starry Cove for some bread. I was eating as if my life depended on it which, funnily enough, it did. And that's when I spotted Rude Bloke's royal blue windbreaker at the dairy counter, his arms full of groceries. As soon as he saw me, he turned around and practically ran for the checkout.

I followed him with my one loaf of bread. In fairness we'd never met face to face so I decided to give him a chance to redeem himself. So I smiled at him and said, 'Hello. I've only got this one item, would you mind if just—?'

But he ignored me, chatting up the adoring checkout girl and plonking his goods down onto the conveyor belt while turning his back to me as if I didn't even exist. Goodness me! Who did he think he was, royalty? It was obvious I was invisible to him.

The next morning, Noah arrived at nine on the dot, bringing in wiring and other electrical materials.

'Mornin', darl!' he said cheerfully. I had not counted on him coming back, to be honest. Not that I had anything against him, but lately my motto was *Trust no one and you will not be disappointed.* Plus, I really didn't want him snooping around, although there wasn't anything to snoop about once I had my documentation and purse on me. Perhaps I was being a bit too suspicious, but better safe than sorry.

'If you're going into the village, I suggest you take a hat,' he said as he began to attack the socket by the front door again. 'It's vicious out there.'

'Oh. Uhm.' I still didn't feel comfortable leaving him in here on his own, but I couldn't stay here guarding an empty shell for the next three weeks, or as long as it would take him to finish the jobs. Of course, there was always the offer to stay at the Old Bell Inn but I liked the independence that the cottage afforded me. Besides, I'd already started to buy things for the place and I didn't want to lug it all over to the inn. 'Thank you, I will. Have you got yourself lunch? There's some cheese and stuff in the fridge,' I offered.

'I'm all right; I brought my own. Figured you'd be job-hunting today. Good luck!'

'Thanks,' I said as I let myself out, pulling my hood closer around my short hair. Noah was right. Although the sky was a clear, bright blue, you could cut the cold with a knife. Speaking of which, I had no plates. Will would be gloating if he saw the state I was living in. But the joke was on him because at least I was free.

Meadow Lane was particularly slippery this morning, so I carefully picked my way past the pretty little terraced cottages, this time noticing they all had names. My side was all named after flowers. On the way down, I spotted a Jasmine Cottage, an Iris Cottage, and even a Dahlia Cottage. When the terraced cottages gave way to semi-detached houses, the flower names turned to trees, such as Maple Way, Oak View, etc. I exhaled, realising I had been holding my breath since I'd arrived. Something had shifted suddenly, and for some reason still unknown to me, I knew I was going to make it.

# 9

Two days later, I received a letter from Mrs Nankivell:

Dear Sophie,

Thank you very much for your lovely invitation. I would most certainly love to join you for a cup of tea. Would it inconvenience you to pop over to mine instead? I live at 5 Seagull Terrace, just at the end of the High Street.

So I went, after stopping by The Rolling Scones to stock up on treats for her, although I tried to get the healthiest ones available. I also stopped by the village flower shop and got her some daisies.

When I knocked on Mrs Nankivell's yellow front door, a middle-aged woman opened the door and let me in, taking the flowers from me with a smile. She introduced herself as Agnes, the carer.

'She'll be happy to see you, Sophie,' she said as if I was a regular visitor. 'Come in, come in, she's in the sitting room.'

'Thank you.'

Mrs Nankivell's cottage was just like her: small, quirky and colourful, with flowered curtains and textiles, but not the old kind you see in shabby homes (or Tulip Cottage, as it were).

Before leaving after her morning shift, Mrs Nankivell's carer Agnes put the daisies in a pretty vase and set them on the side table under the window, and the cakes onto the coffee table as Mrs Nankivell gasped in delight.

'Two of my favourite things. Thank you, my dear!' Then she turned to Agnes. 'You can go now, Aggie. Say hello to that lovely husband of yours.' Then she turned to me. 'Everyone should have a lovely husband. I did. But then he died.'

'Oh, I'm so sorry…' I said.

'Oh, well, it was a long time ago. Life goes on.'

And she proceeded to tell me about her garden, and if I liked, she would let me have a few pots for my own (my own garden, I still couldn't believe it!) and some cuttings for the autumn.

'Oh, thank you, Mrs Nankivell, you've already been so generous with all your welcome gifts. You are truly so kind!'

She blinked. 'All my welcome gifts?'

'The kettle and the toaster and the food…'

'I'm afraid I only sent you the biscuits, my dear. Everything else was Robert's doing.'

Dr A? I'd have to thank him. He needn't have done all that. 'Oh. Well, then I'll be sure to thank him directly again.'

At that, she patted my hand. 'You do that, dear, you do that,' she said. 'And now, can I stupefy you with my musical talent?' she asked, gesturing toward the piano in the corner of the room. I'd noticed it the moment I'd stepped inside the cottage.

'Oh, please,' I said, clapping my hands in excitement.

She grinned. 'Don't clap yet, dear. I could be a total disaster. Sometimes, I am, you know? Sometimes I even forget what I am playing. Call it a senile moment.'

'Nonsense, I'm sure you're great,' I said.

And she was.

With the ease of a virtuoso, she threw herself into Chopin's 'Fantaisie in F minor', one of his most difficult pieces to play. And she was brilliant. I was a quarter of her age, more or less, with ten years of music conservatory under my belt and yet she played much better than I ever had. She played as if 'Fantaisie' was a dear old friend coming over for her daily visit. She played as if she played it every day, every hour. She played it as easily as breathing, a warm, relaxed smile on her gentle face. Mrs Nankivell was a revelation.

And then she stopped as her right hand went to her head. Had she forgotten what was next? I glanced at her, rising from the settee in alarm. That was not the face of someone trying to remember.

'Mrs Nankivell? Are you okay?'

But she didn't answer me.

'Mrs Nankivell? Can you hear me?'

But her head fell onto her chest, her body beginning to sag, and I caught her before she fell onto the floor. With one hand, I fished my mobile out of my pocket and dialled Dr A's number. Thank God he answered immediately.

'Sophie?'

'It's your nan,' I said. 'Come to her house now, please!'

'What happened?'

'She lost consciousness all of a sudden!'

'Okay, Sophie, listen to me carefully. If you can, put her feet higher than her head. Can you do that?'

I put him on speaker phone and pulled the cushions from the settee down onto the floor, gently pulling her down and lifting her legs so they were resting on the settee.

'Done,' I said. 'Now what?'

'Feel her heartbeat. I'm driving as fast as I can.'

I knew he wouldn't be long. 'Her heartbeat is feeble, but regular, from what I can tell.' I was no doctor.

'I'm on my way,' he said and hung up.

'Please hurry,' I whispered. If anything happened to this kind old lady, I would never forgive myself. I checked her pulse, which was getting weaker. Should I call him back? That would only slow him down.

I looked around and grabbed the throw from the settee to keep her warm.

'Mrs Nankivell? It's Sophie. Robert's on his way. You're going to be okay. Can you hear me?'

Nothing.

Five eternal minutes later, the slam of a car door was followed by the front door opening.

'Here!' I called and almost sagged with relief when he appeared in the doorway and fell to his knees.

'Nan?' he called as he attached her to a blood pressure machine. 'Nan, it's me, you're all right... Did she say she wasn't feeling well?' he asked me.

I shook my head, rubbing her soft, papery hands. 'No, she was playing the piano. I don't understand...'

'Nan? Can you hear me?' he called again, but there was no answer.

*Please do something*, I wanted to cry out, but I had to keep calm. She was in good hands.

We waited for the ambulance while Dr A. kept a constant check on her pulse and heartbeat, lightly tapping her on the cheek every once in a while, but to no avail. Surely, she should have been waking up by now if it wasn't serious? But Dr A kept his cool, revealing no emotion whatsoever, whereas I fought not to burst into tears as if she was my own grandmother.

If I thought I could live and not become attached to my new fellow villagers, I was wrong.

When the ambulance arrived I got up to follow, but Dr A. turned and took my wrists. 'Thanks for everything you've done, Sophie. Now go home and rest.'

'But I want to know…'

He squeezed my hands gently. 'I'll call you to fill you in the minute we know something. You need to take care of your baby and not exert yourself. Go home. I'll call you later. Okay?'

I sighed. 'Okay. I'll wait for your call, then.'

He smiled tightly. He was worried, I could see it in his eyes, even if he pretended everything was okay. 'Get some rest.'

But I couldn't, so when I got home, I jumped into my car and headed for the hospital.

An hour later, I was with Dr A by Mrs Nankivell's bed. She was sitting up, scowling. I'd never seen her scowl before but somehow, there was a comical side to it.

'Come on, Nan, just a few more hours as we check you out completely,' Dr A said.

'I can check myself out, thank you, and I'm going to. Get me those papers and I'll sign them d'rectly!'

It was the first time I'd heard her speak in a Cornish accent and I loved it.

'Just give the doctors a little longer and I'll drive you home myself,' he promised.

She scowled at him, then turned to me. 'How do I put up with him?' she asked.

I suppressed a laugh. She was going to be okay. 'You just do, Mrs Nankivell,' I said, taking her hand. 'He's only looking out for you.'

'Just call me Nan, dear,' she said. 'After all, you apparently did save my life. Not that these doctors know what they're talking about!'

Robert's eyes swung to mine and he sighed.

'Okay, Nan,' I agreed cheerfully. 'Hey, how about when you're up for it, you come and play the piano at The Rolling Scones? God knows that place needs some of your musical talent!'

'I'll say,' she readily agreed. 'I've been working on a new arrangement of "Those Were The Days" and it sounds so much better my way. You'll see!' Then, with regret, she looked at Robert. 'This one: he's the only one with no musical talent. God knows we've all tried to teach him at one time or another, but he's as useless as a pair of ice skates on a goat!'

I looked at him and chuckled as he lifted his eyes to the ceiling and sighed, but I could see the glint of humour in his eyes.

'You get some sleep, you old battle axe, and I'll see you in the morning,' he said, placing a tender kiss on her cheek and getting to his feet.

I kissed her other cheek. 'See you tomorrow, Nan.' I liked calling her that.

'Will you come back round for that cup of tea, then?' she asked me.

'Of course!'

'Good,' she said, satisfied, and nestled up for a nap.

Outside, Robert took my elbow. 'Thank you, Sophie. You may well have saved her life.'

'Is she going to be okay? I mean, like before?'

'Yes, absolutely. It was just a minor spell, and with the right treatment, she's going to be okay.'

'Good. I'm glad.'

He blew out a sigh of pent-up stress and smiled at me to reassure me. 'I don't know what I would have done had you not gone to see her,' he whispered, his eyes watering. 'That woman is my entire family.'

'You two seem close.'

'She is my mother and my father,' he said. 'Both my parents died in a boating accident when I was little, along with my aunt and uncle.'

'Oh, God, Robert, I'm so sorry…'

He shrugged. 'Some people in the village seem to think that I'm all cold and insensitive. Well, I'm not…'

I put my arm around him, something I would have never done in a previous life, but the situation called for empathy. 'I know. You've been very kind to me.'

'Even Sheila, my ex-wife, thought I was. I guess I never really showed her how I felt about her… what an arse I am.'

'You can still tell her,' I suggested and he snorted.

'Well, that ship sailed a long time ago. She left me and moved to Truro.'

'Oh. I'm sorry.'

'Don't be. She's happier, being married to a bank

manager. Apparently there's less work, more money and more glory.'

'Robert, your job is paramount,' I said. I really believed it.

He smiled. 'Thanks, Sophie. Go home now. I'll call you tomorrow.'

'Okay. Take care, Robert.'

'Will do.'

When I got home, I found Noah in the garden, working away at the system that fed water to the house. He turned at the crunch of my feet on the gravel.

'Hey,' he said. 'What happened to you?'

'Forget about it,' I muttered as I shrugged out of my coat. 'What are you so happy about?' Scratch that. He was always happy.

He grinned. 'I finally cracked the bastard!'

'Eh…?'

'There was nothing wrong with the cistern or anything except for a bunch of debris, but I've cleaned it out and now your water runs like a waterfall!'

He followed me into the house and turned on the tap as I slumped onto a chair in the kitchen. 'Look, see? Hey, what's wrong?' he asked, hunkering down before me.

'Huh? Oh, it's Mrs Nankivell. We had to take her to the hospital this afternoon.'

'Geez, is she going to be okay?'

'Yes, but I was really worried for a moment.'

'Can I do anything for you?' he asked. 'Get you a cup of tea?'

'Tea would be nice, thanks,' I said, suddenly very down. This was happening to me more and more. I thought I'd been able to shut down the empathy button, what with my own tumultuous emotions taking up the brunt of my energy, but I simply couldn't switch off my caring mode. I tried to ignore it, but it was as if I actually felt the suffering of others in my own heart, and to be honest, it wasn't a gift I was happy with. All I wanted was to make myself a new life, far away from the source of my own problems. I asked for nothing more, except for my freedom and for my baby to be healthy and happy.

'Here you go,' Noah said, snapping me out of my misery. He'd had the time to make the tea and place some biscuits on a plate and I hadn't even noticed.

'Oh. Thank you, Noah...'

'Are you going to be okay?'

'Yes, yes, of course. Have a seat and sip with me,' I said, trying to be flippant, but it didn't work.

He sat opposite me on the armchair and slowly sipped his tea. 'So, I was wondering, would you like to go to dinner some time? With me, I mean?'

I looked up at him. 'Dinner?'

'Just as friends,' he said hastily. 'I'm still new here and really don't know that many people, and you seem like a nice person.'

He was a nice bloke. Well-mannered. Kind. And I could use some company right now.

'That would be great,' I said, tucking my legs under me.

He grinned, his teeth white and straight. 'Yeah?'

I nodded. 'Yeah.' Why not?

'So, I'll give you a bell?'

'That would be nice.'

He drained the last of his tea and jumped to his feet as if his seat had caught fire. 'Great. I'm off, then! See you!'

I sat up. 'Oh? Okay.'

After Noah left, I sat, listless. I had been looking forward to a chat with him. With anyone, really. But I couldn't just ring people up and start chewing the breeze, could I? As kind as Emmie and her friends were, people had their own lives and their own worries. I certainly didn't want to add to their problems.

I fished out my mobile and dialled Tamsin's number.

'Hello?' she said. She sounded as if she was a million miles away, on another planet.

'It's me,' I whispered.

'Kate?' came her gruff voice.

I hadn't heard my real name in what seemed like ages.

'Where the hell have you *been*?' she cried. 'Are you all right?'

'I'm okay. The signal's pretty iffy at best here.' I had been lucky that I'd managed to call Robert about Nan. That would have been terrible otherwise. I'd have had to take action myself and... I shuddered at the thought of not being able to help her.

'If you would only tell me where *here* is,' she pleaded.

'I'd rather not, in case Will or the police ask you.'

'They have asked me.'

'What did you tell them?'

'That the theft and the blackmailing have absolutely nothing to do with you.'

'I'm so sorry I ran, Tamsin!'

'Well, it doesn't make you look good, with Will insisting that you are the thief. I quietly suggested to the police that he was having financial problems... so now they are also looking into him. He had it coming.'

'Thank you for doing that for me, Tams. You always said

I should leave him, but I could never find the courage, until the day I ran. I had gone to his house to break up with him, you know?'

'Good for you, Kate. God, I could kill him...'

'I am okay,' I said truthfully. I hadn't realised *how* okay I was. I was just a little lonely, but Emmie had promised to introduce me to even more of her friends. 'I miss you, though, Tams.'

'Oh, sweetie, we miss you too!'

'How is my little Jake?'

'He's great. He's always asking after you.'

'Give him a big cuddle for me. And Mike?'

'He went in for more chemo yesterday. He'll be okay.'

'Oh, Tams, I'm so sorry for leaving you at such a difficult time in your life, but it all happened so fast and I had no choice...'

'Kate?'

'Yeah?'

'We both know he was bad for you.'

I sighed heavily. Tamsin didn't need to hear any of this. She had her own problems with Mike.

'Well, on top of everything else that you already know, when I got to his home, it was full of women's clothing. And let me tell you, he isn't a cross-dresser.'

'The scumbag!' she spat.

'Yeah...'

'Honey, come home, talk to the police, I'll testify in your favour...'

'Tams, I can't risk it. I'm okay now. Really, I am. I've met some very lovely people who seem to be protective of anyone who lives here.'

'I'm happy to hear that, sweetie. But financially? How long can you live on your savings? Do you want me to send you some money?'

'I'm fine. I've got a job,' I lied. 'And I've rented a lovely little cottage.' If it weren't for her own troubled life, Tamsin could move down here too, and maybe find some peace herself. It seemed that people from broken homes attracted each other in life. 'Maybe one day, you can come and see me?'

She sighed. 'Does this mean you're not coming back at all, not even when your name is cleared? What about… about…' she floundered, looking for my oh-so-many reasons to be happy. '…everything else? Me and Jake?'

'You three are the only people I really care for in the world,' I croaked. But even as I said that, the faces of some of the villagers came to mind. Emmie and her daughter Felicity, for instance, and Mrs Nankivell. Even Robert and Noah.

Everyone else, Mum, Dad and my grandparents were but a distant memory now.

'Can I come and see you?' she asked. 'Just to make sure you're okay?'

I wasn't yet ready to tell her I was expecting a baby. It would be too much and she already had enough to worry about. I'd tell her later. 'The police are probably watching you. I am okay, Tams, really.'

'Okay. But just in case, you know I'm a phone call away. Just so you know, I'm listing you here as Maria.'

I chuckled. 'I've always wanted to be a Maria…'

'No, you haven't.'

'I cut my hair,' I said out of nowhere. Tamsin and I were like that.

'Good job. Although your honey-coloured mane was your trademark; maybe you should dye it too.'

'Maybe. We'll see.' Of course, it would make me disappear completely. I don't know why I hadn't thought of it myself.

'I miss you,' she said.

My throat constricted. 'So do I. I miss you and Mike and Jake…'

'Promise you'll call me, whatever you need?'

I nodded as if she could see me. 'Promise.'

When we rang off, I felt more homesick than ever. I felt *affection*-sick.

I wondered whether Mrs Nankivell was okay, so I texted Dr A.

How is she?

He texted back immediately.

What are you still doing up? She's rallying, thanks to you.
Go to sleep now. Rx

Aw. R for Robert and X for a kiss. How sweet was this man, and how much of an effort did he make to hide it?

# 10

The next day, I got a call from Emmie. 'Hey, Sophie! Are you dressed?'

'Er, sorry, have I forgotten something?'

'You certainly have! My friends want to meet you, remember?'

'Your friends? You mean The Coastal Girls?'

'Yes, but drop that name; it's so eighties! We want to take you out to lunch.'

My first question would have been, *Why?* But then I remembered that not everyone was as suspicious and closed off to the world as I was trying to be. They were very probably good people who were just being warm and welcoming.

So with a bit of trepidation we went to meet them at Pandora's Cove, which was more like a shack on the end of a pier than a restaurant. But inside it was cosy, with a blazing fire and the most comfortable, plush seats ever.

As I sat down, I was met by a group of beautiful and genuinely friendly faces.

'Guys, this is Sophie from London. Sophie, these are my crazy ladies, Rosie, Faith, Nina and Nat.'

'Welcome to Starry Cove!' chimed Nat, a short-haired girl. 'You'll love it here!'

'Good to have you!' greeted a pretty blonde. 'I'm Rosie.'

'Rosie is Penny's stepmother,' Emmie explained. She looked far too young to be anyone's stepmother, with a girlish face and the most beautiful eyes I'd ever seen.

As the introductions were made I tried to keep track. They were all so different and yet that same kindness shone out from them like an internal glow. I learned that Rosie was the mother of the young boy, Penny's brother, who helped tend to the horses at The Old Bell Inn. And that her Irish husband Mitchell owned a string of holiday homes down the coast which he'd bought after giving the inn to Penny.

Then there was Faith, an interior designer who was married to the, believe it or not, famous architect Henry Hudson. They ran a business together and she was stepmother to his boy Orson. I gleaned that the mother was sort of in the picture but not very well.

Next came Nina, whom I knew by fame. She was a Hollywood scriptwriter who preferred to remain in her native UK after having moved down from London. She had three kids, Ben, Chloe and toddler Charlie, and was married to Jack, who ran a cider farm.

Nat was petite like me, with short, dark hair and a fun, mischievous face. She was local but was now married to Shane, an Irishman with whom she'd had baby Hannah. They all lived in Lavender Cottage, which was just down the road from me, but closer to the coast.

They seemed intrigued by my presence, but in a good way. They seemed to understand my desire for a new life in Cornwall without asking me any prying questions about the reason for my move and my lack of a husband. Ideal, as those were the two topics I wanted to discuss the least.

After we ordered they asked me about my likes and dislikes and my opinion on things while offering loads of information on themselves, particularly their weakest points, which I found so heart-warming. They wanted me to know that there was no disgrace in starting over again. I learned that most of them had come from horrible previous relationships and that they had found solace here. That lifted my spirits to no end.

'Are you planning to stay long?' Rosie asked as our food arrived. Mussels and wine for everyone except me; I'd chosen lasagne and ginger ale. If that didn't scream *Pregnant Lady here!* I don't know what did. But no one seemed to notice and I couldn't help but grin. 'I hope so. I love it here! But I'll need to find myself a job.'

'What kind of job were you looking for?' Nina asked.

'Well, anything, really. I'm good at organising and planning.'

Faith hesitated. 'Vanessa's in need of a PA but I don't think—'

'That one's in need of a bit more than that,' Nat interjected, then grinned at me. 'Sorry, but she's the last one you want to work for. She's an interior designer but woah daddy.'

'She's been banging on about wanting a PA, but you probably don't want that job,' Faith agreed.

'I don't?' That would have been right up my street, actually.

'No, Sophie, you don't,' Nina said. 'I might have something, but it's boring.'

'Anything,' I said, veering on desperate.

'Well, my secretary is going away for two weeks and there's a backlog of audio notes that need to be transcribed. You can even do it from your own home if you like. Would you be interested in filling in for her? I promise I'm not as bad as Vanessa.'

I grinned. 'That would be ideal, thank you, Nina.'

'When can you start?'

'Tomorrow, if you like?'

'Perfect! Maybe come by the house and I'll show you my chaotic work process. I'll pay you in cash, if that's okay?'

My throat constricted. Emmie must have mentioned something to her, but she didn't make a fuss of it. She just wanted to make sure that I felt comfortable and that she would ask no questions. It was only for two weeks, granted, but any money would be a godsend. 'I promise I won't disappoint you, Nina.'

'Don't be silly,' she said. 'You won't.'

How refreshing, to have kind, relaxed people about me rather than the high-octane atmosphere at Wise & Templemann. I could feel my mind regenerating already.

As I dug into my lasagne, I looked around the table, thinking that these women could well become very good friends of mine, if I only I had the freedom to be myself.

The next day, I walked down to Nina's house. It was a

beautiful farmhouse that she shared with her husband Jack and their three children. They lived on an apple cider farm, but they also made pies.

After I was shown the ropes of the work, I sat down to the task of typing out Nina's voice-recorded notes on her Dictaphone. I sat at her PA's desk overlooking the immense orchard, the distant laughter of her children lost in the immensity of the grounds. What a way to grow up: happy and free. And how much had Jack and Nina achieved in their lives? Was I ever going to make something of my own life, I wondered? Would I ever be able to provide for Baby the way Jack and Nina had provided for their family?

It wasn't just about the beautiful objects around the farmhouse. It was about the atmosphere of love and togetherness that ran wild all over their home. There was a sense of security, of finality. *Love lives here and no matter what happens, we will stick together because we are a family.*

And to think how she, too, had had some very tough times. Based on what she'd told me about her own past before she came to Starry Cove, we had a lot in common. With a first husband who'd gambled away their kids' college fund, she'd had no choice but to pull up her sleeves and take a job catering for restaurants – alongside writing her novels – in order to haul herself out of debt. At one point, she'd had three jobs and everything would have fallen apart had it not been for her best friend and neighbour, Emma. And Jack, the farmer down the road from her place. When she'd received a call from Hollywood wanting to turn her latest book into a movie, life had finally smiled down on her. And she gave back a hundredfold.

*

It took me about a week to catch up with Nina's notes and start on her new ones. The tiny, battered table and wicker chair in the corner of my sitting room had become my work station. It gave me a sense of power, as if from there, I could manage and control everything.

'I can't believe how good you are!' Nina cried after I dropped by to give her a first sample of my work. I had put my all into it.

I shrugged. 'It's nothing, really.'

'Nothing? My own PA takes forever, but what can I do? I haven't got the heart to fire her. She's a single mum, so…' She cleared her throat. 'Anyway, how are you finding it here? Are you really going to stay?'

'Oh, definitely,' I nodded. 'I absolutely love it here. You people are all so kind and fun to be with!'

Nina cackled. 'Don't be fooled. It's not always like that. Listen, Sophie, I was thinking, when my own PA gets back, maybe you could stay on and share the work?'

My heart leapt for joy. 'Really?'

'Of course! She could continue doing her PA job and you could continue with the notes; how does that sound?'

'Like heaven. Thank you!'

She laughed and squeezed my arm. 'Come on, let's have a cuppa and a chat. I'm sure you need a break…'


The next day, just after Noah had left, the doorbell rang. It was Robert, bearing a huge jar of peanut butter. He knew my weak spot, this one.

'I thought I might come to keep you company,' he said when I opened the door. 'And to thank you for what you did for my nan.'

I grinned. 'You know, you don't have to bring food every time you come over?' I chuckled, stepping aside to let him in.

'Ah, but I come bearing the irresistible peanut butter, your favourite!'

'Well, in that case, you're always more than welcome!' I assured him as he plonked the box onto the table and shrugged out of his coat.

I reached for the sliced bread and popped a few slices into the toaster while turning on the kettle. I was happy about how the cottage was slowly coming along. With the electrics done and the piping completed, it was finally beginning to feel permanent.

Then, of course, the lights flickered and the kettle died as the toaster ejected four slices of untoasted bread.

'What…?' I whispered as the lights went out.

'Power surge,' Robert muttered as he marched to the circuit breaker. 'Surfer Sparky didn't do his job properly.'

'I'm sure he did.'

'Hm,' was all he said as he took the casing off and stared into the spaghetti mess of the cables. Surely, it shouldn't have looked that complicated?

'Why don't you leave it to Noah?' I asked.

He scoffed. 'I think I know how to fix a circuit breaker, Sophie.'

I shrugged. Who was I to argue?

'He gives you any grief, you let me know,' Robert said gruffly when I mentioned how much fun it was to have someone around the house. I hid a smile. *Men and their chest-thumping.*

'Aw, no, he's just so lovely,' I said, but somehow, he didn't seem too reassured. Robert finished fiddling with the wires in silence and the lights sparked back to life. As he replaced the covering, he cleared his throat.

'I came over as I sort of need to ask you for a favour, if it's not too much trouble,' Dr A. said.

'Of course,' I replied.

'My secretary is off sick with chicken pox and it's a madhouse at the surgery. I need someone to organise my appointments and generally hold down the fort while she's gone. Her entire family's got it and I'm at the end of my tether. It would just be in the mornings, and I would pay you for your time, of course. What do you say?'

I really had no reason to refuse, plus I desperately needed the money.

'If it's just in the morning, I can do it.' On top of transcribing Nina's notes, Nat had promised to put out feelers for any piano students I could tutor in the afternoons as I needed to make money anywhere I could.

'Great, thanks. You have no idea how much I appreciate this.'

So it was agreed. I'd work at Robert's surgery in the morning, tutor in the afternoon and Nina kindly agreed to let me work from home in the evenings. At this rate, I'd be bringing in something close to a decent salary.

# 11

May brought warmer days so I was able to finally kick off my shoes, don T-shirts and spend more time in the garden watering and admiring my flowers.

My first day helping out at Dr A's surgery was a hectic one. We barely had time to go over his system before I had hordes of women of all ages dying to get in. And it soon became apparent why, by the looks on their faces when Dr A came out into the waiting room.

They were, to put it mildly, enamoured with the wholesome village doctor. Who wouldn't be? He was a take-charge but kind man, and it was clear he genuinely cared about his patients. A good person to have on your side. And yes, he was quite handsome too. I wondered why he believed that everyone in the village thought he was cold and insensitive when this waiting room alone proved the complete opposite was true. Had his ex really done such a number on him? But that stuff was the last thing on my mind. All I wanted was to provide for Baby, and work was the only way I knew how. I had no time nor interest for anything else.

I spent all morning sorting out the mess that was the scheduling book. There were at least three people in every slot and I wondered what had possessed his assistant to do that. If I'd made a cock-up like that, Will would have had my head.

I tried not to think of him as I worked, but images of him kept creeping to the front of my mind. I didn't know when I would see him again, but I knew I couldn't stay hidden from him forever.

Luckily, Dr A.'s patients kept my mind off it for the most part. They were all lovely, some very quirky and original. Most of them brought in cakes and pies, for which Dr A gave thanks, asking them if they wanted him to become a big boy; they chuckled and gave each other bashful looks like teenage girls.

To be fair, Dr A. was very dishy in that old-English gentleman way, with that wholesome, trustworthy air about him. I could see why the ladies fancied him, flirting with him so coyly yet at the same time so brazenly. They'd throw an innocent-sounding innuendo at him and chuckle. I wondered whether he was seeing anyone, or if he was even aware of what his patients were doing.

After two intense mornings, we were running smoothly: his appointment book was full but operational. He even looked happier, more relaxed, and I felt pride in being able to help him.

'I wanted to thank you for stepping into the breach,' he said as he came into the office with two large bags full of parcels.

I sat back and grinned. 'What have you got there: peanut butter sandwiches?'

He grinned. 'Well, it's not peanut butter sandwiches, but I thought that to say thank you, I would get you something for the baby. Is that okay, or I am butting into your private space?'

'Oh! No, not at all. But you needn't... I mean... that's very kind of you. I...'

'Sophie,' he said. 'Let me be your friend.'

'You are my friend.' *Much more than many have been in my life.*

He grinned. 'Good. Now open up. There's just a few basics, nothing much.'

'Okay,' I said, pulling all the packets out of the bag. There was a cartload of onesies, nappies, cot quilts, a rattle, cot sheets, bonnets, baby bottles and a maternity calendar with medical appointments listed. And bottles of maternity supplements such as folic acid by the bush-load. Everything I could possibly need. 'Oh my goodness,' I whispered reverently. 'You've thought of everything! How can I thank you?'

He grinned. 'By taking care of yourself.'

I grinned back. 'I will. I promise.'

'Good.'

Each day that went by, I learned that Dr A. was a man with many layers, and the more you delved, the better he got.

When I got home, the lane was deserted as usual. The cottages all looked so pretty and well-kept, but in truth, I had no neighbours to speak of. I'd always yearned for a Cornish cottage and nice neighbours to chat with across the fence while hanging the laundry in the back garden. To talk about the weather or a new recipe for a cake. Simple things. Things I hadn't had in a long time.

For example, I'd always wanted a dog, but Will said that he was dangerously allergic, so that dream had disappeared. Now I suspect that, like everything else, it was a lie.

Standing in for Mrs Harris, Robert's secretary, had been more pleasant than I'd thought. In the space of a few weeks, people began to wave at me in the street. Mostly, they were mothers, young and old, who at some point had brought their children or grandchildren in. After they'd been seen to, they would sit down for a chin wag. I got the impression that I was becoming a celebrity: The Woman From Nowhere or something daft like that. I guess it's like that in tiny villages. They wanted to know, but never asked me directly. They were very dignified and warm. I ended up exchanging recipes with a few, while some others asked me to go to their homes and give their children piano lessons. They must have known that I was in dire straits and wanted to help. I couldn't have asked for more. With these three part-time jobs, I was slowly building my little nest egg.

And my students were so lovely! My favourite was Missy, who soaked up everything I told her. It was such a joy to teach her rather than the little brats whose parents had paid for lessons against their will, and who clearly couldn't wait to get back to mindlessly scrolling on their phones. But Missy was a treasure. And she was so intuitive too! She had an innate sense of rhythm and excellent discipline. She would go very far if she continued like that.

Word must have spread around because a woman I'd never seen before stopped me in the street. I mean literally stopped me by blocking my way.

'Are you the woman staying at Tulip Cottage?' she said.

So much for staying under the radar. But I was finding that I liked the attachments I was forming. I felt safe here.

'Yes I am. And you are?'

'Dr Armitage's wife,' she stated, a forceful edge colouring her voice. Even if we both knew she was his *ex* wife. But her message was clear. *Stay away from him.*

'Oh yes, he's my doctor.'

'He's *everybody's* doctor,' she corrected me.

*O-kay there.* 'Of course,' I answered amiably; she made no move to say anything more, so I side-stepped her and continued on my way. Poor Dr A. I guess we all had our problems. What a waste, though. Such a lovely man. Pigs before pearls and all that...

Despite my unpleasant encounter with his ex-wife, I got along swimmingly with the villagers, who were even starting to treat me as one of their own.

Just yesterday, at The Rolling Scones, I got another chance to slot myself into the life of the village. I was sitting at the table by the window, already envisaging the taste of some luscious carrot cake and a nice hot cup of coffee, my second and last for the day. But after about ten minutes of waiting, I realised that Daisy was on her own, boomeranging between the tables, without seeming to be bringing anyone their orders. She saw me and waved over the sea of customers.

'Hi, Sophie!' she called, running a hand through her hair, clearly frazzled. Not good.

I went up to her. 'Hi! Why's it so busy today?' I whispered.

'There's a choir in from Truro and they're ravenous,' she cried at me over their heads as if they weren't even there. Poor Daisy; she was on the verge of breaking.

'Can I give you a hand? I could go in the back and prepare the orders for you while Hugh mans the coffee maker?'

'Oh thank God, thank you, Sophie! Yes, go back there and prepare the orders but please, please don't tell Ralph or he'll fire me! He already calls me Ditsy Daisy and he's absolutely right!'

I laughed as I went to the back to wash my hands. 'No worries.'

*Back there* was an absolute chaos. Everywhere I looked, cakes and other sweets were all mixed up, some still to be iced, some still on their cooling racks. I sighed and got to work, cutting the cakes into slices and checking which cakes were cool enough to ice. The baker was in the very back, swearing at someone about the ovens. This was going to be a long day. But with a bit of organisation and a lot of courage, we could do it.

I spread out the little plates ready with their doilies and forks and spoons, easy for Daisy to access. If I'd had more time I could have been more careful, but on a day like this, it would have to do.

'Where's Ralph?' I asked Daisy when she popped her head through to retrieve her orders.

'He's in Launceston,' she huffed. 'And I've no idea when he'll be back. The baker's been yelling at me all morning and I swear, I'm about to quit this shitty job!'

'Now, now, Daisy, we can do this. Just hang in there a little longer. Look, you see how much easier it is like this? I'll get your orders ready for you.'

'I love you,' she blurted out before she disappeared. 'You are the best.'

'No,' I whispered to no one in particular. 'You are. You *all* are…'

Later that day, I popped into the village shop to get some milk and fruit. Just as I turned into the greengrocer's section, I slammed into a man and my carton of milk exploded in between us.

He looked down at his shirt and jumped back, his mouth a grim line.

'Oh! Sorry,' I said, looking up into his dark face, but I froze when I realised it was Rude Bloke. For a moment, I had doubted it was him because I actually hadn't got a good look at him until now. But there was no mistaking the long, lean body and the wide shoulders. And the silly beanie he insisted on wearing over his dark curls. Despite everything, I had to admit that now I could look at him properly, he was very handsome.

'Watch where you're going,' he muttered as he brushed past me, leaving me there with a squashed quart of milk leaking down my chest.

'Listen, Mr Manners,' I huffed after him, 'the first times we bumped into each other, you were a total arse, but I forgave you because I thought you might just be having a bad day. Now I know for sure that you're a jerk. So if anyone should watch themselves, it's you.'

At that, he looked over at the cashier and shrugged, completely ignoring me.

I watched him pay, have a jolly good laugh with her and leave with his little paper bag. And as he left, I felt a sense of dismay. God, what was wrong with me? Why did I care if he ignored me? Unless I had been *hoping* to bump into him? Why would I be doing that? And then it hit me. Was I *attracted* to this piece of work? Hadn't I had enough of horrible men? And wasn't my life complicated enough as it was? *New goal: avoid cranky but oh-so dishy Rude Bloke at all costs.*

I hadn't long arrived home to the cottage when the doorbell rang.

'Noah, could you get that, please?' I called from the kitchen as I was boiling the kettle.

'Company!' he shouted from the front room.

I hoped it was good company, after my encounter at the village grocery shop, not to mention the one with Dr A's ex-wife. And speak of the Devil, it was him: Dr A (not Rude Bloke, thankfully).

'If Mohammed won't go to the mountain...' he said with an apologetic shrug.

I rolled my eyes and my mouth spread into a smile. I had decided to not tell him about his ex-wife; there was no reason to upset him, or potentially jeopardise our newfound friendship.

'I've come to give you your check-up. Shall we head upstairs, away from prying eyes?'

'Oh! Sure, come on up,' I said, hoping that Noah didn't think anything untoward was happening between us.

Upstairs in my bedroom, he listened to my heart and checked my blood pressure.

'So how am I doing?' I asked as he removed the cuff from my arm.

'Excellent. Your blood pressure's gone down. You're glowing – and if I may say, you don't look so miserable anymore.'

'This place is miraculous.' I beamed at him. 'I'm quite well!'

'I'm glad, Sophie, truly. Listen, I want to apologise about Sheila.'

*Huh?*

He dipped his head. 'My ex-wife. This is a tiny village and people talk.'

'It's okay, Dr A. She was just protecting her territory.'

'But I'm not her territory anymore.' He blushed. Honest to God blushed. 'If it doesn't work, it doesn't work, right?'

'Absolutely.'

'And we have to get on with our lives,' he added.

'Of course. You have the right to be happy.'

His gaze became softer. 'We all do, Sophie.'

I wondered if he had someone else on his mind, but he was always so buttoned up. A real Mr Darcy!

# 12

## May 30th

'Sophie! Guess what?' It was Emmie on the phone, breathless.

'You sound happy. Did you win the lottery?'

'Better! A friend of mine who runs a food company is looking for a PA! I told him about you and he seems very interested. He said to send in your resume!'

'Oh my God, Emmie, what did you tell him?'

'That you are sweet and smart and trustworthy and organised as hell. He seemed impressed.'

'Thank you, thank you!'

'No worries! And the pay is excellent. In cash!'

'In cash? But how—'

'Isn't that what you were hoping?'

It was, but the fact that someone would be willing to oblige such an awkward demand sounded a little too shifty. Before I could question it, Emmie beat me to it.

'I know it sounds odd, but he's a good man. You do the work and he pays you. Trust me on this one, Soph!'

If someone had said that a few weeks ago, I would have

baulked. But ever since I'd arrived in Starry Cove, I'd been met with nothing but honesty and kindness. Perhaps I'd been wrong to be so wary. Being with Will for so long had skewed my ideas about love, about trust. Not everyone was out to get me and it had taken me some time to realise that. So could I trust Emmie? Of course I could.

'Absolutely! Thank you!'

'Okay, then! Write down his email. Have you got a pen?'

'Hang on,' I said, lunging for the biro on the sea chest as she dictated it to me.

'How the hell am I going to thank you for this, Emmie?'

'Ah, no worries! I'm just so happy I thought of it!' Just then, a shrill cry resounded in the background. 'Gotta run, Felicity's wanting her feeding.'

'Okay! I owe you one!'

'And keep an eye on your spam box!'

'Got it!' I grinned and put down the phone. A job! As a PA, my own territory! How funny was life? Just this morning, I was feeling a bit gloomy thanks to Sheila Armitage and now, look at me! Things were definitely looking up!

But oh. There was just one thing. If he hired me, I owed it to him to be upfront about the baby, if not about my real name. My pregnancy wouldn't stop me from working of course, but once the baby was born, things would change, much to his detriment. Maybe I could go part-time? But what good was a part-time PA? *Very good, if you knew what you were doing.* Listen to me, already dictating terms, and I hadn't even got the job yet. As far as references were concerned, I'd already had so many odd jobs around the village that I'm sure Dr Armitage or Nina would provide them for me. Worst case scenario, I could always ask Tamsin to cover my arse.

So I sat down to write a cover letter. But how do you address someone who hasn't even given you a name? I texted Emmie for the info.

She texted back immediately.

Oh, sorry about that! His name is Piers Henshaw. Good luck and keep me posted! Exxx

I stared at my screen for a moment, then started to type.

Dear Mr Henshaw,

Further to your conversation with Emily Moon please find attached my resume for the position of PA. I appreciate the opportunity for an interview with you.

I am reliable, organised and fluent in IT. I am very good at multi-tasking and always welcome a challenge.

My weak points are

I stopped. Where to start? *My weak points are that I am a fugitive from the police. Which is why I cannot provide you with my real ID or National Insurance Number. And did I mention that I'm pregnant?*

Scratch that immediately.

My weak points are that I take my work home with me and that I must learn about work and life balance.

This was absolutely true.

I fleshed out my letter, explaining how I could be an asset to his company, blah, blah, blah, attached my partially-true resume minus my last job for obvious reasons and signed off as professionally as I could, when instead I wanted to draw smiley faces with coloured pens. I didn't want to get my hopes up too high, but I had a good feeling!

For now, I decided to take one day at a time and not worry myself sick with all the tomorrows. A new life in Starry Cove, where one tomorrow at a time was good enough. But most of all, I wasn't willing to jeopardise my baby's life and wellbeing. I didn't want my child to turn around one day and accuse me of lying to her. I wanted something that I had never had for many years: a life without fear. A life where I was free to do as I pleased and not what was dictated to me by Will.

All I wanted was to have a healthy baby and stay hidden here in Starry Cove, away from London and the rest of the world. And maybe one day, make a living off my writing. I had several articles on my hard drive to present to the local rag. Or, when I gathered enough courage, maybe one day, I would actually sit down and write the book that had been in my heart since I was a child. Maybe.

But for now, survival was the priority. I was no idiot. I knew that even my simplest desire was going to be more difficult to attain than for others. For one thing, because I was completely on my own. But what I had been through had prepared me for just about anything. I wasn't afraid for myself, but for my child. I wanted it to be safe no matter what. And if one day, Will did manage to find me, I wanted to be in a position where he couldn't take my child away from me. He literally had no right to it.

No court on earth would grant a man like him any rights, especially once I spilled all the beans on what he'd done to me.

As I was pondering this, I got an email notification. It was Dark Skies! Piers Henshaw! Talk about alacrity!

Dear Ms Graham,

Thank you for your resume. If you would like to come in for an interview tomorrow morning at ten o'clock, that would be most convenient. The position is part-time, preferably in the mornings.

Sincerely,
Piers Henshaw
Rosestones Manor
Starry Cove

An interview! I thought it would take quite a while but here I was, going to my very first Cornish interview! And the job was in the mornings, to boot, so I could easily continue tutoring in the afternoons and doing Nina's transcripts in the evenings. I couldn't have asked for more.

I picked up my mobile and dialled Emmie's number.

'Is this a bad time?' I asked, wondering if she was busy with Felicity. I had recently started to think along those lines. Motherhood must be starting to enter my neurons.

'Of course not, what's up?'

'I got an interview with your friend Piers!'

'Oh, Sophie, that's fantastic! He'll positively love you! When is it?'

'Tomorrow at ten. Can you tell me where Rosestones Manor is?'

'I can do more than that. I'll take you up there myself. You don't want to get there all muddy and stuff. It's in the countryside.'

'Oh, Emmie, you don't have to—'

'Nonsense, I insist! Have you got an interview outfit?'

'Um…' I hadn't thought to pack anything formal when I'd been ransacking Sophie's wardrobe. One of those fancy cocktail dresses might have actually come in handy…

'Okay, don't fret!' she cried. 'Just give me a few minutes. Bye!'

And before I could open my mouth, she hung up.

Ten minutes later, she was at my door with Nat, lugging bags.

'Hi!' they chimed like twins. 'We thought you might need some help!'

'You look like my size,' Nat said. 'Is that okay?'

I let them in, my throat constricting. They must have noticed I'd been rotating the same few jumpers and T-shirts since I'd arrived, and had probably figured that there was not enough time (or money) to go and buy something new.

'You guys are too kind…'

'Nah,' Nat said. 'My husband is threatening to move out if I don't get rid of some stuff, and who better to wear it than you?'

They plunked everything down onto the settee as Nat started rifling through the bags.

'Now, with those eyes of yours, this green dress would look amazing. It has a matching jacket, just to give it that touch of workwear while actually venturing into elegant and classy. What do you think?'

I fingered the dress. It was gorgeous, made of fine wool. 'It's perfect,' I whispered. 'Thank you. I'll have it dry-cleaned after the interview.'

'No, no, you can keep all of this stuff, if you like it, that is,' she said as Emmie pulled out a navy-blue dress and matching coat. It was even more beautiful than the green one.

'But I can't,' I whispered.

'Oh, please, Sophie,' Nat begged. 'I can't bear to see anyone else wear this stuff. Please try them on and see what you think, at least?'

'You guys,' I said, shaking my head. 'Thank you so much. I have to tell you, though. I wasn't planning on saying anything yet, but... I'm pregnant.'

Silence, then:

'I knew it!' Emmie cried. 'How far along are you? You're barely showing, but I could just tell. Mother's instincts.'

'About three months.'

'And everything's good?' Nat asked. Trust her to be so discreet.

'It is.'

'Anything you need, Sophie, you just call, okay?'

'Thank you. You girls are true friends, and it feels so good to tell someone. I have a best friend at home, but she's got a lot on her plate already.'

'You haven't told her?'

I shook my head. 'She's got enough to worry about.'

'But if she's your friend, she'll want to know.'

'I'll tell her when things are better for her; her husband is ill at the moment.'

'Is there anything we can do to make things better for you?' Nat asked, reaching out to take my hand.

'Oh, you already have, infinitely!' I assured them. 'I never expected to find such kindness after… well, it's been tough…'

'Remember, we've all been there,' Emmie said softly. 'And it does get better, I promise you.'

'You girls have made it better. And Mrs Nankivell, and Dr A. He knows about the baby, of course, and he's been keeping an eye on me.'

'He's such a dear, isn't he?' Nat said, a twinkle in her eyes.

'Yes. He's very kind.'

'Will you want to know if it's a boy or a girl?' Emmie asked. 'Jago and I knew it in our hearts before any scan.'

I thought about it. Yes, I wanted to know. No more surprises. I mentioned I had an appointment to see Dr Chenoweth in Truro the following week.

'So I'll ask.'

'Oh my God, that's fantastic!' Nat cheered. 'Do you want company?'

'Oh, no, that's okay. I kind of need to do this one thing on my own.'

'Of course. We understand. I didn't want to tell anyone about being pregnant for months,' Emmie said. 'Eventually, I had to!'

We all giggled, but Emmie took my hands in hers, surprising me. 'Only someone who's been through stuff can understand you,' she whispered. 'And I've been through stuff, before I came to Cornwall.'

My eyes met hers. There was kindness and sympathy. But most of all, there was a kind of acknowledgement of... kinship.

'You're going to be okay, Sophie. You have us now, and we won't leave you on your own,' Nat said.

'You'll have to beat us away with a stick!' Emmie reassured me. 'Besides, these are all wool; they'll stretch and see you through years to come. Come on, try them on!'

There were several elegant outfits, all of which I could wear to work until I started showing. Nat and I were the same size, in effect. I might as well wear them while they fit.

'I'm going to think of a thousand ways to thank you both,' I said as I pulled off the last dress, a cream-coloured, cashmere wool ensemble. Chic yet simple.

'Don't be silly! Just go over there and knock him out! He's partial to elegance, you know?'

'He'd have to be, if he lives in a manor! I'm pretty nervous.'

'That's good,' Emmie said. 'It means you really want the job, and it will show. Piers likes enthusiasm.'

'How do you know him again?' I asked.

'He's a local. He likes his privacy, but he does a lot for the community. Charity and all that.'

Well, I hoped he had some charity while judging me tomorrow. I was already a wreck and had no idea how I was going to get through this night without falling apart from anxiety. I was very antsy lately. It had to be the riot of hormones raging inside me.

'Have you guys got any plans for tonight? Would you like to stay for dinner?' I asked.

'I'd love to,' Emmie said. 'Jago promised me some time with the girls so he's on Baby Duty tonight.'

'Shane's working from home so he'll be okay to stay home with the kids,' Nat said.

'Done!' I said and went into the kitchen to pour them some wine (that I had bought just in case) and whip up some pasta while they made calls home. I was growing fond of them, and revealed more about myself and my past today than I'd ever planned on. It felt good.

If only I could tell them the whole story...

# 13

## May 31st

The next morning, I was jittery and sweating buckets before my interview. Emmie had promised to take me and was due any minute. Just as I opened the door, a black BMW slid into view, softly crunching the gravel on the drive. I instinctively shut the door, my heart pounding. Will! Was it possible? How had he *found* me? Were the police with him? I bolted the door shut and cowered in the corner, tears of horror pricking at my eyes.

The sound of footsteps crunching over gravel was followed by the doorbell ringing.

'Hey Sophie! It's Nina!' came a joyful call from behind the door. 'Let's get you interviewed!'

I gasped. Nina! But Emmie had already offered. I wiped the tears from my face and flung the door open.

'Hey, you,' she said as I stepped aside for her to come in. 'Emmie couldn't make it, so I—What's wrong? Why are you crying?'

'I'm fine,' I assured her, but the look of true concern and

kindness on her face bored a hole in my projected coolness. 'I'm ok-kay…'

'The hell you are,' she said, taking me by the arms and guiding me to the settee. 'What is it? What's happened?'

I wiped my eyes and shook my head. 'Nothing. I just didn't recognise your car.'

'It's my friend Emma's. She's in town to plan a wedding. Sophie, you can trust me. What's wrong?'

'I know, I'm sorry. Later, okay? I'll tell you all later. Promise. But right now, I just need to get to my interview.'

'Then let's make tracks!' she answered with a smile.

I was so grateful for all this kindness. Where I came from, people didn't do people any favours, let alone unsolicited ones. Where I came from, it was mostly about jealousy, envy and scheming against others. As a PA at a legal firm, I was surrounded by it, even complicit in it. I felt ashamed for ever allowing myself to think that these women were untrustworthy.

'You didn't think we were going to let you schlep all the way up that hill on foot, did you?'

I laughed, the tension slowly ebbing out of me. 'Schlep…'

'Yes, sorry. I stayed in the US too long this time. God, I'm so glad to be back here in the land of mud and rain!'

Despite myself, I laughed again.

Nina patted my back. 'That's it. Come on, let's get going. Piers is going to love you.'

'You think so?'

'I know so. Got your bag?'

I nodded, reaching for my resume as well. I had no choice

but to continue deceiving everyone around me. And it was killing me.

To call Rosestones a manor was an understatement. With turrets and moats, enormous grounds with actual ha-has, not to mention gables, it was more like a castle.

'Wow' was all I could say as we neared the property.

Nina smiled. 'Wait until you get inside. There's a Minstrel's gallery, portraits, anything you can think of.'

'Is it open to the public?' I asked.

She laughed. 'God, no!'

Closer to the actual manor I stopped in awe under a huge arch, a topiary marvel made with yew and lavender under which rested a solitary bench that looked perfect for a lazy afternoon of reading. Only I wasn't here to read or be lazy. I was here to try and make a living.

'I know, gorgeous, isn't it?' Nina said. 'The manor is Elizabethan and has mullioned windows. All leaded. Six hundred separate panes. It was bought a wreck and Piers lovingly restored it all.'

'How do you know all this?'

'Because he let us shoot a movie here a few years ago.'

'Wow.'

'Only now he wants his privacy back.'

'I can imagine.'

'But you'll love working here. He's a great employer and a friend to everyone in the village. He also runs the farm, making jams and preserves of all kinds.'

It was difficult to believe that the man living there was as informal as the girls had said.

'Just be yourself and talk to him about your work experience,' Nina said as I stared at the site. 'You know the drill. I'm not saying the job's practically yours, because he wants to meet you first to see if you are a good fit or not. But believe me, you have no reason to be nervous. He's a real gent. So just relax, okay?'

*Relax*. This was my first job interview in more than half a decade and I had no idea what to do. Had interview protocol changed? I hadn't been able to glean much from my internet research last night. But I guess it was time to throw myself into the mix again. Survival of the fittest and all that.

'Okay, thanks ever so much.' I took a deep breath.

'You'll be fine,' she said, patting me on the back. 'Call me when you're done and I'll come pick you up. Good luck!' And with that, she drove off.

At the front door, I used the brass knocker and adjusted my silk scarf.

The door opened to reveal the most beautiful woman I'd ever seen in my life.

She was the kind of woman who was perfectly put together from head to toe, from her long, elegant neck to her waspish waist line, while her tan, suede skirt hugged her perfect hips all the way down to her tan stilettos. She wore tons of obviously expensive jewellery, and it all came together flawlessly.

Somehow, she seemed out of place in Starry Cove. Not that people weren't well-groomed, mind you. But she looked like a celebrity, and I wondered whether she might actually be one, and whether I should've known who she was.

'Hello, I'm... Sophie Graham,' I said and consciously ran

a hand over my own short hair, wishing I'd made more of an effort with it. She assessed me pointedly, then sighed.

'Please follow me.'

To keep up with her, I had to practically jog after her down a lengthy corridor as her long, black, silky hair swished from side to side.

If she saw I was lagging, she made no effort to wait. With each step, I convinced myself that I wasn't good enough to work in a place like this, with these practically perfect people, and by the time we got to the door at the end, I was freaking out.

'Come in,' she said, pushing the door wide open. 'Have a seat.'

As I did so, checking my surroundings, she sat opposite me.

'Mr Henshaw will not be able to take this interview,' she informed me.

'Oh. I understand.' Which I didn't, really. Hadn't he sent me an email to confirm?

At that, she smiled. 'I'm afraid you don't, Ms Graham. Mr Henshaw has very high expectations for his workforce.'

I opened my mouth to protest. I couldn't let it go. The old me would have, but not this one. Not the new me. 'I was sent by a mutual friend.'

'That may well be,' she condescended. 'Still, Mr Henshaw is not required to satisfy just anyone's request at the drop of a hat. We here at Rosestones Manor have very high standards. And I don't think you meet them. I'll have our chauffeur drive you back into the village.'

I stood up. 'That won't be necessary, thank you. I'll see myself out. Good day,' I chirped, and turned to leave before she could humiliate me even further. She had made it as clear as the waters in Starry Cove bay that I was not fit for the job, based on absolutely nothing except the way I looked.

What was it about me that had disturbed her so much that she wouldn't even reschedule an interview that her boss had set up? So much for being a gent, this Piers Henshaw. And his assistant, or wife or whoever she was, was no better. She hadn't even introduced herself.

I practically stumbled down the hill, dizzy with humiliation, my eyes stinging with unshed tears. But I would *not* cry, not this time. I had been through too much to let some lanky-haired snob make me feel ashamed of myself.

But in truth, she was the least of my problems. There must be some kind of misunderstanding. Mr Henshaw had been expecting me. I had come recommended from Emmie and the girls. What reason would he have not to see me? One thing was certain. I was not going to be treated the same way I had been when I worked with Will, as if I was invisible.

I lifted my chin up against the cold wind, my still unshed tears threatening to freeze in my bottom lashes. Let her have her moment of glory, whoever she was. She probably had nothing else in her life besides that pompous job that made her feel important. Well, I had bigger fish to fry.


'I can't believe it!' Rosie cried from across my tiny dining table while the rest of the Coastal Girls shook their heads in rage.

Nina had called my mobile when I was not waiting for

her outside Rosestones Manor so I'd had to explain what had happened. In my shock, I had completely forgotten that she had promised to return to fetch me.

'The *nerve*,' Nina said, shaking her head.

'I'm calling that piece of work up to demand an apology,' Nat seethed.

'Girls, please. It's not necessary. Obviously, he doesn't need anyone that badly.'

'Oh, but he does,' Faith interjected. 'That Patsy was wrong for him from the start. How dare she take a business meeting for him!'

'Well, it looks like Patsy knows his business very well. She carried herself like a celebrity.'

'Nonsense,' Nina said. 'She has no business whatsoever treating you like that. I'm calling him to let him know.'

'Please don't, Nina,' I begged. It was humiliating enough showing up on a recommendation and then being rejected, let alone having someone standing up for me like that.

Faith put her hand on mine. 'It's not just for you, Sophie,' she said. 'Patsy's had it coming for ages and I think it's only right that she be called out. Piers will not be happy when he finds out. She had no right to do that.'

I was suddenly getting very tired of all this.

When they left, I kicked off my shoes and slid onto the settee in one smooth move. Here I would stay for the entire weekend. No strangers, no walks, no novelty of any kind. I was done with trying, at least for today.

I settled down to watch some old reruns of *Dr Who* on an old telly Noah had found, the ones with David Tennant. I loved that man. He was so talented yet so humble. A bit like Dr A. I wondered how he and his patients were doing.

When I got over feeling sorry for myself, I'd peel myself off the settee and pay a visit to the clinic. Some of the women were very elderly and didn't get around all that easily, and it seemed like they'd enjoyed having a friendly face to chat with. I'd bake a few biscuits and maybe take them over there to keep them company.

The next morning, I got a call from Nina. I smiled, wondering whether she was still on the war path and loving her for it. They were all great girls, every single one of them, and I was lucky to have met them.

'So, I've got some news,' she said. 'Piers had been called away on an emergency and is livid that you were treated that way. He sends his sincerest apologies. He would like to get you in for an informal chat, whenever you want.'

'What?' If he'd been that livid, why hadn't he called me himself? You don't apologise through other people. What was it with this bloke, and why did everyone think so highly of him?

'He says to email him with a time and he'll have his chauffeur come and pick you up.'

'I… thank you, Nina. This whole thing sounds so weird.'

'Piers will be blessed to have you instead of that Patsy.'

Great. Just what I needed in this minuscule, idyllic village. A brand-new enemy. But I did need a job, and badly too. 'Thank you, Nina. I'll email him.'

'Good. Do you need anything? Jack is on his way into town.'

'I'm fine, thank you. I feel so lucky to have you all on my side.'

'It's nothing, Sophie, seriously. Now try to relax.'

'I will. Thanks again.'

The least I could do was appreciate her gesture of friendship and make good on it. So I emailed Mr Henshaw, who wrote back immediately:

Dear Ms Graham,

Delighted to put this unfortunate incident behind us.

Please accept my sincerest apologies and my chauffeur's assistance in escorting you to the premises on Monday morning.

Sincerely,
Piers Henshaw

# 14

## June 3rd

On Monday morning, I woke up at 5 a.m., showered for as long as the hot water lasted and then ran to my bedroom already freezing like a lolly. So much for the soothing effects of hot showers. So much for the Cornish summer so far.

I laid out the cream cashmere dress on my bed next to the file containing my resume. I'd chosen to leave the references as 'available upon request', as I still hadn't quite figured out what to do about them. But I'd cross that bridge when I got to it – I needed to get my foot in the door first.

Eating breakfast was absolutely out of the question, just as coffee was, so after a few hours of nail-biting and rehearsing my possible interview questions, I decided I was ready.

'You can do this,' I said to the nervous wreck in the mirror. 'Just get over there and stupefy him with your experience and skills.' After all, this was for Baby. And a future without Will. Without fear.

Justin the chauffeur picked me up at 9 a.m. sharp, and

the small talk he made on the drive did little to soothe my apprehension as we drew closer to Rosestones Manor. 'Mr Henshaw will see you now, Miss Graham,' he said as we arrived. 'I am to escort you to the meeting. Please follow me.'

'Thank you.'

I followed him down a long corridor full of portraits where ancient, pasty faces in wigs and people on horses smirked. Generations and generations of filthy rich people stared down their aristocratic noses at me like I was a useless waste of space until we reached a set of double doors at the end. The sheer scale of the place was intimidating, not to mention the luxury of it.

Justin gave a curt double rap and when a deep voice answered, he opened the doors and I was ushered into what seemed like the private offices of The Boss, and I didn't mean Bruce Springsteen.

'Please come in, Miss Graham,' the voice said and I stopped in my tracks. If I had been expecting a rich farmer with a flat cap and a pipe, I'd been dead wrong. Mr Piers Henshaw of Rosestones Manor was anything but a country squire. In fact, he was the horrible man with the cutest dog on earth, a.k.a Rude Bloke. Who apparently didn't even recognise me, or was choosing not to acknowledge all the times he'd been an arse to me.

Wearing a pair of jeans and a navy-blue jumper, he stood and offered me his hand with a kind smile. A *kind* smile? The gall of the bloke! Did he think that I was blind or that I had lost my memory? Was this how he wanted to play it: by pretending he had never seen me before? But I'd sussed him out, all right. And I knew what an arse he was. And yet,

I needed this job like I needed my next breath. And if I could pretend to be someone else for my own personal purpose, then I could also pretend I didn't recognise him either. My finances, and thus my future, depended on it. And as he was being kind and welcoming, I had to assume he was going to give me a chance.

He was taller than I'd remembered. Without the beard, the beanie and the shades, his face was lean and dark, with exotic eyes that studied me warily. Had he been spying on me? *Of course not*, I scolded myself. Was I paranoid or what? Why would a billionaire spy on someone as inconsequential as I was? There was no chance on earth he knew who I was. All in all, he looked like a no-nonsense bloke.

And yet, there was no mistaking, under that polite façade, the fact that he had an opinion on me and, just like Patsy, I could tell that it wasn't a good one.

'Please come in. I thought we could have an informal breakfast together in the orangery, if that sounds okay?' he enquired, politely enough.

*Orangery? Pulling out all the stops.* 'Ah, thank you, that's very kind of you.'

Mr Henshaw gestured for me to follow him and we passed several open doors onto magnificent salons, drawing rooms, lounges and even a library. All had crystal chandeliers and exquisite antique furniture. Slack-jawed, I took it all in. There was a serious amount of history here and I couldn't wait to learn about it. If I got hired, that was.

At the end of the corridor, we emerged into a bright room with huge potted plants that basked in the light that streamed in through the glass roof and enormous windows.

This place looked like something you'd find in a corner of Kew Gardens.

Mr Henshaw gestured to the large glass table that occupied the centre of the room. 'Please sit, Miss Graham.'

I took a seat and trained my eyes on him, trying to look serene. He studied me in turn and finally smiled, shaking his head. 'I can't apologise enough for what happened. I had no idea you hadn't been informed I couldn't make it. Please, can we start all over again?'

His smile was now genuine and far from the condescending one I'd expected. I could have mentioned the elephant in the room, that he had been absolutely hideous to me on several occasions, and why would I want to work for such a heel? But I needed this job, so I kept my mouth shut. If he had decided to pretend he'd forgotten our not so cute meet-cutes, what was the point in reminding him that I'd told him off at the grocery shop?

'Of course, Mr Henshaw.'

'Piers.'

I bit my lip.

'Look,' he said. 'Don't get the wrong idea about this place. This is a serene work environment. All my employees are nice people – you'll have to forgive Patsy's behaviour the other day as well. I have farmers; some take care of the livestock while others grow the vegetables. Others make the preserves that do very well in the open market. We are also a dairy and we make yoghurt, ice cream and Yarg, our Cornish cheese. As you can imagine, we are thriving, but I need someone trusted to coordinate all operations as I have suppliers and clients who all need attending to. That's the gist of it.'

'And what is your role? I mean, are you involved in the daily workings of the business or do you just let others—?' I asked before I could stop myself.

He looked at me in surprise and then grinned. 'You know, Ms Graham, I'm still trying to figure that one out. But in the meantime, Nina and the girls have told me that you're super-organised and trustworthy. That's pretty much all I need on a daily basis. No protecting me from bad news. You give it to me straight every single day. Okay?'

Of course. I was done lying and pretending everything was all right when it most definitely wasn't. So when Mr Henshaw asked me if there was anything he should know about me, I was going to be as honest as I could be without giving myself away entirely.

The arrival of two breakfast trays on a cart could have been the moment to be distracted and not tell the truth. But I soldiered on as Justin proceeded to dish up succulent sausages and bacon and pretty little omelettes and croissants and buttered toast, along with a pot of steaming coffee, the smell of which brought me to my knees.

'Thanks, Justin,' Mr Henshaw said as Justin withdrew the cart. 'This looks good! I hope you're hungry.'

'Yes,' I managed, wondering whether I was going to have morning sickness. I'd read that it was supposed to ease off by this point in my pregnancy, but combined with the stress and anxiety I'd been experiencing about the interview, I wouldn't have been surprised if it made a reappearance. That would have been a real treat, for me to heave up last night's dinner on today's breakfast table. But luckily, I managed to keep things under control and actually began to feel quite peckish. After all, I had been up since five and it was now ten past ten.

'And speaking of being totally honest, Mr Henshaw – Piers – I must tell you. I am pregnant, so I don't know how long—'

'That's not a problem,' he said as he dug into his omelette. 'I won't be needing you indefinitely.'

Well, at least he was upfront, too. 'Oh. Okay. I just wanted to be honest with you.'

'Thanks, much appreciated. Is honesty one of your best qualities?' he asked.

'I try...'

'And what about discretion? You come highly recommended, but I need to make sure.'

'In the sense of can I mind my own business and keep a confidence? Absolutely. I'm great at keeping secrets.' If only he knew.

When his left eyebrow went up, I rushed to make amends, but his upper lip had followed the rest of his face into a smile. 'That's good to hear. Not that I have any that would interest anyone. But I like my employees to be discreet. I don't want other people to know what I eat for breakfast or what I read in bed.'

As if I would be allowed anywhere near his private quarters. But still. 'You can count on me, Mr Henshaw. Piers.'

For a while, we ate in silence. He seemed to be deep in thought, and I didn't want to interrupt and potentially say something that could ruin my chances.

After what felt like an eternity, Piers put his cutlery down. 'Okay, then. Welcome to the club. You're hired.'

'I am?' I couldn't believe my ears. I had a job!

'You start at 9 a.m., Monday through Friday. Lunch is at one, but as you only work mornings you can leave then if you like. You can have as many coffees or snacks as you like. Just ring Justin if you need anything. *Mi* kitchen *es su* kitchen.'

I felt a huge pang of regret for lying to him when he was being so kind. No one wanted to hire someone who was wanted by the police. But I had no other choice. 'Thank you. I won't disappoint you.'

'No, I hope not,' was all he said. 'If you're finished, let me show you around.'

The word 'around' had been aptly used, as it seemed that we were going around in circles as he led me down wide corridors, up and down majestic marble staircases, past round rooms that appeared to be the inside of the turrets. I had kept up with the geography of the manor up until a few staircases ago, but now I was completely lost.

'And this is the parlour, where we have our gatherings,' he said.

On the threshold, I stopped with a gasp. A luxurious grand piano commanded the room, so black and shiny it reflected all the light. I made a step toward it as if approaching a glowing spaceship.

'Oh my God! Is that… a *Steinway*?' my voice came out a whisper.

Piers looked up, hands in his pockets. 'Huh? Oh, that. Dunno, it was here when I bought the house.'

'Do you play?'

'Me? Nah. You?'

I nodded, feeling the joy splashing my insides. 'I studied at the Conservatory.'

'Wow. So what are you doing being a PA then?'

I shrugged. 'I don't know. Lack of confidence, maybe. I haven't played in years. Except for when I teach my students, but not in front of anyone else.'

At that, his face lit up. 'Well. Maybe you can come in here and play sometime and I'll sneak in and listen to you.'

I was caught off guard and couldn't think of anything to say back.

He smiled. 'Come. There are a few rooms that are non-entry. Can you respect that?'

Not exactly the way I'd have phrased that question. 'Yes, certainly.'

'Good. You will be asked to keep anything you may learn about me strictly confidential.'

Now he was beginning to sound like a gangster. It was a good thing that the girls had vouched for him, otherwise with all this secrecy, I'd have been out of there like a shot.

As if I was one to talk.

'No worries, it's all above board, Sophie,' he said as if he'd read my mind. 'Nothing illegal. I'm just a farmer. But you must understand that I value my privacy very much, and that my business depends on it. Do you understand that? Can you respect that?'

Again with the respect. 'I can assure you that I am 100 percent trustworthy.'

'Yes, the girls said so. They think the world of you. And I need someone like you.'

'Thank you.'

'Can you start today? I'll show you the ropes.'

As he walked on, I tried to size him up. He seemed kind enough, likeable enough. But beyond that, I couldn't glean anything else besides the fact that he was wild about his privacy. Did he have business enemies? Was he working on a new, secret ice-cream flavour and was afraid of industrial espionage? I had no idea, but as long as it was above board and paid well, I was in. The girls would have never suggested this job to me if it was shady.

So I spent the rest of the morning going over my new routine in what was to be my office, a room that backed onto a secluded garden in the rear. It had a large desk and a beautiful, blue velvet sofa, and armchairs with gold-coloured threading that reminded me of Morocco. Hanging on the walls were antique prints and photos of actual Middle-Eastern landscapes, deserts and sand dunes, images that collided with the luscious English garden outside the enormous, floor-to-ceiling windows. And yet, it all came together very tastefully. There was a coffee table and a table in the corner by the window, presumably where the previous PA, Patsy, used to eat. Unless, hearing what the girls had said, she preferred to lunch with the boss?

'You can move the furniture around so it's comfortable for you. No one else will be working in here but you. I'll pop in from time to time.'

To see if I was earning my keep. Fair enough. 'It's perfect,' I said in earnest. 'Thank you.'

'Thank *you*,' he corrected me. 'I'm so glad to have someone I can count on.' Meaning that he hadn't been able to count on Patsy? Probably not, if the way she had treated me was anything to go on. I decided that it was none of my business: one of the reasons I was being hired was my discretion, which suited me fine. I wasn't interested in anyone's business but my own.

'And by the way, Sophie? I apologise for being an absolute jerk with you on several occasions when you first arrived in Starry Cove.'

*What?* So he *had* recognised me after all…

'I thought you were just passing through. But now that I know you're going to be part of the community, I have to come clean and tell you that I only did it to protect my privacy.'

'No worries, I understand,' I assured him. And I did. Maybe it wasn't the best way to go about protecting himself, but after today I couldn't help but warm to him, and if he valued his privacy half as much as I did, we'd get along splendidly.

He studied me. 'The girls were right. You can keep a secret.'

Better than he would ever know.

# 15

'**I** got it! I got the job!' I cried into my phone to Emmie.

'Oh, Sophie, congratulations! I knew you would!'

'And I have you girls to thank! We need to celebrate! Can I make you all dinner?'

'Aw, you don't need to do that...'

'But I want to! You've all been nothing but generous with me and I want you to know how grateful I am.'

Only... I was giving these kind people nothing in return. Not my truth, not even my real name. I was betraying the friendship and their trust in me, I knew. But it was all to protect Baby and our new start.

'I've been there, I told you,' Emmie said. 'You will get through whatever is ailing you. You have us now. You're going to be okay.'

I nodded, willing the moisture out of my eyes. 'I know that now. Thank you. Now, let me call everyone else—'

'No need to. I've just added you to our WhatsApp group called Coastal Girls. Whenever you need any or all of us, just send a message to the group.'

This was beyond kind. This was indeed what friendship felt like. So I went onto WhatsApp, found the group and typed in a text message:

Hiya! Got the job, wanted to thank you all by cooking at my place tonight, are you free? Bring partners and kids!

To which I got five immediate beeps.

NAT: Oooh, I'm in! Bringing cakes!
NINA: Bringing apple ciders!
ROSIE: Bringing party favours!
FAITH: Bringing a table big enough!

So I went out and did a food shop for two meat and one vegetarian (just in case) lasagnes, loads of grilled vegetables, and a huge mixed salad. For the kids, I made chips, and for dessert I got two huge pies, one apple and the other cherry, from The Rolling Scones. I didn't worry about how much it would cost me: soon I would have a regular income, even if it was only for the next few months.

For the kids, I made cupcakes with little frosted sailboats and beach huts, all in the old Cornish spirit. I even managed to make a couple with Squally Isle in the background, and a couple with the breakwater. For Emmie, the lovely girl who had opened her heart and shared her friends with me, I made an entire batch featuring her place, Books On The Barge, to which she later said, 'Ooh, they're too beautiful to eat!'

While I was finishing up, Faith dropped in with a

handsome, dark-haired man lugging what seemed to be folds of a table.

'Hi! Congratulations, Sophie!' Faith chimed and threw her arms around me. 'I knew you could do it! This is Henry, my husband.'

'Hi,' he said with a grin as he attempted to balance all the pieces of table. 'Nice to meet you.'

'You, too! Come in, come in! I know you mentioned a table but this is huge…'

'It folds down to a tiny two-seater!' Faith exclaimed. 'Isn't my husband an absolute genius? He used to be a carpenter. Shall we set it up in the garden? I've also got a chimenea in the car in case it gets a bit cooler later!'

'Ooh, great idea, thank you,' I said, beginning to wonder whether I was going to make a fool out of myself. I had invited all these people with nowhere to sit them, really. It was a good thing I did have a garden.

'And this strapping young lad,' she said while embracing a young boy under her arm, 'is Orson, my favourite boy in the whole wide world!'

Orson blushed and held out his hand with a bouquet of wild flowers. 'For you, Sophie.'

I bent down to him. 'For me? Thank you so much. You are a true gentleman, Orson!'

'Listen, we didn't know if you had any plates so Rosie gave me some to give you. She threw them herself in her own kiln!'

'Oh, wow,' I enthused, ashamed of my basic white plates and few pieces of cheap cutlery. I hadn't been planning on hosting any parties when I'd bought them, and they paled in comparison to Rosie's home-crafted ones.

'Orson, do you want to help your dad set up the table in the garden?'

'Sure!' he said and skipped off out the back door.

'Well, he's adorable,' I cooed.

Faith gushed. 'I know, right? I cherish him. He lives mostly with us.'

I remembered something about Orson's mother not being well but decided not to push. In good time. And again, I felt the sting of my deceit when they'd all been so open with me. I hated keeping things from them, but it was the way it had to be, at least for a little while longer.

'Why don't you finish up and I'll set the table? I've got all sorts of pretty samples of stuff in the car.'

'Oh, wow, thank you, that's so thoughtful of you,' I said. I wished that, rather than borrowing these beautiful plates and glasses and trays that Faith was unloading onto the table outside, I'd actually had the money to buy some decent stuff for this dear little cottage that I had grown to love. It had all I needed, i.e. privacy and safety from Will. I'd accumulated most of the basics over the past few months, but anything else would have to wait as I was saving up for Baby's crib, bassinet, clothes, and everything she would need for the future. There was no money to be wasted on anything else.

It was a wonder I'd landed a job at all, and I had my new friends to thank. They had opened their hearts and homes to me and for now, this was the best I could do for them.

The doorbell rang and in spilled the rest of the gang: Emmie, Rosie, Nina and Nat, all smiles and laughter as they brought their partners and children in. It was beautiful to see how love clung to these genuine people who hadn't let fame and success go to their heads. I was literally opening the door for national treasures such as authors, journalists, designers and architects, receiving them in my garden and feeding them my lasagne.

'Congrats, you!' Nina chimed, holding her toddler Charlie while following her two older kids, Ben and Chloe. Jack brought up the rear with a crate of his own apple cider. If only I could drink!

'Thank you,' I chimed back as Rosie hugged me with one arm while her son Danny arrived astride Mitchell's shoulders. Once he'd put the boy down, he gave me a squeezing hug as if he'd known me all his life. 'Well done, Sophie,' he said with a grin.

Next came Emmie and Nat together with their babies and Shane's girls, Amy and Zoey, who gave me a huge biscuit tin with a row of beach huts printed on it, the words *Starry Cove Delights* hand-written on the label. They were delightful children, all of them, who seemed really happy to be here at a stranger's house for dinner when they could have been doing their own thing at home or at a friend's. But here they were, so well behaved. It was obvious that these kids had been raised with love and respect.

'Just so you know, the kids have been instructed to not post anything about us online,' Nina assured me as they took out their phones and started snapping pictures of each other. 'They all have pseudonyms and know that we all need our privacy respected.'

'Thank you,' I whispered, relieved. They had gleaned that I had left ugliness behind me in London and were always swift to reassure me.

What a way to live, with terror sitting on your shoulder

all the time. But tonight wasn't about me, even if we were celebrating my job. Tonight was about friendship, and it had been such a long time since I had felt this rush of affection for anyone, but these amazing women and their families literally took the proverbial cake.

I simply couldn't deceive them any longer. It was killing me.

And another thing. Tonight was fantastic, and I was grateful. But seeing other families, happy families, only made me more acutely aware of my own situation. Because after I said goodbye to my friends and locked up for the night with no one to say, *They're all so nice, aren't they, honey?* to, I felt the loneliness descending upon me as thick as the darkness of the night sky.

## June 4th

The next morning, Justin arrived in a hatchback to pick me up. I hadn't expected anyone to come and get me, but I sat in the back while we listened to Vivaldi's 'Primavera' from *The Four Seasons*. It was very relaxing. Classical music had always been my favourite, but I loved almost every kind of music, as long as it was well-written.

After the last bend, Rosestones loomed ahead atop the giant hill, and my stomach gave a sudden lurch. My first day had just been getting familiar with the premises and the job tasks. But would I be efficient enough? Intelligent enough? I knew nothing about the job really, apart from the fact that I had to tackle daily issues regarding the running of Piers's companies.

'Mr Henshaw says to enjoy a nice breakfast in the orangery while he finishes up on the telephone. Mrs Watts, the housekeeper, will be waiting to meet you.'

'Thank you,' I said graciously. Justin was so gallant; he brought the best out in me.

*Another breakfast in the orangery?* I thought as I made my way down the familiar corridor. At least I had this part of the manor down pat. What was he trying to do, kill me with kindness? Or was this simply how the other half lived? I could get used to this, even though I knew I shouldn't.

'Good morning, Miss Graham,' came Mrs Watts's soft voice as I entered the orangery. She was perhaps around fifty, and petite, with intelligent eyes and a small mouth, probably what you needed to work for someone as successful as Piers. 'Pleased to meet you. Please come and sit down. We didn't know what you liked so I've made you a bit of everything.'

Just like the first day. 'Oh, Mrs Watts, that's so kind of you; you didn't have to do that.'

'Mr Piers's orders. He wants you to feel at home.'

'Thank you. It all looks delicious.'

'Do let me know if you need anything else,' she said before disappearing back to the kitchen.

'I will, thank you,' I half-called after her. The woman was a whirlwind despite her small stature. Efficient as hell. Like Justin. I was beginning to think that perhaps I had got in over my head. Could I be as efficient as they were? They didn't talk much, but they got the job done well, judging by what was under the lids of all the plates laid on the table. It was beautifully set, with linen and lace tablecloth and what looked like very antique china and silverware.

Mrs Watts had not exaggerated. There was a bit of everything, from yoghurt and muesli to ham and eggs to French croissants, omelettes and pancakes and humongous muffins that made my mouth water. A generous selection of jams and spreads and toast sat next to two large pots: one of coffee, the other of tea. There was also a selection of orange juice and apple juice and a red juice which I guessed was cranberry or something terribly healthy. This would do Baby a world of good! But could I be so brazen as to accept this again if it continued? I didn't quite know how to behave.

I thought I wouldn't have the stomach to eat, as nervous as I was this morning, but after my first bite of the fragrant croissant and a sip of the decadently delicious tea blend, I couldn't stop myself from sampling everything else, too. Just a bite at first, but by the time I'd finished, I was absolutely full. And then I panicked. What if I got sick all over the Persian rug? At least it looked Persian, and Faith had told me that only the best furnished Rosestones Manor.

I sat up and took deep, deep breaths, trying to not be sick on my first day on the job, which would have been my last as well.

'Morning. You're early,' came a deep voice at my back.

I jumped. 'Oh!'

It was Piers. 'Sorry, I didn't mean to startle you, Sophie.'

'Oh, no,' I assured him. 'I was just planning things out in my head. Lost in thought, you know,' I fibbed. *Great start.*

'Excellent. I *like* planners,' he said, plunking down a folder that was thicker than a doorstop. 'All the info about our company is in this binder. We call it the Bible. Codes, prices, our customers' contacts, our freight details, publicity. If you need help, here's a list of the departments and the numbers of everyone else who works here. You'll meet them at the weekly meeting tomorrow. Anything else, just call me on extension 100. Got all that?'

'Got it.' Where was everyone else? Were they working from home? 'So, am I to understand that I am the only one in the company, aside from Justin and Mrs Watts, working here on the premises?'

He grinned. 'Sophie, you are officially Headquarters. We should call you Miss HQ.'

I gulped. 'Great. Let's get to it, then.'

'Have a great day,' he said. 'See you later.'

As it turned out, I managed to get through a full morning of phone calls without asking anyone for help. Granted, they were easy questions about delivery schedules of our goods. I mean *his* goods. All I had to do was look at the online spreadsheet that the Freight department had uploaded and relay the information. A piece of cake.

And speaking of, I'd completely forgotten to end my workday at lunchtime because Justin had brought me a delicious meal of roast chicken, potatoes and peas on a tray. I was ravenous. If I didn't eat anything, I would seem ungrateful, but if I ate it all up now, before leaving, I'd seem like I was a down and out. *Not too far from the truth until a few days ago*, I mused with a snort.

I was still there because after lunch, one call to a supplier had led to another and I found myself prepping my groundwork for tomorrow. It would be easier that way. When I put the phone down, as a reward, I popped a mini quiche into my mouth. The last one of the day, I promised myself.

'Sophie?' came a voice from behind me.

I whirled around, my mouth still full of quiche. I tried to swallow as Piers came into the room with a grin. 'Sorry, didn't mean to scare you. Again.'

'Hmmm...' I uttered, trying to chew as fast as I could, waving my index finger. 'Then you should knock.' *Chew, chew, chew*. 'Not that you need to knock in your own house, but still, a girl could have a heart attack.'

He laughed as he came to sit on the edge of my desk. Or rather, *his* desk.

'So how did it go? Getting the hang of it?'

'Easy-peasy,' I lied. The day, although successful, had taken it out of me. I was absolutely depleted, knackered, exhausted, but I wasn't about to tell *him* that. I wondered how I was going to manage to make it to the end of the week if every day was this hectic. I'd had no idea that apples and fruits and potatoes and stuff had all these uses, even cosmetics. Clever man. No wonder he was so successful.

'Why are you still working?' he asked casually.

'Well, you know, I had a few issues to solve that needed time.'

'Thanks for doing that, but you didn't have to stay. I'm sure whatever it was could have waited until tomorrow. Although I like your enthusiasm. So I can count on you coming back?'

'You bet. Today has been... rewarding.'

'Great. Ask Justin to drive you home when you're ready.'

'Oh, no, that's okay. I'll walk.'

'You sure?'

'Positive.'

'Have it your way. See you tomorrow, then. Remember we're having a meeting tomorrow at nine, first thing.'

'Right.' I smiled. He smiled back. And it became kind of awkward. 'So I'll be off, then,' I said.

'Right.'

I gathered my bag and coat, and was off, conscious of his lingering gaze.

Once outside, I made my way through the front grounds to the main gate. Out of the fairytale and back on the dirt road, I scarpered back down the muddy hill and into the village. Might as well stay active while it was easy.

And oh, was I ever glad I did walk, because everything around me was magical! The air was crisp and clean, fairy lights and gas lamps flickered all along the way into the village, welcoming me in the warmest of hugs. Perhaps the girls had been right. Perhaps now I could begin to finally round the corner in my life. It was amazing how good a healthy dose of optimism could do to your soul. I felt like a million pounds. I couldn't recall the last time I had felt so good about myself.

This called for a nice cup of tea and a slice of cake. A *slab* of cake, even! So I snuck into The Rolling Scones and found a table by the window. As I waited for Ralph to come round to me, I had a good look about the place. In the corner at the old piano sat an elderly woman playing some old classics.

I watched her, pleased at how well she played, despite her obvious physical afflictions. A huge hump kept her bent forward in a very uncomfortable position, her face almost touching the keys as if she was trying to see the atoms moving around. How could she bear sitting in that position for so long, poor dear? I wondered about talking to Dr A about her, but then thought to myself that I should really mind my own business.

And yet, she played so beautifully that I had to wipe a tear from my eye. What the heck was wrong with me lately? Was it my pregnancy hormones wreaking havoc? Or was I not quite as serene as I told myself I was? Of course, I was worried about Baby's future, about how I would support her and all, but I thought I'd talked myself out of all that. I was smart. I was resourceful. I was going to make it.

'Well, as I live and breathe!' came a laugh from behind me. I whirled around to see Noah. 'Does this mean I can buy you a cup of coffee?'

'Noah, hi!' I chimed. 'Only if I'm buying! Please, sit!' I needed someone to share today's success with. I had actually made it through the day without making any mistakes. I'd come off as confident and competent as I had been on my old job, despite Will's efforts to convince me otherwise.

'What are we celebrating?' Noah asked as he slid into the seat opposite me, his eyes mischievous.

'My new job!' I blurted, then paused to try to remember. Was I allowed to say I worked with Piers? He hadn't actually said that I couldn't, had he? Or what if he had, and it came out that I'd blabbed his confidential secrets (not that I knew any) all over town? No, he'd told Emmie about the job, and the girls and their families knew. Besides, I didn't think Noah had anyone to tell even if he wanted to.

'Well, congratulations, then!'

'Hello, luvvie,' said Ralph as he got to our table and set

his eyes on Noah. 'Isn't it enough that you see Sophie every day at the Nankivell place? Why are you bothering this lovely young maiden on her tea break?' he asked of him, then slid me a grin. 'Beware of this sly fox, Sophie,' he said. 'Noah's too charming for his own good.'

At that, Noah spread his arms in a fake plea, his smile bright. 'Who, me? C'mon, Ralph, everybody knows I'm harmless! Plus, I have a girlfriend!'

'Now *that* would be the day!' Ralph answered, then winked at me. 'Have a care, luvvie. There ain't no one immune to his charms! So what are you wanting today?'

'I'd love a cup of your lovely tea with maybe… a slice of your delicious carrot cake?'

'Gotcha. And you, lover boy?'

'Same again,' Noah said.

'We just run out,' Ralph said, not looking up from his writing pad.

Noah looked over at the counter where there was an entire carrot cake, then back at him. 'Ralph. Seriously?'

'Nah, just kidding you,' Ralph answered, nudging him. 'But you shouldn't be bothering maidens who have already been spoken for.'

Something akin to terror shot up my legs, landing in my stomach with a thud. How could he possibly know about Will? Or had he simply found out I was pregnant and figured I was already taken?

'I'm not spoken for.' I laughed to allay the arctic atmosphere that had suddenly descended upon our table. 'Nor am I looking, so it's all good!'

'I heard otherwise, luvvie. Some'un's on your tracks.'

I felt my mouth fall open. 'Who…?'

Ralph shrugged. 'I'm not minded to say. But you can believe there is.'

He said it conspiratorially, like I was in on the secret, but I thought I detected a hint of malice. Was it Will? Had he finally found me? Or was I being paranoid, reading something into this conversation that wasn't actually there?

I *knew* I wasn't going to be able to live without looking over my shoulder for the rest of my life! It was impossible, even for the most hardened criminals. Perhaps it would have been better to call the police and tell them I was wanted in London, but that I was innocent. But what proof did I have, and against Will's word? Not a good idea after all. I couldn't *believe* how short-lived my joy had been! I gathered my coat and bag and stood up, all the energy and enthusiasm instantly drained from me.

'You know what, Ralph, please cancel my order.' To Noah, I said simply, 'I'm going home, sorry.'

Noah followed me out of the café. 'Hey Soph, did I do something wrong?'

'No,' I said, but what the hell did I know? For all I knew, he could have been a private detective hired to find me. Showing up to this town out of all of them, with this supposed 'girlfriend' of his nowhere in sight.

'Can I drive you home?' he offered. 'It looks like it's going to rain.'

I turned around and faced him. 'I'll be all right, Noah. Thanks anyway.'

'What about our dinner? Is it ever going to happen?'

'I'll give you a call,' I said over my shoulder as I opened the door.

'Sophie, remember, I'm your friend.'

'Yep.'

All I needed was to find out who this person Ralph mentioned was. Anyone could be a threat to me at this point. Especially Noah, who I'd let have unadulterated access to my home with hardly a second thought.

# 16

I spent an age talking myself off the ledge. Yes, I had to be careful of who I got close to. But Noah was a good bloke; there was no mistaking the kindness in his eyes and in his voice. What a way to live, suspecting everyone around me.

And as far as a secret admirer was concerned, there was no way on earth that I was going to get involved with someone new any time soon. Not after what Will had done to me, and certainly not when I had Baby to take care of. I was going to put all of my time and energy into raising her, and that would leave me no time to seriously date.

As I was heading home, I heard my name being called. I whirled around to see Dr A.

'Hello Dr Armitage!' I called back, stopping for him to catch up with me (I could never call him Dr A to his face). 'How is your grandmother?' I asked. 'When can I come and visit her again?'

He grinned. Such a rare sight, and good to see. 'She's getting better every day. Of course you can come and see her. I'm on my way there now, if you'd like to join me?'

'Oh, yes, please!'

'But I've told you before, please call me Robert. I think we're friendly enough for that now, what with you seeing my embarrassing excuse for organisation down at the clinic.'

I'd never been on a first-name basis with a doctor before. I blushed; I don't know why. 'Okay, then... Robert.'

'Come on, then,' he said, taking me by the elbow. 'I'm in desperate need of a good cup of tea.'

The afternoon was a pleasant one; Nan regaled us with stories of when she was young and all the lads she had enthralled in her day, her wrinkled eyes twinkling with nostalgic delight. When Robert offered to walk me home to help me carry all the parcels she had bestowed upon me, I refused, telling him to stay and enjoy his quality time with her.

'Are you sure?' he asked, rather miffed, it seemed.

'I'm sure. She needs you.'

He shrugged, and together they stood on the stoop, waving. Nan was beaming, and I had the distinct feeling she was trying to play matchmaker, but rather than finding her invasive, I found her endearing. Just an elderly grandmother who wanted a girl for her grandson. I would cherish her just as he did.

I turned around to wave once more, almost dropping the carton of eggs she had slapped down onto the pile in my arms as a final gift.

The warm day had turned into a very cool evening. It looked like there was going to be a thunderstorm. Would summer ever properly arrive? When I got home, I took off my boots and changed into a pair of leggings, the thickest wool socks I could find and a huge jumper, ready to batten down the hatches against the worsening weather and the storm that was looming, not to mention the one looming in my life. Was there someone out there looking for me, as Ralph had seemed to imply, and could it be Will or the police? Which reminded me: time to give Tamsin another call.

I padded into the kitchen and flicked on the kettle. It seemed I was running on tea, lately. Better get some decaf tea. I would feel better once I'd spoken to my only friend from my past.

It rang a few times before her voicemail kicked in. I cleared my throat. 'Hi, uhm, Tams...? I hope you're all okay? Just wanted to let you know that I'm okay, too. Better than the last time we spoke. I'm really sorry not to be able to tell you anything else, but I can't compromise you in case Will asks again.' I laughed bitterly. 'Because he will ask you again. Not that he cares, of course. He just wants to find me and have me thrown to prison in his stead. To show me that he's smarter. That I have no say in my life.' The kettle boiled and flicked off loudly in the quiet kitchen. 'Well, you know what? He's not the boss of me. I've got a job, and a house. I'll be okay. Talk to you soon. Give my love to yours. Bye...'

I hung up before the knot in my throat grew. I didn't want to go down that road again where I started thinking about her and how I'd disappointed her by running away. I should have been able to tell my best friend what was happening in my life. But for her sake, it was best if I kept it from her. At least for now.

I poured the tea and peered into the fridge. Not much dinner material in there. Perhaps I could make myself a sandwich, or even an omelette with Mrs Nankivell's eggs? She may be batty, as some affectionately say, but she did have a heart of gold and she was the first to glean that something was amiss. I had to learn to look confident. Happy, even. I would be happy, if I didn't have this sword of Damocles hanging over my head.

## Wednesday, 5th June

The next day, at nine o'clock sharp, Piers buzzed me from his office.

'Morning. Ready for the meeting?' he asked, his deep voice reaching some hidden part inside me where dreams and happiness still managed to exist. Goodness me, where had that come from? What did Piers have to do with my happiness?

'Certainly.' I was actually rather nervous about meeting everyone else; I got the impression that everyone else had been here since forever. What if they didn't like me? What if they thought I wasn't good enough to be Miss Headquarters? 'Where is it?'

'On Google Meet. I'll email you the code.'

'Oh.'

'You didn't think it was going to be in person, did you?' he asked.

'Uhm, no, I guess not.'

He chuckled. 'We're a modern company, Sophie.'

'But if everyone is local…?'

'Ah. Local but very busy. Sending you the code right now. See you online.'

Before I could answer, he buzzed off, and my laptop pinged with an email. I clicked on the code and then on *Join*, and was amazed to see how many picture boxes appeared: at least thirty. All these people worked for Piers? Doing what? Perhaps I had underestimated the scale of the company. Perhaps I really wasn't fit to coordinate everyone else. Reality started to sink in and I had to force myself not to slump in my chair as Piers greeted everyone and introduced me as the new voice from yesterday: Miss HQ.

They all introduced themselves and their departments in turn as I thought, *Oh God, all I wanted was a simple job, not to be coordinator of the Cornish Del Monte!* I was way in over my head.

I tried not to panic and concentrate on the conversation, which was mainly about the chase-ups made on Monday by every department and where we were at with produce, shipping, etc. It sounds boring but I was fascinated by how many people around the world were interested in buying Cornish products, and particularly his.

And then a familiar, friendly face popped up. Nina's husband. 'Jack!' I almost cried out. Good thing I'd muted my microphone.

'Hi, everyone, sorry I'm late. Hi, Sophie! Fancy seeing you here!'

I felt instantly at ease. I wondered why Nina hadn't mentioned it before, but maybe it was supposed to be a nice surprise, to see a friendly face. Jack was one of the good ones. Not that anyone had been bad. I just had issues with dealing with new faces, and so many of them all at once. God, just how many faults did I actually have?

As it turned out, I impressed even myself with how well

I handled the meeting. When asked about deadlines and shipment updates, I actually had answers, and without even having to look them up! I remembered the names of the companies I'd dealt with and even whom I'd spoken to from said companies. I was on a roll, feeling my ears burn with something between shyness and pride as I related the info. When I was done, I sat back, turned the microphone off and let out a sigh of relief, hidden behind a cough.

'Excellent,' Piers said before grilling someone else. *Yes!*

Around lunchtime, Piers buzzed me again. I could definitely get used to this, hearing his voice every other minute. What was going on with me?

'Yes?' I answered.

'It's sunny outside, so I thought we could take advantage of it. I've got a couple of sandwiches here. Mind if we go for a walk around the grounds?'

Uh-oh. Something was up; I could tell from his voice. Had I screwed up?

'Of course not, that would be great,' I croaked, my heart rushing to my throat.

'Okay.'

Why this sudden outdoor lunch? Was he about to fire me and wanted to get me as far as possible from the house? I'd heard about people not going willingly and making a scene, but really?

And I suddenly realised that perhaps I'd allowed myself to get too comfortable too soon. I had projected a confidence I didn't feel, and now the gig was up.

'Meet you at the front door in five?'

'Sure,' I said, my stomach churning so badly, I knew I wouldn't be able to eat a thing.

As it turned out, Piers had a huge picnic basket. 'I hope you're hungry,' he said with a grin that had nothing apologetic about it. Not even a tiny bit of remorse for wanting to fire me?

'Starving,' I lied as I followed him out the huge double doors and out onto a gravel path. Actually, I was so tense, I was afraid I was going to throw up right into his perfect borders.

'Have you had breakfast? You look pale,' he said.

All this worrying and fussing was only making it worse. 'Is everything okay?' I blurted out. Might as well make it short. 'Am I not doing well?'

He stopped, his face blank. 'You're doing wonderfully,' he was quick to reassure me. 'Did I give you the impression that you weren't?'

I shrugged. 'I'm not sure.'

'Or was my invitation too forward? I just want to get to know you a bit better, Sophie. I'm on solid ground with all my employees and I wanted to do the same with you.'

*Ohthankgodinheaven!* I still had a job! I could keep the cottage! I didn't have to run away again! Trust me to still assume the worst of every situation, when Starry Cove had shown me time and again that good things really could stick.

'That's very kind of you,' I murmured, unable to muster a proper voice.

'So, Jack tells me that you helped Nina with her work.'

'Oh? Yes. She's amazing. They both are.'

'They think the same of you. As a matter of fact, everyone who knows you thinks the same.'

I felt my cheeks burn. I wasn't used to compliments,

especially from someone so important. I really must have done something right to impress someone along the way, but I couldn't figure out what it could have possibly been. Of course I did my job, but who doesn't?

'They tell me that Dr Armitage seems to think the world of you, as well.'

'Well, I think he's great, too,' I confessed. 'He got the cottage sorted out so I could stay, even if it wasn't in mint condition when I got there.'

He chuckled. 'Old Nankivell is a dear. Batty, but a dear. Like grandmother, like grandson. Not that Robert is batty. He's actually very competent.'

I wondered where this was going. 'Is he your doctor too, I'm assuming?' I asked, seeing as he was the only one in the village.

'I haven't seen a doctor in years,' he said. 'Are you seeing him?'

I stopped amidst the copse of evergreens. I'd already told him I was pregnant, so he must have meant... 'Do you mean like *that*? No. Dr A and I are only friends.'

'Right. But you know, things happen. Sometimes friendships turn into something more.'

Where was he going with all this? It sounded like he was asking me how well I knew Robert. Why didn't he ask him?

'So you two aren't friends, I take it?' I asked.

'It's complicated. So, the two of you are not going out, then? Sorry, it was a bit naughty of me to ask out of nowhere. Apologies.'

I slid him a glance. 'I'm not dating anyone,' I said softly. 'My life is a little complicated at the moment. I've no time for romance.' And yet, as I said it, I knew I was lying.

I wanted nothing more than to have someone caring to share my life with. Yes, I was busy all day with the job and piano lessons and transcribing and all, but when I got home after a long day and closed the door behind me, it always sank in deep. I hated to admit it, but I was lonely.

He was silent, which was just as well as we meandered through the long and winding paths that weaved from copse to copse, stopping to admire this border or that bush.

In a romcom, this was the moment in which the bloke would have stopped and taken the girl's hands, his eyes boring into hers, and he'd have given her the mother of all kisses. Just for the sake of it. But because this was reality, and particularly *my* reality, every time Piers asked to speak to me in private, I was afraid the gig was up and that he'd send me packing.

'These grounds are amazing,' I said to distract myself as we came upon the ha-ha.

Piers stuffed his hands in his pockets. 'Yeah, I guess it all kind of grows on you. Come this way.'

I followed him in silence until we reached a gazebo. Although gazebo was an understatement. It was a round structure with a huge chimenea in the centre and lined with two half-circle-shaped sofas absolutely drowning in cushions. In front of each sofa, there was a coffee table and foot stools. All around were fairy lights and if ever there had been a winter wonderland, this was it. I almost expected Santa to fly over us even if it was nowhere near Christmas.

'Oh my goodness,' I breathed. 'This is beautiful!'

He grinned and took my arm. 'Come,' he said and we sat on the sofa as he began to divest the picnic basket of its contents.

'I'm glad you're starving, because I've got loads here. But first, a nice iced tea to cool you down?'

'Ooh, yes, please!' I chimed, wiping the sweat off my brow. Despite the summer storms, June was slowly starting to sizzle, catching me unawares. Plus this pregnancy thing was messing with my body every day now. I went from hot to cold, tired to energised, in two seconds flat.

'Here you go, then,' he said as he poured me a huge glass from a thermos and added a slice of lemon.

I watched, transfixed, as he pulled out a couple of deep ceramic bowls and silver spoons and linen napkins, crunchy bread, a selection of cheeses and quiches of every shape and size. There were also mini meat pies and an assortment of fancy vegetables on the side. How exquisite!

'This is tabbouleh, an Arabic dish. I hope you like it?' he said. 'If not, there's mushroom soup or simple tomato soup. Mrs Watts is an excellent cook.'

My stomach grumbled and I laughed. Now that my livelihood was no longer on the line, my appetite was back with a vengeance.

'Tabbouleh is perfect, thank you. And so, so kind of you, Piers,' I said as I took the tray from him.

He shrugged. 'It's nothing.'

*Do you do this for all your employees?* was a question that came to mind, but I thought better of it. I couldn't deal with either answer. It would be disappointing if the answer was yes, but also if it was no. My unrequited need to be acknowledged and appreciated all these years had led me to be somewhat insecure about myself, I knew that. But I was no good at flirting in general, let alone with my own boss. Not happening. That was how I'd got into trouble in the first place. I'd tried to resist Will's charm, but he'd been an avalanche of wooing and roses and fancy dates. In the end, I'd simply capitulated, convinced I had feelings for him. Well, that had served me right. This time I'd be careful.

Piers and I ate and chatted, touching every topic in the book. He asked me about my childhood and my family, where I went to school and where I used to vacation. Hobbies, likes, dislikes, he asked me everything. Piers was incredibly charming, and talking with him felt natural, as if I'd known him for a long time; I had to be careful not to get too comfortable, lest I revealed anything that could tie me back to London.

When, in turn, I asked him about his childhood, he was a little reticent of sharing too many details. I guessed he'd had a terrible time growing up and didn't want to relive it. I knew, from looking at Will's life, that money did not perform miracles. He'd had a terrible childhood and it showed in everything he did and said. It was only later in our relationship that this anger was turned on me.

'You okay?' Piers asked. 'You've suddenly gone quiet.'

'Oh!' I said. 'I'm sorry, it's just that I haven't spoken about my childhood in ages.'

'Do you still miss your mother? Have you forgiven her for walking out on you and your father?' he asked softly.

I sighed. 'I didn't think I'd ever forgive her. But now that I'm expecting, I wish she were here. I wish I could talk to her, but she's disappeared off the face of the earth.'

'Have you tried hiring a private investigator?'

I shook my head. 'No. If she doesn't want to be found, I have to respect her wishes.'

'So you're telling me that you're not angry with her?'

'I was. I was livid. I couldn't understand why she left, and I still don't. Dad was a lovely man. Also, I don't think I would be able to look her in the eye. I'm just too hurt. The divorce was a huge shock to me.'

'I know how you feel.'

'Thanks, Piers.'

'Talking to you is very easy. Everyone loved you at the meeting.'

'Really?'

'Oh yes. Major consensus!'

For the umpteenth time that day, I blushed while he grinned, his eyes searching my face as if he wanted to say something, but thought better of it.

*And you?* My words seemed to hang in the empty space between us. *Are you part of the consensus?* But of course I didn't. That would have been all kinds of conceited.


Thursday, June 13th


After nearly two weeks of running the tightest ship I could, gently getting a couple of the slackers to pull their socks up, I allowed myself a ten-minute breather by looking out the window onto the beautifully landscaped grounds.

I loved this place, with its ornamental trees of every kind, but also fruit trees that were beginning to yield. As I took in all the beauty, a tiny robin flew straight through the open window, landing on my windowsill, blatantly staring at me just like the one that had visited me on my kitchen windowsill in Tulip Cottage.

'Well, hello,' I whispered. 'Look at you. My, you're cute, aren't you?'

It had something in its beak that appeared to be stuck. I couldn't understand if that was the case or if he was just carrying his food somewhere else. But he began to flap his wings wildly and I soon saw that he was indeed in trouble.

On instinct, I grabbed a letter opener from the desk and gently caught him in my left hand while I pried a tiny cherry pit from his mouth as he patiently waited.

'There you go, my friend. You'll be okay.'

But instead of flying off, he just stood there, slumped. The poor thing! What could I do?

I grabbed some tissues and lined the smallest drawer of my desk and gently put him in it, leaving it open. Then I removed the cap from my bottle of water and filled it for him to drink. He seemed too exhausted or perhaps still in shock, so I gently caressed his little feathered head to reassure him. After a few moments, he lifted his wing and tucked his head under it.

I knew how he felt. Dazed. Scared. Exhausted. But he'd get over it, I hoped. We all have to. It's the way of life.

The day went well, except for a hiccup with a Californian company that bought our gooseberry jam. All day, I waited for them to get back to me as I had a deadline and needed confirmation of their final order before I expedited it. No biggie, if they hadn't been the last order of the month which needed to be included in the monthly reports. Of course they were eight hours ahead of me so I waited. And waited. Until I fell asleep. And woke up to find that it was 3 a.m.

and that I had a blanket on me. Justin must have come in and not wanted to wake me. How embarrassing!

And the next morning, I got a text from Piers:

I heard about last night. That wasn't necessary, but thank you. Let Justin take you home to catch up on your sleep. You won't be needed for the rest of the day.

Piers.

*OhGodohGodOhGod.* Had I just got a warning? Was he going to fire me? I couldn't afford to get fired! I rubbed the sleep out of my face and texted him back.

I apologise. I'm mortified. No need to go home. I can keep working, no problem.

To which he answered:

Absolutely not. Go home.

Then, as if he'd read my mind and wanted to reassure me I wasn't out on my arse, he added:

Next time you're expecting a call, we can arrange a guest room for you. No need to stay up to wait. See you tomorrow.

So my livelihood was safe after all! At least for now.

# 17

## Monday, July 1st

As the weeks rolled on, so did my belly. It was finally the end of my first trimester and I was a bit anxious about showing up at the maternity shop out of the blue and surprising everyone.

I was officially starting my fourth month now and had been back to see Dr Chenoweth who confirmed I was in my nesting phase. She said everything was in tip-top shape. My blood pressure was good and I was gaining weight at the proper rate, which was a miracle in itself with all the food I regularly managed to tuck away. I had changed my mind about finding out the sex of the baby. I'd spent my whole pregnancy referring to it as a girl, but it wouldn't change the way I felt if it turned out to be a boy. I would leave it as a lovely surprise on my due date.

Things were going well. I was getting very comfortable with my job and Piers always praised my work. We had our daily cuppa together and gradually got to know each other more and more. I liked talking to him. And as I got to know him, I realised how charming he really was. He had this boyish, mischievous attitude mixed with this sheen of a lack of confidence that I found endearing.

He may well have been lord of the manor, but Piers and I were very similar. We'd been through the same growing pains and had been angry for years. But we'd managed to move on. We often talked about our similarities. And yet, there was so much more I was dying to know about him, but a part of him was inaccessible.

'How long have you lived in the area?' I asked Piers one day out of the blue while we were having a cup of coffee.

His eyes shot to mine. 'Why?'

I shrugged. 'I just wonder how much you know the villagers.'

'Specifically, which villager?' he asked.

I looked up to meet his inquisitive, dark eyes.

'No one specific. Everyone seems to think the world of you.'

'And I of them,' he said, beginning to relax.

'You know, Piers, you remind me of someone.'

He lowered his eyes and chuckled. 'I get that a lot. You know what they say: seven doppelgangers in the world. Or I guess I just have a very common face.'

Actually, his face was anything but common. He had a lovely smile and his eyes were the kindest I'd ever seen. Dark, but twinkling at the same time, set in a lean, expressive face that could slide into a smile as easily as a frown. I never knew what was coming, and whilst it annoyed me, it also fascinated me. And under all that millionaire shield, I'd come to learn he was painfully shy. I actually felt for him when he turned red and began to flounder for words. Sometimes, I was surprised he didn't stutter.

'I get that too,' I admitted. 'Do you believe in fate?'

'Okay, what's with all the questions?'

'Oh? I'm sorry, I'm just making conversation.'

'No, I'm sorry. I'm just a bit on edge today, I guess.'

I opened my mouth to ask why, then rolled my eyes in self-chastisement.

He grinned. 'Sorry, I don't want to come across as a tosser.'

'Oh, you're so not,' I assured him. 'You've been so kind to me, a total stranger. All of you here in Starry Cove have. I should have known.'

His eyebrows lifted in a silent question.

'It's always in Cornwall that I got treated the best. When I was a girl, my parents used to vacation here. We became chummy with a family, and they had a son about my age. He was the nicest boy I ever met. To this day.'

'To this day, eh?' he said expectantly.

I grinned and rolled my eyes. 'If you're fishing for a compliment, you're not getting one.'

He laughed. 'So who was this bloke, then?'

I laughed at myself. 'Long story.'

'I'm listening.'

'Okay. Well, I was being bullied on the beach. A group of boys knocked my ice cream into the sand, so he chased them off and bought me another one. Then he brought me back to my parents and his parents came along and we all became friends. I had this huge crush on him and—' I stopped short, wondering whether this was an inappropriate thing to discuss with my boss.

'And?' he prompted.

'Nothing. He invited me to become part of his band and

we played for a few summers. His name was Banjo. We took pictures of ourselves, thinking it would be cool to look back at when we were rockstars.'

'That's cute.'

'It was a very long time ago and I haven't heard from him since. He probably left the village years ago.'

'Many people leave Cornwall. For the life of me, I can't see why,' he said. 'And we are pretty insular here, but once someone becomes one of us, that's it. Cornwall is like that. Have you still got the picture?'

'I keep it safe back at home, because it's the last family picture I ever smiled in.'

His face went soft. 'How come?'

'When we got back from holiday… that's when my mother left.'

'I'm so sorry.' He studied me in silence, his face mirroring his voice. I half-expected him to reach over and hug me. But that would have been a bit awkward considering that, despite all our deep conversations, we were still firmly in employer-employee territory. We'd never seen each other off the manor grounds.

Correction: temporary, part-time, lying employee who was going to get the boot the minute the gig was up. And I was sure whatever he thought of me was very far from what was slowly beginning to stir inside me. Willingness to trust a bloke again. The enthusiasm of being next to someone new. Missing them when they're not around, and almost having a coronary every time he entered the room. There was no doubt about what was going on inside my heart and mind. But Piers was way out of my league in every way, and beyond that, it was hugely inappropriate to come on to my boss. Perhaps it was time to come to grips with reality and look to settle down with someone more akin to my lifestyle. Or, even easier, just continue to live my life this way.

I shrugged. 'Thanks. It was a lifetime ago. I'm a big girl now.'

An awkward silence followed.

'You'd better get a move on and go home to rest before your lessons start,' he finally said. 'And then you have Nina's transcribing to do, don't you? You are one busy woman.'

'I certainly am, but I like it that way,' I answered, fetching my bag. Work gave me less time to think.

He stood up and stuffed his hands in his pockets. 'Great. See you tomorrow, Sophie.'

'See you tomorrow,' I said and left him sitting on the corner of my desk as he always did whenever he dropped by.

On my way home, I passed what seemed to be an animal fair on the common. There were pens everywhere. Once I veered closer, I could see that there were a large number of dogs, cats, budgies, rabbits and so on.

Without even thinking twice about it, I marched over to the woman who appeared to be in charge.

'Hello,' I said. 'May I see your puppies, please?'

'Of course,' she said, delighted. 'Have you got a particular breed or age in mind?'

'I'd like the one that's been waiting for a home the longest.'

She smiled warmly. 'That's sweet. Then I would have to say that's Trixie. She's a little mutt that no one wants because she cries a lot, I'm afraid.'

There, we already had something in common. 'I'll take her, if she'll have me.'

'Oh, you kind heart,' she said. 'Come this way, please.'

I followed her to a pen where several dogs were playing around, nipping at each other's tails and rolling on the grass. In the corner, with the saddest eyes I'd ever seen in my entire life, was Trixie.

She looked up at me, but then looked away, almost turning her back on me. Was I the umpteenth person who'd come to see her but ultimately rejected her? That was not happening again.

'What happened to her?' I asked the lady.

'Her owner abandoned her on the A30 almost a year ago. She was nearly run over.'

'Oh my God!' I whispered, reaching down to gently pet the furry head. She responded coyly, nudging her head further into my hand by the tiniest amount. 'You're coming home with me right now,' I promised her. 'You'll get lots of love and good food and a comfy bed.' She was so tiny, she'd fit into a serving bowl. I wondered if she was malnourished. How could anyone do something so horrible to such a sweet, sweet creature like this?

'Well then, all you have to do is fill out these forms. She's microchipped and vaccinated but will be needing her follow-ups very soon.'

'Got it. Have you got a carrier or anything for me to carry her in?'

'I've got a cage,' the woman volunteered. 'But you'll have to bring it back.'

A cage? That was the last thing this little sweetheart needed! 'No, thank you, I think I'll just hold her.' God knew by the way she was suddenly clinging to me that she craved kindness and human contact. It made my blood boil to think that some people believed they could get away with such behaviour. An animal is a living thing that adores its owner. She would never have abandoned her person. They're just not built like that.

I lifted Trixie closer to my face and plonked a huge kiss on her head, whispering silly sounds into her ear until she looked up at me. But her face had not changed expression. She probably didn't believe in people anymore. I could understand that. But not all people were the same, thank God. Look at my new friends.

I filled in the forms one-handed, still cradling Trixie in the other. 'Okay, I'm ready to take her home now.'

'Bless you,' she said. 'Thank you for your kindness. Trixie's luck has just changed.'

At home, I made Trixie a makeshift bed by the fire with an old cushion and one of my sweaters. Perhaps she could get used to my smell and feel safe? Then I got out two old bowls and filled them with kibble and clean water. I watched her near the bowl with kibble, sniff it, and finally dig in.

'There you are, sweetheart,' I cooed, caressing her fur. Surprisingly, she didn't shy away, so starved for affection, poor thing.

Satisfied she would be okay for a few minutes, I snuck upstairs and slipped into my usual glad rags. Then I crept back downstairs and made myself a cup of cocoa. After nightfall, it wasn't that warm anymore. I was getting sick of tea and the mention of ice cream to Piers had subconsciously made me peckish.

Who was I kidding? I was always peckish; I hoped Baby was enjoying herself in there.

The next morning, Piers called my mobile as I was getting dressed. 'Morning, Sophie. Just calling to check if it's okay with you to take some more international calls tonight?'

'Of course, certainly.'

'So can you sleep over? Mrs Watts would prepare a room for you.'

'Right. There's just one thing. I have just adopted a tiny dog and I can't leave her on her own. She's very quiet and just needs to lie in a basket in the same room with me. Can I bring her in? She won't bark or make a mess, I promise.'

'Fine by me as long as you keep her away from Wolf. He hates other dogs.'

'Oh! Okay. Then I'll close my office door from now on.'

When I took her to the car with me, she panicked, but I let her sit in my lap all the way and even when I sat behind my desk, she clung to me. 'You're not going anywhere, sweetheart,' I whispered into the top of her head before dropping another huge kiss on it. Which reminded me to check my drawer. Little Cherry, as I'd dubbed him, seemed to have gone. I only hoped he hadn't died in the night and that Justin hadn't disposed of him.

Back to work. I had barely slept the previous night and was struggling to keep my eyes open. The hardest part about being pregnant was the drowsiness vs being wired. I was tired, but then when in bed, I couldn't fall asleep. I used to have allergies as a teenager and had had to take Dramamine for a while which made me constantly sleepy. This was pretty much the same feeling, only back then, falling asleep on my desk and not getting my homework done wasn't such a tragedy. Could you imagine me falling asleep on the job? Piers did know I was pregnant, but the last thing I needed was for that to happen again.

My gyno had told me I would be getting more and more tired throughout my pregnancy, but today was the worst so far. Still, work was work. Of course, I had promised to sleep over, should the need have arisen, but now that I was actually going to be sleeping there, a frisson of excitement and curiosity coursed through me. I had never slept in a manor before, not even a hotel manor.

'Good morning again, Sophie,' Piers greeted me from the table as I walked into the orangery for a cup of coffee with my little dog bag.

'Morning. Please meet Trixie.'

'Hello, new puppy!' he said as he peered into her face. 'Hey, she's so ugly, she's actually cute.'

'Don't say that,' I hissed, covering her ears. 'She's very sensitive, you know?'

'Okay, okay, sorry!' Piers laughed. 'Will you or Miss Universe here be needing anything specific for tonight?' he asked.

'No thanks, she'll be fine. I have her blanket, her food and her vitamins. Everything she needs.'

A strange light appeared in Piers's eyes. 'And you?' he asked softly.

'What do you mean?' I asked as I sat down opposite him. With him, it was always better to make sure.

He shrugged. 'I don't know, do you have any special pregnancy needs?'

I couldn't help but giggle. 'No, no pregnancy needs, thanks. Just a firm mattress.'

He grinned sheepishly. 'Sorry for being so ignorant. I know absolutely nothing about these things.'

'Oh, no, please don't apologise; that's actually very considerate of you to ask.'

'So you'll be okay? Are you okay?'

'Absolutely, thank you.'

'So, when is the baby due?'

'In December, around Christmas.'

This was the first time he had ever actually shown any real interest in my pregnancy; he'd only ever asked if I needed anything. In that way he had always been very attentive, a good employer, but it was never anything beyond surface level. But then I realised this sudden interest in my due date was probably linked to the timeline of his business. He wanted to know when I'd be having my baby so we could aim to get the work done before I left the job.

Which made me wonder, how was I going to manage to survive for all the months that I couldn't work because I was taking care of my baby? I would have to work. But then who would take care of her? There was no way I could ever leave her with anyone. It would kill me to do so. Besides, I didn't have the budget for childcare. Even if I continued to work elsewhere, I'd never be paid as well as I was here.

'Right. And... I hope you don't mind my asking but... will the baby's father be joining you at any point?'

I didn't quite see how that information could be of any importance to him, but when his face began to turn a shade of red, I suddenly realised that perhaps he was asking me once again if I was seeing anyone. The first time I'd told him I wasn't, and now it seemed he wanted to make sure.

But there was something there, in his stance, on his face, the way he avoided looking me straight in the eye. And in the tone of his voice, aloof and almost insecure. Could it possibly be that he was growing as fond of me as I was of him?

For me, it was only normal to develop a crush on him. Piers was kind and intelligent; he owned his own business and was highly regarded by Emmie and the girls. But were my instincts wrong in telling me that he might actually be interested in me, his employee who was carrying another man's baby to boot?

Piers and I came from two completely different worlds. He was a successful businessman while I was soon to be out of a job again. The thought that I was bringing a baby into this world, in the state my life was in, suddenly seemed like idiotic to me. Just what made me even think I could do it on my own? What had I been thinking?

Of course, I was so much better off without Will. But had I actually thought it through when I ran? I could have handled it differently. Gone to the police. Who knows which way these things can go sometimes? But the thought of not having my baby had never even occurred to me. It would have made my life much easier, I suppose, with only myself to worry about, but from the moment I saw those two pink stripes in that stick, I was no longer alone. Whatever happened from now on, I would have Baby, and Baby would have me.

'I'm so sorry, I can see that I've upset you,' Piers whispered from across the table.

I looked up. 'Oh, no, Piers. You haven't. I'm on my own and it's tough, but so am I.'

He studied me in silence for a moment, his eyes probing, pondering.

*Just kiss me, Piers*, I willed him silently. *Just reach across the table and kiss me. Take the risk…*

'Yes, Sophie,' he whispered.

I snapped out of it, wondering if I'd said any of that aloud, when he leaned in close. Almost close enough to kiss me. 'You don't look it, but you are tough. I can see that.'

He could see my strength, but he couldn't see what was right under his nose. He couldn't see how I was terribly attracted to him. And I suddenly realised what a lost cause I was. He would never see me as I saw him. He would never be attracted to me, let alone act upon it. We were in a stalemate, caused not only by my being Piers's employee, but also by my expecting a child by another man. And yet, I longed for love. I yearned for a new start, a new life shared with someone as fascinating as Piers. But as usual, my affection was one-sided. Would no one ever love me again?

For the rest of the day, I worked pretty much undisturbed except by Mrs Watts, who came in offering coffee and sandwiches, which I readily accepted. I was always ravenous lately. Savoury, sweet, you name it, I'd eat it. Which reminded me. If I was sleeping at Rosestones, did that mean that I would be having dinner with Piers? Or would I eat in the kitchen with Justin and Mrs Watts? After all, I was staff.

As I was finishing up a phone call to a strudel company in Germany, I heard a soft flutter. I looked up from my screen to the window and lo and behold, Cherry was back. It had to be her. Just to make sure, I opened the desk drawer and she flew right inside, cocking her eye up at me.

'Welcome back, you…' I whispered, giving her a capful

of water, which she readily drank. 'Are you hungry? I've got some sunflower seeds here; would you like some?'

She studied me for a minute as I created a tiny path on my desk leading to me. She hopped out, cocking her eye at me again, just to be sure, before deciding it was safe and proceeding to eat. It was such a pleasure, to be able to feed an animal. I even got a kick out of watching Trixie eat. I only hoped that she wouldn't wake up from her sleep in her basket and give Cherry a hard time. But she continued to snore as if all was right with the world. I turned to look at Cherry, shrugging. 'Lucky her, eh?'

Later that day, Piers stopped by my office. It was getting difficult to ignore the hitch of my breath every time he was around. 'Sophie, about this morning,' he said leaning against the table. 'I truly apologise for butting into your private life.'

'That's okay, Piers, no harm done.'

'Good, I'm glad. I just felt it was important to know, as a member of my staff, that you were okay.'

Right, I was just his employee. I knew this. Even Trixie must have known by now. I looked down at her and she raised her eyebrows at me and I couldn't help but laugh. She would definitely agree that that wasn't what a girl wanted to hear. I knew he was satisfied with my work so far, but evidently that was it.

'Some inside joke between the two of you?' he quipped, watching our silent conversation.

I giggled. 'Trixie gets me. Again, no harm done, Piers.'

He cleared his throat. 'Good. I'm, uh, glad.'

Today, I'd had a momentary weakness: you know, when your hormones are running amok and you actually come to believe that anything is possible? Well, that was this morning. Now, having actually thought it through, and thanks to his comment just now, it was all clear that it wasn't. Which was just as well. My main objective had been to start a new life here in Cornwall, and I'd done just that. The picture was complete even without a man.

The rest of the day seemed to fly by, and at around eight, Piers popped his head back into my office. 'Hi! Are you and Trixie hungry yet?'

'Oh! Always!'

'Care to come down to the dining room, then?'

I jumped to my feet quite quickly, even for me. 'Yes, please.'

'Can I pet her?' he asked, eyeing Trixie in her bag.

'Of course,' I said, opening the bag. 'You can hold her if you want.'

'May I? Really?'

'Yes.'

As he gently and slowly reached for her, I couldn't help but notice the wonder on his face, and the chuckle that escaped him when she licked his nose. 'Aw, you really are a cutie, aren't ya? Yes, you are!' It seemed even men like Piers weren't immune from baby-talking animals.

He carried Trixie all the way to the dining room, but we decided it was best to keep her in her bag high off the floor in case Wolf happened to bound in. As we sat down in the luxurious room decorated with priceless antiques, Mrs Watts came in with a trolley full of trays with lids on them.

'Ah, thank you, Mrs Watts!'

'Yes, thank you,' I chimed in.

'I've left your dessert in the fridge as it's still setting,' she said.

He nodded. 'Perfect, thanks.'

'And Miss Graham, I've turned down the bed in the Gold Room for you.'

The Gold Room? That sounded rather grand, indeed. I couldn't wait to see it.

'I'll show you where it is later,' he assured me and I felt a wave of warmth in my cheeks as a naughty thought brushed my mind.

'Thank you, Mrs Watts,' I said.

'Have a lovely evening,' she replied and trotted out of the dining room.

'Good night, Mrs Watts,' Piers and I said in unison but she was already gone. 'She's a bloody prodigy,' he whispered as if he was afraid she could still hear him. 'There isn't anything she can't do.'

'You're very lucky to have found her.'

'I am. And I'm lucky to have found you, Sophie. You're doing a great job.'

The warmth was slowly spreading to my chest. 'Thank you...'

'So how about we do her work some justice?'

'Let's,' I agreed, relieved to change the subject, and off came the lids to reveal an onion soup, followed by a gorgeous Beef Wellington, green beans with garlic, truffled mashed potato, and a crisp green salad. 'Ooh, yummy!' I swooned.

'She is amazing, isn't she?' Piers marvelled as he swallowed his first bite.

'Mmph...' I agreed as we ate, communicating with our eyes, too hungry to speak. It was like we had developed our own code in the space of a magic moment, bringing us closer without even uttering a word as we searched each other's faces. It was recognition of the fact that we were, in spite of our efforts, getting to know each other on a deeper level and it provided a warmth that enveloped me completely, like enjoying a beautiful sunset in total silence. Every now and then I fed Trixie a tidbit of beef which she slurped down happily.

'Can't say she hasn't got an appetite,' Piers said, amused.

'I know, she can eat her weight in food,' I said with a chuckle.

And then he gave me a strange look which made my insides melt, but I forced myself to look away.

As the night unfurled and it was time to retire, I was struck by a feeling of desolation. I didn't want to leave his presence; it had filled me with such a sense of pleasure and security. Piers radiated an invisible force-field that made all those within it feel safe and secure. I didn't know if it was his larger than life presence, or the low, deep voice, or the way he looked at me. All I knew was that I didn't want to give up that sensation, but if I stayed any longer he would see right through me and that was the last thing I needed.

So I stood up. 'I'd better get some sleep,' I whispered. 'Just so I'm fresh for those calls…'

He got to his feet. 'God, yeah, I'm so sorry I've kept you up.'

I felt my cheeks warming again. 'No, don't be. I've enjoyed your company.'

His eyes searched my face, his voice an octave lower than usual. 'Yeah?'

I nodded, afraid to look up. 'Absolutely. All I need now is to sleep.'

'Come,' he said, taking my elbow. 'It's just up the stairs. The mattress is brand new and the light in there in the morning is incredible. That's why it's called the Gold Room.'

I scooped up the bag containing a now sleeping Trixie and followed him up a wide staircase with an ornate wooden banister and down the central corridor. I only hoped I'd find my way back to my office from here tomorrow morning.

'Here's the office phone, it's fully charged,' he said, placing it in my hand, his fingers long and warm around mine. And with that, he paused, perhaps a moment too long.

He cleared his throat. 'Uh, good night, Sophie. Sweet dreams…'

'And great deals! Good night,' I chimed, trying to take the magic out of the moment or I'd simply melt into this sudden, ridiculous sensation of belonging. He was my employer. End of. And when I closed the door behind me, I knew I'd managed a tremendous feat.

The bedroom was not as large as I'd been expecting, but it had an elegant double bed with a cream upholstered headboard and a thick, fancy duvet cover, all between two large, high windows, adorned with golden-coloured drapes. Goldenrod plush rugs were scattered here and there, covering a flagstone floor. A very far cry from my bedroom in the eaves of Tulip Cottage, it felt like the room of a princess. And for a few hours, it would be mine.

Mrs Watts had put my overnight bag on the bed and my toiletry bag in the ensuite bathroom, which was covered from top to bottom in what I surmised was Carrara marble. I knew that because I'd seen something similar in one of those home fashion magazines. It was beautiful.

I set Trixie's bag next to the bed and slipped into the

*real* Sophie Graham's best silk pyjamas, but skipped the wool jumper that I usually added back at the cottage as the manor was well-heated. I looked at myself in the mirror as I brushed my teeth.

My scratches had thankfully left no scars, and my short hair wasn't so short anymore, assuming its natural waves again. I wondered whether my baby would look more like me or Will, though it was irrelevant. My baby was only mine, now.

'I love you more than you can ever imagine,' I whispered to my belly. 'Now, let's get some sleep.'

My stomach was comfortably full, and the mattress was firm but comfortable. By all rights I should have fallen asleep in an instant, but instead I stared at the swaying shadows created by the trees in the wind just outside my window. Safe, warm and happy. This was how the other half lived, without a care in the world.

As it turned out, it was a good thing that I'd stayed the night for those calls, as I became aware of a major flaw in an order that had been placed previously by Patsy. A company in Germany had asked for a shipment of our baked and seasoned apples for tarts, but Patsy had prepared an order for fresh apples. Imagine the look on the freight receiver's face when a truckload of fresh Bramley apples were delivered to them! So I intercepted the shipment and hijacked it to another company that had literally just ordered them. I would have one extremely satisfied company and be only just a little late with the other.

The next morning when Piers asked me how the calls

had gone, I merely nodded and told him that everything was okay. No need to tell him about Patsy's mistake. She'd already paid for all of them by being fired.

I would miss this job, the people, even my beautiful Moroccan-style office with the oh-so-comfy velvet settee. I intended to make the most of it before Baby came. So on my lunch break, I toured the grounds, taking selfies to show her one day. I wanted her to know only the happier parts of my life.

'See, sweetie?' I said into my mobile as I made a video of the grounds. 'This is where Mummy worked for a few months while expecting you. It's so beautiful here!'

I swirled the camera around to show more of the grounds.

'This is the perfect place to come and hide if you don't want to be found!' It was true. Rosestones Manor was so far removed from the gritty, ugly world that it seemed that nothing bad could ever happen there. Its beautiful stone walls would protect you from every harm.

'And today is a gorgeous day! There are so many plants and animals here! And I've just discovered a new nest of choughs, the Cornish bird. If you look closely,' I said, zooming into a patch of trees sheltering the window of the dining room, 'you'll just be able to glimpse the very reclusive specimen right… *there!* I can't zoom in anymore, I'm afraid, but I think he might be having his lunch. We all know that he likes his privacy and I've been hoping for him to make an appearance.' I prattled on, thrilled at the idea of my own baby seeing this one day and calling me a bird nerd.

'It's very rare to see them so I guess that today is our lucky day! I just wanted you to know that from now on, I will share these gems with you, because my time at Rosestones

Manor is not forever, especially when I get caught dilly-dallying out here instead of working away in my office as I should be. Jokes aside, my boss is a lovely person. He has a heart the size of this manor. So will you, one day, even if right now you're only as big as a bean – or a baby chough, even, a little creature that can't help himself from...'

I stopped, feeling a lump rising in my throat. Gosh, what a time to get emotional in front of your unborn baby! Really! So I took a deep breath and collected myself. 'But I will protect you and love you. Because I already love you so, so much...' And then, because I felt my eyes moistening, I decided I wasn't reporting material right now so it was probably best to call it a day. I wanted her to see me as happy as possible. I wanted her to know that I was so looking forward to meeting her in person. Besides, I had to get back to work.

Noah's renovations were taking far longer than expected. The initial three weeks had somehow expanded into three months, with new problems seeming to crop up every time an old one was fixed. Sometimes I wondered if Noah was just looking for excuses to stick around so he could drag me to that dinner. Every once in a while, Robert would come over while Noah was working just to check on the progress. He seemed happy enough with it, and for a moment, I hoped that the veiled animosity between them could come to an end. It had almost become like a game, this sparring, with Noah fending off Robert's questions and demands with a courteous demeanour.

It was hard not to like Noah. He was always cheerful and

always had a kind word for everyone, despite the fact that he was an outsider. Perhaps that was why we felt we had something in common as I, too, was an outsider, but thanks to the girls I'd made it to the Inner Circle of Respected Villager. As far as dinner with Noah... it felt wrong. He had a girlfriend and even though he meant nothing by his invitations, I knew it would be wrong to accept. The last thing I needed was to lose a new friend over a silly misunderstanding.

On Friday evening, after a long, hard day, I found Noah waiting for me at the cottage to show me his progress. The piping had been completed, and the electrics, plus all the plastering. And while this was going on, I kept getting offers from Robert to put me up at the inn, which I'd refused. It hadn't been that disruptive; I'd actually enjoyed the company of having Noah around most days. Plus, I needed to call this place my home from the beginning. Next, Noah would be painting. It was a joy to see Tulip Cottage in such great shape! Of course, it was still relatively devoid of furnishings because I was saving every penny for the nursery and things for Baby. But the quality of the work was truly stunning.

'Noah, I have to say, hats off to you. You are an amazing builder!' I swooned.

He shoved his hands into his pockets and grinned. 'Yeah, I know...'

And then we laughed. He would never lose that Aussie swagger.

'Dr A said he wanted the best materials and stuff, so it was easy to do this little place justice. It's like a hidden gem, isn't it?'

'It is; it's my safe place,' I agreed, then bit my lip. 'Would you like a cup of coffee? Or tea?'

He shrugged. 'Sure, if I'm not crowding you?'

'I'm always glad of the company,' I said as we stepped into the kitchen, where I filled the kettle.

'Don't you see a lot of people at the place you work?' he asked. 'I figured, all the staff and the owner…?'

I rolled my eyes. 'Please. I'm alone most of the mornings, either going through orders, accounts, or on the phone with buyers. Not that my boss ignores me. He is actually very considerate. He usually has a coffee with me and sometimes even breakfast.'

Noah's eyebrow went up. 'Really?'

'Yes. And just before I go, he comes to see if I need anything.'

'Sounds like a real gent.'

'I guess so. And it's good money. It's a shame I won't be working there after my b—' I took a deep breath. I had never acknowledged the pregnancy in front of Noah, and I wasn't sure I wanted to get into the whole thing with him right now.

'After what?' he asked as I poured him a mug of coffee and set it down before him.

'Oh, it was just a temporary job. I'm going to have to start looking for something else next year.' This conversation was getting all too personal. I pushed the Hobnobs toward him. 'Do you like these? I have other biscuits too, if you like?'

Noah took a sip of his coffee and snagged a couple. 'Thanks. So, let me get this straight. You'll be out of a job in a few months but you're going to start looking next year. What are you, pregnant?'

I blinked. *Busted.* 'Yes, Noah, I'm pregnant. Not that it's anyone's business, but I am.'

'You're acting like it's a bad thing. Is it a bad thing?' he asked softly.

'It's the best thing that could ever happen to me,' I whispered.

He looked as if he wanted to say something, but changed his mind and instead said, 'So I guess the second bedroom is going to become a nursery, right?'

'Right.'

'Cool.'

'Great,' I confirmed.

Anyone in my place would have told him before this, because I considered him on the way to being a good acquaintance, if not my friend. But my circumstances had dictated privacy. My future depended on it. If he only knew the rest...

'Does that mean that you can't eat?' he asked with a grin.

'Eh?'

'Come to dinner with me already. You've got to eat, right? Why not with me? If you come, I promise you can have my dessert.'

I sighed. He was indeed good company. Plus, I needed to distract myself from thoughts of Mr Manor...

'Oh, go on, then,' I said with a grin.


Sunday, July 7th


On Sunday afternoon, I kept my promise and went back to see Mrs Nankivell at her cottage.

'Well, there she is, my own little Florence Nightingale!' she cooed, lifting her arms up to me from her position on the settee.

'I'm so happy to see you,' I gushed as I wrapped my arms around her. It was so good to see she was doing well, with her usual rosy cheeks and the mischievous glint in her eye. This woman still had so much to give. She couldn't have died. The entire coast of villages, from Little Kettering to Starry Cove, would have forbidden it.

'Sit, sit,' she urged, gesturing to the nearby armchair covered in delightful flowered material with blue piping. 'I want to know everything you've been up to. Robert tells me that the cottage is coming along nicely and that you have a job?'

'Oh, yes!' I chimed. 'It's all going very well and the cottage looks amazing and I can't wait until Christmas!'

'Marvellous, marvellous!' She giggled. 'I can't wait to show you Christmas in Starry Cove! It's such a delight! The children running about the streets, or skating in the rink behind the church. All the festive lights and the tallest Christmas trees dripping with decorations, and the carolling. And the cakes! You wouldn't believe the cakes! And speaking of: Agnes!' she called to the back of the house. 'Would you bring in the cakes you baked for Sophie, please?'

I gasped. 'For me?'

'Just for you,' she said, beaming as Agnes appeared from the kitchen with a pot of tea and a cake stand loaded with delights of all colours and sizes. I swear, once the baby was born, I would have a tough time returning back to my normal size.

'She had me bakin' all mornin' and made sure it passed

muster,' Agnes said with a grin as she gently placed the ensemble on the coffee table. 'Shall I be mother?' she asked Mrs Nankivell, who waved her on while turning back to me. 'I want to know everything. How is working at Rosestones? I bet that they're positively thrilled to have you! Maybe they'll throw a grand Christmas party!'

I laughed at her enthusiasm. I couldn't remember the last time I was that happy about anything. She was like a six-year-old on Christmas Eve. It was still only the summer and way too early for Christmas, but it would indeed be nice to celebrate Christmas in Cornwall with all these lovely, warm people that had become my friends.

Agnes finished serving us our tea and cakes and discreetly left us to our banter.

'So, tell me all. Who is it going to be, the hot builder, the handsome doctor or the hermit up at Rosestones?'

I blinked. 'Sorry?'

'Don't give me any of that useless coyness, Sophie! You've got a decision to make! Time's running out!'

I put my cup down. 'I'm sorry, it's not like that, Nan.'

'Pshaw!' she said. 'Are you telling me you don't fancy any of them?'

I laughed. 'Really, Nan, I didn't take you for such a gossip!'

'Me? Can I help it if people come to talk to me?'

'People come to talk to you—?'

'And tell me their bits of news. It's not my fault. I'm just an invalid sitting at home listening to the world going by!'

I giggled. 'Oh, Nan, I'm afraid someone's yanking your chain! First of all, one is my boss, the builder is nothing more than a friend and Robert is also a friend. A very dear one.'

But she shook her head. 'What are you waiting for, luvvie? Time's running out!'

'What do you mean…?' I said, but I was getting a distinct feeling she knew about the baby.

'I mean that love is never to be wasted, nor is time! And that we all need to belong to someone.'

I sighed. 'I don't have any prospects right now, not with Robert nor my builder nor my boss.' *Unfortunately*.

'You have feelings for none of them?' she insisted.

I shrugged. 'They're all amazing people, but really, none of them have expressed any interest in me.' And as far as Piers was concerned, I was simply his employee. Nothing more. He'd told me so, no matter how it may have seemed at times.

As much as I wanted a companion, I couldn't see any of them likely to become such. So after about another hour of denying the gossip and eating the cakes, I got to my feet and kissed the lovely yet batty Nan goodbye.

As I was leaving, Robert arrived and offered to walk me home. 'But you just got here,' I protested. 'Your nan was looking forward to your visit.'

'I'll be right back, Nan,' he apologised to her.

She grinned from ear to ear. 'Oh, by all means, you walk our lovely friend home. I'll be here when you get back, love.' And with that, she practically shooed us out the door, grinning like the Cheshire Cat as she waved us down the road.

On the way home, I told Robert that I might be away from the cottage at night from time to time in case he came calling. Not that he'd come calling at night, of course, but I felt better if my landlord knew I hadn't jumped ship. In London, I had arranged to pay my rent and bills online so no one would come looking for me.

He groaned. 'I thought you were comfortable at the cottage.'

'Oh, I am! Everything I own and love is at the cottage. But Mr Henshaw—'

Robert sighed. 'Is this about him?'

I frowned. 'What do you mean?'

'Have you already fallen under his spell?'

I crossed my arms in front of my chest. 'I haven't fallen under anyone's spell. I just want to do my job well. There will be some times when I'll be required to deal with different time zones and work nights.'

'All the while enjoying the perks of hobnobbing with the filthy rich.'

'What the hell does that mean? And why are you being so unfair?'

He put his hands up. 'Sorry. I just don't like seeing women always falling at his feet, is all. Have a care you don't fall in too deep so as you can't find your way out.'

I sighed. 'You know what, you've just managed to say a load of rubbish all in one breath.'

As soon as I said it, I was sorry. It wasn't like me to be rude, and I had a feeling that Robert was disappointed in me. In any case, no one could tell me what to do or where to go. This was part of my job. End of.

'So you're not an item?' he insisted.

'We are not an item.' *Unfortunately*. 'And even if we were, I don't see how it's anyone's business.'

He shrugged. 'It's your life. But after he's reeled you in, used you and spat you out like everyone else, don't come crying to me.'

'Oh, I'll remember not to, no worries,' I retorted. Why was he so adamant about this?

'Good,' he said loftily as we reached my front door. 'Now you have a lovely evening.'

'Thank you. I will,' I reassured him, and closed the door in his face.

*Men.*

# 18

## Monday July 8th

Justin came to pick me up on Monday morning. As I was staying for the night and had an appointment with my gyno, Piers had given me the morning off and asked Justin to drive me to Truro.

As we sped past hedgerows that seemed to be closing in on the car, I settled comfortably in the back seat, feeling like I was moving to another country. And I was also glad that the girls knew my whereabouts. I felt better knowing that someone who cared about me knew where I was. Robert also knew about the apartment, and even after our spat last night, I knew he'd be there if I needed him. Even if he was not happy with my decision to work at Rosestones. What did he have against Piers? What bad blood ran between them? Everyone else, including the girls, seemed to not want to talk about it.

When I got to Truro, I sat in the gyno chair and blurted out, 'I'd like to know my baby's sex.'

'It's a girl,' she beamed.

'You already knew?'

'I did, but you said you wanted to wait.'

'Oh my God,' I whispered. 'I'm going to have a baby girl... a daughter!' *I knew it!*

'Congratulations, Sophie! Now, let's get you checked...'

I spent the entire afternoon in a daze. Not only was I going to have a baby; it was going to be a girl. All I could think of was explosions of pink. Actually, every colour of the rainbow!

When I climbed back into the car, Justin noticed my happy face and smiled, but said nothing. He was the epitome of discretion.

I leaned in. 'Justin, do you think we could make a detour to some shops in Starry Cove before we go back home?'

'I'd be happy to, Miss,' he obliged.

It was time to spend some of my hard-earned money on the nursery. Other things, such as rugs and pictures and everything that makes a home a home, would have to wait. After the most important thing arrived: my precious little bundle. So I went out and bought a few items for her which Justin carried back to the car and helped me unload back at Tulip Cottage. Five more months and she'd be in my arms. I couldn't wait to have my very own child, a *person* to love.

## Tuesday, July 9th

The next day, Piers came in, very uptight. This hot and cold thing was not giving me good vibes at all. Will used to do that. He could go from lover to enemy in a split second. Even Trixie sat up, aware that the atmosphere of the room had shifted.

'Piers, hi.'

He put his mobile down on my desk. 'I saw you were in the grounds at lunch the other day.'

'Yes, they're so beautiful.' And then a lightbulb moment. 'Is it not permitted to wander there on my own?' Gosh, I hadn't even thought to ask! So much for being discreet.

'I don't mind if you wander during your breaks, of course not. But what I do mind is you taking video footage of my home. The day you came in to interview, I did explain that my privacy was my utmost priority, did I not?'

'Of course,' I said. 'I'm sorry. But those videos were only meant for private use.'

He raised an eyebrow in question and I felt silly.

'They're, uh, for my baby. I wanted to document my life for her before she was born. I meant no harm to you, Piers.'

His face softened. 'I understand. I'm sorry for being so harsh, but you know by now how important my privacy is.'

'I'm sorry,' I whispered.

He nodded. 'I know you did it without thinking. Let's put this behind us, okay?'

'Okay…'

And with a nod, he left the room. Apparently, I was back in the dog house.


'I feel like an idiot!' I cried into my fist as Emmie poured me a cup of tea and put an éclair in front of me, her soft face saddened. 'I just wanted to document the start of my new life for my baby to see one day, you know?'

'I know,' she whispered. 'You didn't do it on purpose.'

'But I did the one thing he asked me not to,' I insisted as I tore into the éclair with the voracity of a starving tiger. 'It's a miracle he didn't fire me on the spot.'

'He wouldn't do that to you. He's happy with your work. And you.'

I washed it down with a huge gulp of tea. 'You think so?'

'I *know* so. He just values his privacy is all.'

'I understand I was out of line, Emmie, but why is he like that? Why is he so obsessed with his privacy?'

Which was one hell of a question to ask about others when I was just as bad.

She looked at me pensively before she took a long sip of her drink. 'For the same reason you are, more or less, Sophie,' she answered simply. And I understood that, however good a friend she was proving to be to me, her loyalty was with Piers. 'Would you like to stay for dinner? I've got a nice shepherd's pie in the oven,' she offered.

'Ah, that's very sweet of you, but I was thinking of calling on Mrs Nankivell. I heard she is a bit under the weather again. Maybe some other time?'

'Absolutely. Give her a hug for me, will you?'

'Of course.'

And with that, I thanked her for the respite and set off to see the dear old lady, stopping by The Rolling Scones to bring her some mini cakes in the hopes of cheering her up.

Later that evening, I called Tamsin. I really missed the sound of her voice.

'Kate!' she gasped. 'Are you okay? Why don't you call me more often? I need to be able to talk to you!'

'I'm sorry, Tams, but it's for your own good. If Will gets wind that we talk—'

'But that's the thing: we don't talk!' she cried. 'I'm out of my mind here worrying about you.'

'Oh, please don't, Tams. I'm fine. Really, I am. I'm working. I've made some friends. I'm finally on my way to being happy. Is there any news about the investigation?' I asked, dreading the answer.

'No, nothing. The company seems to have run out of ideas, at least for now. Honestly, I think it might just all blow over.'

Now that was a nice thought. 'What about your suggestion of looking into Will?'

'I think they have, but there's no proof.'

Of course, he must have destroyed the documents. Or hidden them somewhere else. The thought of the police entering my home without my permission and looking through my personal things just made me want to scream. Luckily, I was too far away to do anything. And, truth be said, all I needed and loved was here, right inside me.

'I've got to say, you really do sound happy, Kate. I wish you would tell me where this Nirvana is,' she scolded me gently. 'Come back. We'll sort the tosser out and send him to jail once and for all.'

'Ha, that's not going to happen,' I retorted. 'People like Will don't go to jail. But it's all behind me now. I've never been better. And… I'm pregnant.'

Silence, then, 'Oh my God, you're going to have a baby? Who is he?'

My skin suddenly went hot. 'I haven't met anyone,' I replied. 'It's Will's. I'm four months in.'

'Oh, sweetie… how do you feel about it?'

'I'm great now,' I assured her. 'I freaked out when I found out. But now I'm over the moon. This is my baby. Not his.'

'Then you need to make sure that he can't get to you in any way. Come back, talk to the police and tell them what you saw. Tell them what he was doing to you.'

'No, I don't want him to take up any more of my life. He doesn't deserve it.'

'But you need to protect yourself, Kate!'

'I am protecting myself, Tams. And I'm not coming back. I'm going to have this baby here.'

'When can I come and see you?'

'Soon. I promise. Take care of Mike first. And please send him my love. And to baby Jake.'

She sighed. 'Jesus, Kate. You were there for me when I was pregnant with Jake. I should be there for you!'

'But you are,' I insisted.

She sighed heavily. 'Promise to call me more regularly at least?'

'I'll try.'

'Okay, then, sweetie. Take care of yourself! Keep me posted about the baby! I love you!'

'I love you too,' I whispered, feeling my throat constricting. 'Got to go. Bye!'

And before she could say anything else, I hung up.

Now that she knew, I felt better. If anyone deserved the truth, it was Tamsin.

I had promised to meet up with Rosie for a cuppa at The Old Bell Inn. I was a bit early, so I went to Reception to say hello to Penny, Laura and Marie. Only Marie was on her own and quite frazzled.

'Hi, Marie, what's going on?'

'Penny and Laura are both at a conference in Truro. They'll be there all bloody day and I'm—'

'Miss, can we get some attention here please? We've been waiting for quite a while now and—'

'In a *minute*!' she yelled and covered her mouth in horror as the guest shrank back. 'Oh my God, I'm so, so sorry!'

'Marie,' I said, leaning over the counter. 'Go into the back office and get yourself a cool drink of water. I'll help these nice people out.'

She looked at me as if an alien had just landed from the sky right at her feet. 'I—are you sure?'

'Go, go,' I said, waving her away as I turned toward the guests. 'I'm so sorry, Marie's just had some terrible news at home.' A little white lie always helped to smooth things over in situations like these.

'Oh.' The guest nodded kindly. 'I understand.'

'Thanks ever so much. How can I help you?' I asked.

'Well, my wife is a vegetarian and she keeps getting meat brought to her and she is terrified of the sight of it.'

'Gosh, I'm so sorry,' I said. 'Let me take care of that for you.'

I leaned over the counter, picked up the phone and glanced at the Kitchen extension number. A deep, gruff voice answered.

'*What?*'

'Reception here. I'm with Mrs…' I glanced at the wife.

'Halverton,' she replied.

'Mrs Halverton, one of our most esteemed guests,' – I was

throwing everything in there today but the kitchen sink – 'is a vegetarian and has had to send back every single meal as it is always meat. Do you think that you could ask the chef to prepare something super special to make it up to her?'

'Who the hell are you?' the voice demanded.

'Hotel inspection, actually,' I lied. I was getting good at this!

Silence. Then, 'Of course, so sorry.'

'Thank you. I'll be waiting with them at their table.'

'Right.' And then he hung up. I had a feeling he *was* the chef. Just instinct. Which meant that Penny needed to straighten this person out. No respectable hotel should have an ogre answering the phone like that.

I managed the phones for a few minutes while Marie pulled herself together. Poor thing, she was still new, but something told me she'd be okay. She was sweet and smart. The rest, she could work on.

About half an hour later, with plenty of time to spare for my meeting, Rosie, Penny and Laura burst into Reception.

'Marie, we heard, we're so sorry!' Penny called as she came round the counter desk to hug her.

Marie looked up from her Bookings screen, frazzled but not as much as before. 'Eh?'

'Your brother…?' Laura prompted.

Marie's mouth fell open. 'My brother? What's *happened* to him?'

'Sally told me that you got a call from home…'

'No, no, that was just me trying to gain a few minutes of peace,' I explained. Wow, news really did travel fast in small towns. Even made-up news. No wonder Mrs Nankivell had the low-down on every man that had spoken to me since I'd arrived. 'Marie was all on her own and I just happened to be here. I hope it's okay?'

Penny blinked at me. 'Okay? Sophie, you're a bloody star! Marie, I'm so sorry to have left you on your own: my mistake. I'll make it up to you. How's dinner for your family here tonight, on the house?'

Marie was almost in tears, though I didn't know if was due to her boss's generosity, or the shock of thinking that something had happened to her brother. 'Thank you, Penny.'

'And Sophie, you should have dinner here, too. Rosie and Dad will be there. Please say you'll join us!'

The prospect of eating on my own tonight did not appeal to me. On the other hand, the idea of seeing some of my new friends cheered me up immensely. 'I wouldn't miss it for the world, Penny, thank you!'

What a lovely girl. No wonder Rosie was crazy about her. These were good people. And yet, here I was, still lying to them about who I really was. I didn't deserve such good friends.


The next morning, I found Piers in my office, his back to the door, looking out onto the grounds.

'M-morning,' I said as I put my handbag down on the floor while keeping the one with Trixie close to my chest. Something told me that this was going to be a very short conversation.

He whirled around. 'Morning. Sorry, I didn't hear you coming.'

I shrugged. 'Look, Piers, I want to apologise again—'

He raised his hands. 'No, wait, please. I'm the one who needs to apologise, Sophie. You've been doing an amazing job here and I was an absolute arse with you. You didn't deserve it and I'm really sorry. It's my fault because I'm a privacy freak. It won't happen again.'

'Thank you. And I'll be more discreet.'

'Thank you.'

'So I still have a job?'

He grinned. 'Your job was never at stake. You're the best I've ever had.'

*Better than Patsy?* I wanted to ask, but that would have been pushing it.

'So are you,' I replied, thinking how true that was. Working for the firm and Will had never been a walk in the park at the best of times, so working for Piers and Whisper Farm here at Rosestones Manor had given me the sense of belonging I'd sorely lacked.

'What I mean is,' he cleared his throat, 'I'm happy you work here. I enjoy our banter. I enjoy your company.'

Oh? I must have really been love-starved if these kind words made my skin tingle to the point that I couldn't say anything remotely intelligible. So he enjoyed my company? Many people enjoyed the company of others without it actually meaning anything, right? So why was the moment so awkward? I had to say something to cut the tension.

'S-so do I, Piers,' was all I could muster. And when I finally managed to look up into his face, there was a tenderness that I hardly recognised. Was it a tenderness based on pity? He knew I was a single, soon-to-be mum who'd moved away from her home and who was desperate for a job. Did I scream down and out that loudly? Come to think of it, almost everyone I'd met had shown me instant kindness. And then I knew. They pitied me, maybe even because of the baby! *Piers* pitied me…

'I need to get started,' I whispered, reaching over to grab something from my bag, but he gently caught my hand.

Surprised, my eyes swung to his.

'I just want you to know that… I'm here for you, Sophie. Whatever you need. I'm not just saying that as your employer. I'm saying it as a friend. Hopefully, a good friend?'

'Yes, of course,' I whispered, unable to bear the tension. It felt like he wanted to stay a little longer. Probably to make sure I was okay. God forbid he had any other kind of interest in me. 'Thank you. I—'

'Sophie?' he said softly, gently squeezing my fingers. 'Would you like to stay for dinner?'

'Dinner…?'

'Yeah. Just you and me again, how's that?'

'Uhm, that would be… lovely.'

He grinned at me beseechingly. 'Yeah?'

I grinned back. 'Yeah.'

'Okay, then. Tonight when you're done, come to the kitchen with me and I'll whip you up the best dinner you ever had.'

'Okay,' I said, feeling my face going red.

How I managed to stay concentrated on my work for the rest of the day, I don't know. I had at least a dozen calls to make between orders and issues and chase-ups. Even the extra hours passed in a blur: all I could do was think about dinner.

At one minute past six, I appeared in the kitchen where he directed me to a stool.

'But I want to help,' I said.

'Nu-uh. You are my guest and I am your cook.' And everything suddenly shifted. I can't explain how, but being alone with him again while he cooked me a meal spoke of a normal domestic life. A life I had tried to build with Will but had never attained. And now, an amazing man I'd met mere months ago was treating me as if I was very important to him. I just wasn't used to all that kindness and attention. Nor being waited on.

'So I can't even peel or dice or…?'

He washed his hands, turning to smile at me over his shoulder. 'Woman, I'm offering you a moment of rest. Take advantage, will you?'

I laughed. 'Okay, then! So what are you making?'

'Ah, but that is a *surprise*!' he said in a mock French accent.

'I will be able to guess when I see your ingredients,' I countered with a laugh.

'Ah, but will you?' he insisted.

'I'm no cook, but yeah, I think I will!'

'But the surprise is part of the pleasure!'

'Oh, go on, then, surprise me,' I said, turning around on my stool to look out the window instead. Outside the fairy lights began to twinkle amongst the flowers and shrubs and down the winding paths. It was a beautiful scene, but I couldn't well watch it all evening while an even more beautiful man was right next to me preparing dinner.

'So… talk to me,' he said.

'Can I turn around now? I promise I won't even try to guess. I'm a horrible cook anyway.'

'Well, it's fortunate for you that I'm here now,' he

answered, not looking up from a potpourri of vegetables which I tried to not identify, but there was a lot of green and red. Wait, what? Fortunate for me that he was here now? What did that mean? Because it sounded as if... I shook the thought out of my head. What a crazy idea. And yet, Piers was a very difficult man to resist under any circumstance, let alone being alone with him in his home.

These thoughts stayed with me as he made a mock-show of dicing and kneading and flipping dough (at this stage it had become obvious that he was making pizza). The simplicity of the meal made him all the more endearing to me. Anyone in his position would have tried to impress a girl with, oh, I don't know, some complicated French menu or something seen on one of Gordon Ramsay's shows. But no. He made wonky, individual pizzas that tasted like absolute heaven.

'You like?' he asked as we finally sat down and I took a huge bite out of my slice.

'Mmph-ph...' I assured him as I chewed in pure delight. 'You put Mrs Watts to absolute shame.'

He laughed, watching me eat. But I didn't mind. I was on my second slice before he even began to eat.

'You like your Italian, don't you?' he teased.

'I sure do!' I said as I took another bite.

He threw his head back and laughed. 'Are you going to come up for air any time soon?'

I shook my head and closed my eyes. All the freshest ingredients, the tomato sauce, the green and red peppers, the mozzarella cheese... delicious. And hand-made with love to boot. I could tell he enjoyed cooking almost as much as I enjoyed eating.

It was a lovely evening. We talked about a million things and I was surprised to see how similar we were beyond our lifestyle choices. He was a millionaire and I was a part-time worker. But besides that, we had the same taste in music, movies and books.

'I'm a real girl at heart,' he said. 'Like romantic movies? I'm bawling my eyes out ten minutes in.'

'You say it like it's a bad thing to cry.'

He took a sip of wine. 'You must be joking. It's cathartic. I cry all the time.'

'Really?'

'Romcoms, dramas, even documentaries. Trust me to always find the sentimental side.'

In my experience, the crying finally happened when I realised I needed healing. I wondered what he was healing from. What could he possibly be missing? He had a beautiful home, a flourishing business with staff that looked up to him and trusted him with their livelihoods. Perhaps he lacked... companionship?

'What are you thinking?' he asked.

'Huh? Oh, nothing. Just how similar we are.'

'We are, aren't we?' he agreed. 'I've never met anyone who also likes grape jelly on their meatballs.'

I laughed. 'I know, right?'

'It's hard to make friends when you're so busy with... life,' he sighed. 'You'd think that we'd make time for one of the most important things, right? But no, we have to go and put everything else first.'

'I've done that, too,' I confessed. 'When my ex-boyfriend and I started going out, my entire life changed. I forgot about my own interests, my friends, everything.'

'Well, we certainly won't be making that mistake again, will we, Sophie?'

'No, we won't.' What did he mean by *we*? The chemistry was certainly there. I could cut through it with a knife. And, as far as I was concerned, I fancied him madly. But could he really fancy me as well?

'Sophie?' he whispered. I looked up into his dark eyes.

'Yes?'

He studied me, then took a deep breath. 'Oh, to hell with it, I'm just going to come out and say it. I don't know what's happening to me. I mean, you come here to work and all I can think about is, what excuse can I make up to come and see you in your office? I can only ask about the German account so many times. And I don't want to look like a tosser or come across as a creep, but... these days with you? They're wreaking some serious havoc with my serenity. I think about you all night, in the morning, when I take Wolf for walkies, when I'm on the phone to my accountant, and it's driving me bonkers.' I couldn't think of a single thing to say back, too shocked by this seemingly impossible revelation. He must have read my silence for fear, though, because he continued, 'Sophie? I'm so sorry, I've scared the crap out of you, I know it. Please say something so I know you aren't going to run out of here screaming. I'll understand if you do. I just came across as absolutely obsessed. But I do really, really, really have feelings for you.'

I watched him, my mouth opening and closing. Piers had feelings for *me*? Real feelings?

'Sophie?' he whispered. 'Please say something.'

'I... I... uhm...' I stammered. Unable to speak, I simply nodded.

'Oh my God, what does that mean? You have feelings for me, too?'

Again, I nodded. I just couldn't believe it: he had feelings for me. The help. It was like in Cinderella. The girl who gets Prince Charming…

He slid off his stool. 'Sophie, I… I should like to kiss you. May I?'

Kiss me? Piers wanted to actually kiss me? And he'd actually asked? I don't think I'd ever been asked before, and it made me want it even more. I nodded again, still unable to say anything, feeling like an idiot, but fully aware of the magnetism drawing us together.

'Sophie, please say yes so I know I haven't misunderstood,' he whispered.

I looked into his dark, liquid eyes, unable to believe this was happening to me. 'Yes,' I whispered back. 'Kiss me.'

His mouth descended on mine delicately, tentatively, like a butterfly that had just been released from captivity; I was grateful for his hands cinching my waist, as standing on my own two feet had suddenly become very difficult. What was happening to me? I hadn't felt attraction like this for anyone, ever. It had enveloped me like a thick fog and the intensity of it almost scared me.

After a long, thorough kiss, I came up for air. 'I need to take it slow, Piers. I just got out of a horrible relationship, and I came to Starry Cove to get away from it.' And that wasn't even the half of it.

'I know…' he whispered, caressing my hair. 'And I'm…' he swallowed. 'I'm a bit of a mess myself right now. I have been for years.'

'I'm so sorry. Can I help you in any way? I'm a good listener.'

He chuckled, playing with a strand of my hair as his eyes flicked between my eyes and my mouth. He was an unique mixture of boyishness and maturity, so irresistibly sexy.

'I promised myself that I would leave you alone, that I wouldn't make your life even more complicated by dragging you into this, but... I find that I'm really, really happy when you're around, Sophie, and I got the feeling that you might be, too?'

I swallowed. *Busted*. I nodded, not trusting my voice, and he lowered his lips to mine again Oh my God, it was like the first time I had ever been kissed! The sparks everyone talks about, I'd never felt them before, but now? My whole head was full of flying, bright colours, clashing, psychedelic rainbows and nothing else, while my legs shook and I literally had to hang on to him for support.

When had all this happened? When had I fallen for him so completely? I had been in denial about the true depth of my feelings up until this moment. I always negated my feelings, but now, after all I'd been through, I couldn't hide from myself anymore. I was *terribly* attracted to Piers. Reality had made me dismiss it as a tiny boss crush. We all had those, right? I'd had one on Will and look where that had got me. But now I couldn't deny it.

'I'll tell you my secret if you tell me yours,' he whispered against my lips.

I bit my lip, pulling away an inch or two. 'I—I can't, yet, Piers. Please don't take this the wrong way. I haven't told anyone.'

He nodded. 'Okay. You're not ready, I understand. Perhaps it's for the best. Maybe soon enough, we'll share our stuff.'

'What if we can't?' I asked in anguish. 'What if it changed everything between us?'

'Did you do something wrong?' he asked. 'Did you hurt anyone? Not that you ever could, Sophie, I know that.'

I shook my head. 'Have you?'

'No. But some people think so.'

'Can't you straighten them out?'

Piers looked down at me with infinite tenderness. 'If only I could. But with some people, you just can't change their minds.'

'I know,' I agreed. 'But if you've never harmed anyone, what can be so horrible that we can't talk about it?'

'And you?' he countered softly. 'Couldn't I argue the same thing?'

He was right. He could be trusted, I knew that. I nodded. 'Just give me some time. Okay?'

'Okay. Of course,' he whispered, kissing me once more.

Perhaps it was much too early to start over again with love. I still needed to heal, to make space in my life for myself and my baby. I needed to attain the quality of a good, normal life. My happiness did not depend on a man. I told myself this every day. But every night, when I turned out the lights and huddled into bed, I thought about all the mistakes I'd made, and how the choice to stay in a relationship that resembled more a war than love had weighed me down. And the sense of serenity that I had been feeling for almost the entire day would always dissolve into thin air. I was lonely, no doubt about it.

And I hated it, because I wanted to feel empowered like all those kick-arse women that didn't need a man. I was sure that *they* didn't long to feel the joy of someone's company over the breakfast bar, or that they didn't mind returning to the echoes of an empty house. How do you get to be strong and happy on your own when it was only natural to share your thoughts and your dreams with your loved ones?

Then I thought about the Coastal Girls. They were strong and independent and happy. Nina was in love with an amazing man who kissed the ground she walked on. Nat's husband's eyes lit up whenever she walked into the room, and Rosie's husband couldn't bear to be away from her. Even Faith and Emmie's husbands, Henry and Jago, were so obviously head over heels for their wives. Hopefully, now with Piers around, I wouldn't be lonely anymore.

The next afternoon, there was a knock on the door of my office. It was Piers carrying his laptop and the look on his face boded nothing good. By now, Trixie was used to his visits, but she could smell Wolf on him and sniffed his ankles. Had I done something wrong? Had we upset a client?

'What's wrong?' I asked.

He stepped toward the desk, his face pale.

'There's, uhm, something I need you to see.'

'What is it?'

'It's about your boyfriend.'

'What? You mean my ex-boyfriend?' I asked, my insides already liquefying.

'It appears to be that he's looking for you. Along with the police...'

My limbs went numb, the horror slithering up my thighs and settling into my stomach like a pool of venom. I should have known yesterday was too good to be true. How would Piers ever want to be with me now that all my lies had been exposed?

'H-how do you know that?'

He looked up at me again, as if trying to gauge how resilient I was. 'He's posted a video on social media about you.'

'*What?*'

With a long sigh, he put his laptop down before me and lifted the lid.

'I had a tough time deciding whether to tell you, but here it is: "Missing: Kate Miller, twenty-five years old, last seen in London. Miss Miller is wanted by the police for theft and blackmail." This *is* you here, isn't it?'

There was no denying it was me, of course, and now I was sure that I was about to have a bloody heart attack. Months of pretending, hiding and hoping Will would leave me alone so I could build myself a new life away from him. And now this.

I nodded.

'I'm sorry for lying to you, Piers. I am innocent. Truly, I am. But I had to run away to protect myself and my baby from *him*. He stole confidential files on his clients at the firm we both worked at. And he blackmailed them, framing me by planting a copy of those files in my home in London. It's a filthy mess but I've got absolutely nothing to do with it.'

'There's more, I'm afraid.'

'What? What could be worse than this?'

He took a long, deep breath and exhaled loudly, pushing Play and, much to my horror, Will came to life, showing the camera a picture of us on one of our very first dates five years ago. Oh my God…

'This is my fiancée, Kate Miller. She's been missing for some time now, but the police have no idea where she is. They don't even know if she's alive anymore!'

*What the actual…?*

He rubbed his forehead, seemingly trying to pull himself together. 'We had an argument about something stupid—I can't even remember, maybe it was about a party I didn't want to go to… but she left while I was at work. I'm worried sick about her.' I rolled my eyes, and Piers gave me a look I couldn't decipher. 'To signal her whereabouts, please contact the nearest police station.' Then he leaned closer to the camera. 'Please, Kate, come back. I promise everything will be all right! I just need to know you and our unborn baby are alive… I don't care about the documents. Just come back.' He began to really bawl. 'And please, please don't hurt our child!'

And then the image winked off.

'I don't believe it,' I cried, dropping my head into my hands again, panic squeezing my throat. 'He mustn't find me! He mustn't find me!'

'And the baby? You said he didn't know about the baby,' Piers whispered.

'He didn't! He doesn't! There's no way on earth he could know!' Tamsin would have never told him in a million years.

'So he's just shooting in the dark?'

'Yes!'

'And the theft? And the blackmailing?'

'Lies! All lies! Piers, I promise I can explain everything if you'll just let me.' Piers was silent, and so I did. I explained the years of Will's abuse, how I had gone to his house that day to end things for good. I explained how Tamsin had called me, how he'd framed me by hiding the documents in my place, and how I had escaped to Cornwall on a whim. Piers listened intently, giving nothing away.

'But I had no time to run home and pack, so I took some of his fiancée's things. His real fiancée. Her name is… Sophie. Sophie Graham.' The fact that I'd lied to everyone, as horrible as it was, only came second to my baby's safety. 'If he finds me, he'll have my baby taken away from me!'

Piers's face paled instantly. 'Jesus wept…' He stood up and took my hands. 'That is not going to happen. You have my word.'

'But… But…' I was sobbing so hard by this point that I could barely speak.

'Come on, look at me. Do you actually think I'd let anything happen to you? I'll protect you. I have excellent security. No one will get in without my permission.'

I shook my head, swiping at another tear. 'You don't understand, Piers. He's already won. Sending me into this panic, terrifying me, it's what he does. Now anyone in Starry Cove with internet will know the truth. I can't lead a normal life for fear of being found. If I know him as well as I do, he's already got a private investigator on my tracks. I should have never come here; what an idiot I am! I came here for a new start and it's all falling apart!'

Piers's dark eyes searched mine. 'Do you trust me?'

'Yes,' I said in earnest.

'Okay then, Soph—sorry, Kate: listen to me. We *will* get through this. I promise you.'

He pulled out his mobile phone.

'What are you doing?'

'I'm calling my lawyer.'

I shook my head. 'That's no good. Will is a lawyer. A very important one. He belongs to a huge firm. He'll eat us all up for breakfast!'

'From now on, I'm taking care of this. You can leave it with me.'

'But…'

'Trust me, you'll survive this. This isn't going to be easy, but you will get through this. Because otherwise, you're letting him win all over again. Hang on, it's ringing… Lee? It's me. I've got a bit of an emergency at Rosestones. It's a private matter. How soon can you get here? In thirty minutes? Perfect.'

He hung up and smiled at me. 'We're going to find out exactly where we stand. See if we can get some leverage.'

'Leverage?'

'To get him off your back.'

'You mean blackmail?'

'Leverage, blackmail, tomato, *tomato*…'

I stared at him blankly. Wasn't I already in trouble for blackmail? Why make my fake crime a reality?

'Sometimes, you have to do anything you can to protect yourself. You wouldn't do this for your baby?'

I sat up. 'Absolutely, I would. I'll tell your lawyer all I know. Only…' I didn't have that kind of money.

Piers read my mind and lifted his hand. 'No worries. I've got your back.'

'Thank you for understanding.'

'I actually do... understand what you're going through.' I wondered what that meant, but I was in no state to ask questions. I knew Piers and I would have to have a conversation about what this meant for us at some point, but right now, I was just glad that he was taking action.

'Thank you. I can't believe you have your own lawyer on call, though. Who the hell are you: the prime minister?'

He chuckled. 'We need to get you sorted so you can live your life in peace. Now go and wash your face. I'll see you downstairs in the drawing room, okay?'

'Okay,' I whispered as I made my way to the door.

'Hey,' he called after me.

I turned.

He was smiling. 'Chin up, Kate Miller. We're going to get you through this.'

Through my tears, I smiled back at him. It was good to have someone who really cared.

# 19

When I came down, Piers's lawyer was already in the study and they were discussing my situation.

'Kate, come have a seat. This is my mate, Lee Simmonds. Lee, this is Kate Miller. I'll leave the two of you to it.'

It was strange, but also a relief, to see how quickly Piers had taken to my new identity. 'Stay,' I whispered. 'Please.'

Without saying anything, he sank back into his seat as Lee opened up a legal pad.

'So,' he said. 'Piers's been filling me in on your situation. Mind if I ask you some questions?'

He came with Piers's guarantee, so I nodded.

'Okay, so how long had you and your ex-boyfriend been together?'

*Forever*. 'Five years.'

'And how was the relationship in the beginning?'

I bit my lip. 'It was great. Like any other happy relationship.'

'Any major fights?'

'No, never.'

'Nothing at all?'

I shrugged. 'No. Will started off as a really happy bloke. Then at one point, he began to come home more and more stressed each day. I'd ask him to open up but he'd say he didn't want to talk about it. So I'd leave it at that.'

Lee began to scribble away. 'And then?'

'And then, one day, when he came over really late and I asked him where he'd been, he told me to mind my own effing business.'

Next to me, I could feel Piers tense as he ran his hands up and down his thighs, but he said nothing.

'Did you ever suspect that he had someone else?' Lee asked. You could tell he was used to all this kind of stuff. Ugly stuff.

I nodded. 'Just recently. Does it make any difference?'

'Not in your case, no. Not with a baby on the way.'

At first, I resented Piers for revealing my business to his lawyer, but I reasoned with myself. It had to come out sooner or later, and it was for the best.

'Is he the father?' Lee asked, never lifting his eyes from his agenda.

*Of course he is*, I almost snapped, but bit my lip. 'Yes.'

He put his pen down and looked at Piers, then at me. 'Unless we can prove he is violent, he has the right to see his own child. I imagine he'll push for that pretty hard.'

'Well, he's never been physically violent, but he's threatened to hurt me before. I have screenshots of his texts.'

Again, Piers's hands slid along his thighs.

'Did you tell the police?'

I shook my head.

'Did you tell anyone at all?'

'No.'

Lee looked at me directly. 'I'll be frank with you, Kate. Threatening texts aren't enough to stop him from seeing the baby on a regular basis once it's born. Unless you sue him for sole custody.'

Buckets of ice-cold water splashed down my spine and I gasped.

Piers took my hand, holding it in his. 'We'll get it sorted, won't we, Lee?' he said flatly. Obviously, Piers was not used to being denied much from his lawyer.

Lee's eyes swung down to acknowledge the gesture but he said nothing and I could feel my ears slowly beginning to burn.

I fished my mobile out of my pocket and tapped on the screenshots of Will's messages that I had sent to my new phone from my old one.

The minute they came up on the screen, I flinched, almost as if he was in the same room with me. I leaned over and passed it to Lee, wanting to spare Piers the ugliness of it all. But I could feel Piers scanning Lee's face, whose only reaction to Will's violent nature was the shooting up of his eyebrows, but he said nothing.

'Don't forget that Will stole the company documents. She saw them in his home,' Piers said.

'Without any witnesses or proof of that or of any physical abuse, this isn't enough to hold up in court. Right,' he said giving my mobile back to me and shuffling his documents.

*No, no, no!* This couldn't be happening! I had to stop Will from ever laying eyes on Baby.

'I'll get on it and let you know what's what.'

*That's it?* I wanted to cry. *You can't do anything more to protect my baby?*

'Thank you, Lee,' I heard Piers say. 'We appreciate your help.'

He lifted his thumb and nodded at Piers, who got up to follow him to the door.

Barely sitting upright on the settee, I was spiralling, desperate to protect my baby. Maybe the solution was to run away again. I didn't want to leave Starry Cove and this semblance of a life I'd finally managed to eke out, but there was no way I could risk my baby's life.

When he was gone, Piers turned back to me and kneeled before me, taking my hands in his. 'Hey, are you all right?'

I knew he wanted to help me. But he couldn't. Nobody could. I had to get through this alone. No more depending on a man or even expecting anything from them. No more doing their bidding just because they seemed charming. I would never again fall into that kind of trap.

'I have to go,' I said, getting to my feet.

'Go where?'

'I don't know. Far from here. My baby and I aren't safe here.'

'Of course you are. Will nor the police have no idea where you are.'

'They'll find me!' I cried, now out of control. If it had only been about my life, I would have accepted my fate. But not my baby. She wasn't going to live in fear as I did!

'Now listen to me a minute, Kate. We're going to go to Tulip Cottage to grab some of your stuff. You're staying with me, okay? I can't even think of you anywhere on your own. You'll be safe here.'

For how long? There was nothing he could do if the police came knocking on his door. But I didn't want to be on my own tonight. I needed one last night before I took the matter into my own hands.

And I also needed to come clean with the girls now. It wasn't fair that I kept this secret from them any longer; I hoped that I would get to them before they saw the video of Will. Even without knowing my story, they had sensed that I was vulnerable and had grouped to help me, the first being Emmie. She would listen to me. Even if she decided not to forgive me, at least she would let me explain. I owed her, and all the girls, that much.

I phoned her to let her know I wouldn't be able to make it to our lunch.

'We heard. It's all over the internet, I'm so sorry. How *are* you?'

'It's all lies, Emmie…' I assured her. 'I didn't steal or blackmail anyone.'

'Oh, I know that! Your ex is just one of those typical monsters who think they're entitled to anything they want just for existing. I had one of those too, I told you.'

'Yes, but this is a mess. I'm sure he'll try and sue for full custody of the baby. If he finds me, I'm dead.'

'He won't find you, Sophie. I mean, Kate. Weird calling you that.'

'I'm so sorry I lied to you all.'

'We understand, really. But you're safe now. Piers will take care of you. We all will. No one from outside is getting to you. You have our word.'

I swiped at my eyes for the umpteenth time that day. I didn't deserve such nice people around me.

'Tell you what,' she said, and I snorted amidst my tears. 'What's so funny?'

'You sounded like Robert,' I said.

She chuckled. 'I did, didn't I? By the way, he's been fishing around here for news about you.'

'Well, now he's got it. Missing and dangerous. Yay me.'

'Rubbish. I'm coming over. Plus, it will be good to see Piers as well. Just let me close the barge for the day.'

'You don't have to do that,' I protested, but inside, I was grateful that she wanted to come and see me. I missed her lovely company. I missed all the Coastal Girls.

'I want to,' she assured me. 'It'll do Felicity and me some good to see you. See you in a bit!'

'Okay,' I agreed, hanging up and heading for the kitchen to tell Piers that she was coming.

'You look better,' Piers said as I entered the kitchen. He and Justin were wearing aprons and peeling potatoes for Mrs Watts while Wolf examined their every move in the hope of some scraps. It was a good thing that I kept Trixie upstairs where she was safe.

'I am, thank you. Emmie Moon is coming over, if that's all right?'

'Of course. Is she bringing Felicity? I love that kid. Justin, please go dig up some more spuds. Emmie loves a shepherd's pie like you wouldn't believe.'

Justin nodded and wiped his hands on his apron. 'Yes, sir.'

'Oh, I don't know if she can stay for dinner,' I said.

Piers grinned. 'We'll convince her.'

A few minutes later, when I threw the door open, Emmie was bobbing up and down with Felicity in her arms.

'Hi-lovely-to-see-you-need-a-pee-desperately-please-hold-this!' she babbled, passing Felicity to me before shooting off down the corridor.

'Oh, sure, it's down the—'

'I know!' she called over her shoulder and disappeared. I looked down at the gurgling beauty in my arms. 'She knows,' I told her. 'And how are you, Little Miss Moon?' I cooed. 'Are you doing well? You're certainly heavier than the last time I held you. Mummy must be feeding you well.'

Felicity spewed some stuff up which I readily used her bib to wipe up while I attempted to remove her little cardigan one-handedly. Which wasn't as easy as I'd thought. And then I began to panic all over again. Would I be able to do this for my own baby? How was I going to manage raising her on my own? And work? I'd have to find a job that would let me do both. Even if I figured out a way to stay in Starry Cove, Piers had already made it clear that this position was temporary. And the fact that we had confessed our feelings for each other didn't mean that things would progress between us. Not after this bombshell.

'Hey, look who's here, Little Miss Moon!' came Piers's voice from behind. The apron was gone but he had a tea towel over his shoulder and a genuine smile on his face. 'May I?'

I nodded and surrendered my charge to him, my arms aching. I was going to be absolutely crap at this mother thing, I just knew it. Even Piers looked like a natural, and when Felicity gurgled again, she did it on the tea towel on his shoulder rather than down the front of his shirt.

'There you go, Missy,' he cooed and Felicity looked up into his face and giggled.

'Where's your Mummy?' he asked her.

'She went to the toilet; she'll be right back,' I informed him.

'She'll be ages in there,' he chuckled. 'Apparently, she loves all the pretty little soaps that Faith gave me during the renos.'

'Oh, she did the work?'

'Wouldn't have done it without her. I'm glad she got rid of Gabe and married Henry instead. Rockstars are unreliable,' he said. 'Let's go back to the kitchen and warm a bottle up for our little treasure here, shall we?'

In a daze, I followed him. Warm a bottle? How familiar was he with Emmie and everyone else? Was he not practically a hermit?

'Hey you, Elephant Man,' Emmie called as she followed us into the kitchen where he proceeded to boil the kettle.

'Hiya, munchkin,' he said back as he kissed her cheek, all while I watched them in stunned silence. Then he turned to me. 'We go way back to even before Emmie arrived in Cornwall. We met at a…'

'Soap shop,' Emmie offered sheepishly. 'That's where we, uhm, all met him, actually.'

'You all met him at a soap shop?' I repeated as they shifted their attention to Felicity.

*Okay. Weird.*

'Here, stick the bottle in this,' Piers offered her a ceramic cereal bowl which he filled with some hot water from the kettle. 'That should warm it up.'

'Thank you,' she whispered, eyeing me.

'So,' she said, seating herself in the bay window to the right of the island to feed Felicity. 'How are you coping? I can't imagine having to deal with something like that. But you're safe here. Isn't she, Piers?'

'Of course,' he said, keeping his eyes averted from me. *Hm.* 'I told her so.'

'I know, and thanks again, but we know that I can't stay here forever.'

'Don't worry about that for now.'

'Th-that's very generous of you, but I can't accept— it goes against my principles. I can get along just fine by myself.'

'Kate,' he whispered and Emmie looked up at us. 'Stop worrying. He can't get to you here.'

'And good luck penetrating the Starry Cove Force Shield,' Emmie added. 'We take care of our own down here.'

'But that's just the thing,' I argued. 'I'm not one of you.'

'None of us were,' she answered simply, giving Felicity a respite from the bottle. 'Look at me. Look at Faith. Nina. Only Nat really has lived in the area, but she used to live up on the cliffs with that jerk of a surgeon husband who always kept to himself.'

'Yeah, well, Neil is odd,' Piers said. 'But he's not a bad man, really. They just weren't a good fit, is all.'

'How is it that you know everybody, always holed up here?' I asked before I could stop myself.

'It wasn't always like that,' he whispered as Emmie shot him a glance. 'I used to be one of the boys before I... went away.'

Went away where, exactly?

'Jago, Henry, Jack, Gabe. We all went to school together.'

'Whenever Jago bothered to show up,' Emmie added with a giggle. 'Thank God things are different now.'

'Things change, yes,' he said. 'And people change.'

What secret was Piers so desperately trying to keep, I wondered?

'And then came Mitchell from Ireland, luckily for Rosie. And Shane too.'

'This place,' I said. 'It's all so strange, with all its celebrities hiding away from the rest of the world. No wonder the villagers are so protective.'

'Well, they've earned their place here,' Emmie said and Piers nodded. 'They've donated consistently to our school, to the church, to the town. Nina insists on her movies being shot here to create jobs in the area. There's actually a filming studio on the edge of town, and Piers used to let the Manor be used as a set before—' She bit her lip, and an awkward silence descended on the kitchen.

'How about I make us all a nice cup of tea?' Piers offered, clapping his hands before he began to open and shut cupboards, then opened the side window to call into the vegetable patch. 'Justin! Where are the *good* goodies? Stop holding out on me!'

'In the pantry, in the Tupperware containers, sir!' was the answer.

'Ah! Yes, now we're talking!' Piers cheered, rubbing his hands together, and disappeared through the side door to return with his arms full of plastic containers which he proceeded to open. 'I knew it, you old dog!' Piers chimed as he lifted a container and held it to his chest like Emmie held Felicity. 'And here, ladies, and baby, with an array of the most exquisite apples from my old friend Jack's orchard, may I present to you Justin's ultimate masterpiece, the apple pie?'

By this time, Wolf was on his hind legs, practically begging. 'Sorry, old friend. This stuff is bad for you.' Instead, Piers pulled a chewy biscuit out of his pocket and Wolf did something akin to a triple somersault to make sure he didn't miss it. He was so adorable. I wished that he liked other dogs. He and Trixie would have had a whale of a time.

'Piers, I forgot,' Emmie said haltingly. 'My tyres look a bit deflated. Can you come outside and give them a proper kick?'

At that, he looked at her, somewhat resigned. 'Yep,' he said tersely and followed Emmie and Felicity out the door.

*Of all the lamest excuses*, I said to myself, but my own thoughts were interrupted by a hissing. Piers had left the window open in his haste to grab the goodies.

'When are you going to tell her? How long are you going to string her along for like that? It's not fair on her. And it's not fair on us.'

He groaned. 'I know.'

'We deserve better, Piers.'

'I said I *know*, Em. But I'm not ready.'

'Not ready? This woman is falling in love with you, can't you *see* that?'

'Yes.'

'So what are you going to do about it?'

'I don't know yet.'

'You have feelings for her too, don't you?'

He was silent.

'Tell her the truth. Don't put me in this position, or anyone else, for that matter. Tell her. You can trust her.'

'I know. But it's myself I don't trust.'

'You make it sound like it was your fault.'

'Wasn't it?'

'Piers, you know we love you, but you have to get on with it. Sophie – I mean Kate – clearly cares about you.'

It was true. I did care about him. More than I realised. But did he care at all for me now, after my revelation? And even though I'd shared my biggest secret, there was something he still wasn't telling me. Based on my behaviour of lying and keeping secrets, I guess I couldn't very well blame him.

Emmie didn't stay long after that. Something had shifted in the atmosphere and she thought best to dissolve, but not without a promise to come back with the rest of the Coastal Girls.

As for me, I spent the rest of the evening moping in my office. She had referred to something he needed to get over. Probably another woman. Perhaps he was treated badly like I was. But surely now that he knew about how Will had treated me, he could confide in me about his own past relationship?

Or was I being selfish and presumptuous? I didn't know what he'd been through, to be honest. It could have been way worse than my predicament. Something much more painful. Mine was all about my fear of losing my baby. Perhaps Piers had actually lost someone dear to him? And perhaps he wasn't over it, and never could get over it. Maybe that was what was stopping him from having a real relationship with me or any other girl? Because his pain was bigger than his love? If that was the case, who was I to stand here and expect him to be a part of my life, if he needed to sort himself out first? It wasn't fair on him.

I huffed and sat down to pay Piers's company bills and tidy up the office as if it was my last day there. And perhaps it was. I had betrayed everyone, even if I'd had my good reasons; the reality of it was that instead of Sophie, they now had Kate foisted upon them. Kate, thief and blackmailer extraordinaire. How could I ask them to trust Kate when she'd done nothing but lie? And how could Kate expect Piers to make good on his promises to take care of her? Based on what, the fact that she had a temporary job with his company? No, I couldn't depend on him.

These thoughts swirled through my head for the rest of the day. Just as the sky was turning purple outside my window, Piers walked in.

'Hey,' he said, leaning on the mahogany desk, his arms lifting to embrace me but falling to his sides when I made no attempt. *Stay cold, stay distant.*

He stopped and studied me in silence as I faffed around with my file folders as if my life depended on them. 'Hey,' I said, piling all the recent correspondence to my left next to the phone, unable to meet his eyes.

As I tidied up all the pens and pencils, just killing time now, I wondered whether Emmie had finally convinced him to confess to me whatever his secret was. But who was I to judge? I'd been duping everyone since the day I arrived. I'd got a cottage, a doctor and a job, all with no ID. Such was their trust, and look how I'd reciprocated. The least I could do was make it easy for him.

'Piers, I… I'm going to go…'

'What? Go where?'

I shrugged, taking the pencils out again and putting them back in, tips down. 'I'm not quite sure yet, but I've taken advantage of you and Starry Cove enough.' And I meant it. I needed to disappear. I just needed to be careful wherever

I moved to, to not become too friendly with anyone. Not to care for anyone too much. And not to love anyone too much.

He stepped forward and we were face to face. 'But why? I told you I'd protect you.'

'I can't do this right now, Piers,' I said, grabbing my bag. Where had Trixie gone off to?

'No, Kate, you can't go. I don't want you to. I care about you.'

'Even after…'

'Yes.'

He lifted my chin so I had to look up at him. 'I'm not the best with words. Nor am I particularly open about my feelings. I'm a private bloke; you know this. But I can tell you that I do care about you and I will protect you.'

Perhaps he could protect me, if only for a little while.

'Will you stay? Please?' he whispered.

I certainly couldn't go back to Tulip Cottage now, in the middle of the night. I sighed and finally nodded.

The next day, I received a visit from old Nan at Rosestones. Even if she hadn't seen Will's video, I now knew that she was an incorrigible gossip. Someone else in the village would have told her. She was pulling a trolley full of goods and looking much better than the last time I'd paid her a visit.

'Hello, love, how are we doing today? Something for when your tot arrives.' So everyone did know now. 'There hasn't been a birth in Starry Cove since little Felicity Moon. The whole village is ecstatic.'

I pushed back a sob and hugged the old dear. She smelled fresh, like a sheaf of mint just picked from the garden. 'Nan, you're spoiling me rotten…'

'Nothing but the best for our newest Starry Covian.'

At those kind words, my eyes welled up completely. But her message was clear. That whatever anyone said, it was the villagers' duty to protect anyone living here. That was a great code to live by, and I had to give back somehow. I had to reassure her that her kindness, even in the face of scandal, hadn't been misplaced.

'He's lying, Nan,' I blurted out. 'My ex-boyfriend,' I assured her, wondering how many people would doubt me now. 'I would never blackmail anyone. I only ran to protect my baby. Please believe me…'

Nan sighed. 'Oh, pet! I knew the minute I saw you that someone had hurt you badly. Your little forlorn face was a portrait of dereliction and fear when you arrived here. And now look at you! You've come such a long way with a little love and kindness. This is your home now.'

'But don't you understand, Nan. If someone gives me away, he'll find me, and he'll just take my baby away from me. I couldn't bear that!'

'Well, that is simply not going to happen,' she assured me right back. 'Piers has got proper security and he won't let anything happen to you. He's not a bloody world-famous rockstar for nothing, you know!'

# 20

A rockstar? Piers?

How had I never even heard of him? I liked to consider myself pretty knowledgable on celebrities; even if he'd been a child prodigy, he was still young, so it couldn't have been that long ago. In any case, not long enough for people to forget. What the heck was going on?

After Nan had taken her leave, I made a beeline for Piers's office. He was on conference calls and, Justin told me, would be so for most of the night. I wanted to tell him I knew, to hear it from his own mouth. But when I went to bed, his conference call was still going. So I gave up and brought my phone with me as I knew that there was no way I was going to sleep without putting my detective skills to the test to find out which famous rockstar had turned country squire. I typed in his name, Starry Cove, Cornwall and all sorts of key words, like *mystery famous rockstar, rockstars who have disappeared off the face of the earth,* etc., and thousands of websites popped up.

Most of them were dedicated to Blade, the faceless lead

guitar and singer of the rock band Kyllyx Attica. His identity had always been concealed due to the fact that he always wore a mask and make-up to cover up his face.

How was this possible? Piers Henshaw, CEO of Whisper Farm and Lord of Rosestones, was also the lead singer of a famous rock band? It simply didn't compute in my mind. Apparently, I wasn't the only one with a double identity. Fancy that!

I'd had a passing fascination with Blade when he came onto the scene; like most people, I was intrigued about the man behind the mask, and why he chose not to reveal himself. That night, I stayed up and read everything I could find about him, watched every video, every interview and listened to every song. And then, only looking very closely, did I recognise his hands. He had large hands, with long, strong fingers. But apart from that, nothing else gave him away. I sat there, stunned, and continued to read.

People were crazy about him all over the world, and I'd been living in his home completely unaware. His real name was Kevin Sharpe, the websites said. Was it true, and Piers Henshaw was a pseudonym? Or was it the other way around? I typed in Piers Henshaw and only documents pertaining to Whisper Farm appeared. So Kevin Sharpe was a made-up name. How clever was that? He had a pseudonym for his pseudonym.

The die-hard fans had even resorted to identikits to try and posit what he looked like under the make-up, and the drawings were surreal. Some even went so far as to say that he was disfigured like the phantom of the opera, and all sorts of drawings popped up in my search. His face was unfathomable. No one knew his real eye colour, or the real shape of his mouth. If he really had any eyebrows. And yet, beneath the get-ups, the garters or the heels or whatever he chose to wear on any given night, he was perfectly masculine.

If they only knew how beautiful he was in real life.

Though it was only two years since he'd left the stage, it seemed like a lifetime had passed. I could scarcely recognise Piers in the made-up face contorted by pure passion for song. He wasn't afraid of showing his softer, feminine side.

In a tuxedo, he was to die for. Looking at the footage, you would think he had it all. Tall and fit, anything looked good on him, even the trashy newspaper headings he wore as a loincloth in the video of the song 'Trash', whose lyrics were in defiance of the press who seemed to be obsessed with him. One day, they hated him, the next, they crawled back to him, begging for more reasons to hate him and write about it. Whichever way you looked at it, he was their meal ticket, although he didn't care about them one jot.

He was a completely different person in his onstage outfits. Black leather pants, bare-chested, he was halfway between Tim Curry's *The Rocky Horror Picture Show* and any one of the members of the band Kiss. There was an almost insurmountable difference between his stage persona and the humble and grounded person I knew, who was capable of saying and doing things so profound. You would have never thought he was the same person stripping on stage while licking the microphone.

He was every star rolled into one, and yet, he was like no other. He had done every look, from schoolboy to Clark Kent to warlock, and had invented a thousand more. He had even done a drag number where you recognised him only when he opened his mouth to sing.

How many times he must have performed each song over and over again. It must have made him sick to the back of his teeth. But like every showman, he did it, making it better and different every time. Without flinching. Without tiring. On the outside. Judging by his sudden exit from the industry, and the fact that he was clearly desperate to keep it hidden from me, it was a different story on the inside.

There were crazy, high-octane songs that only true fans were familiar with, where his voice reached the highest octaves humanly possible, according to the press, who tagged him with irreverent yet awed rag titles and comments. The articles were endless. And as I studied the footage, I couldn't help but agree with the press that his flamboyance went beyond confident and arrogant. He was at one with the camera, but even more so with his fans, who adored him like a god. They knew every song, every pause, every silence. And all he had to do was raise an eyebrow or smile and the crowd would go ballistic. I personally never subscribed to that kind of fangirlish behaviour, but I had to admit that he did have an undeniable, inescapable allure.

In one video I watched, just as one song ended, he swayed on the stage in a tiny, latex loincloth with rhinestones that even Tarzan would have been shy in, the footage suddenly skipped to a darkened stage where he sat on a stool, lit by a single spotlight, in yet another outrageous outfit, delicately plucking away at an acoustic guitar or the piano while singing a delicate ballad.

Nothing could have been more of a mixed message, an anachronism. Your eyes saw one thing, yet your ears heard something completely different, and it was a few moments before you could even put the two together.

He and his band mates seemed to have been very close, practically living in symbiosis, more than brothers on the road, happy and carefree with their music. And yet, today, he lived like a recluse. So where were the others, his friends for life?

As far as his rapport with his fans went, he adored them. He was a real crowd-pleaser and communicator, stopping concerts to check on the wellbeing of his fans and helping Security to drag someone in trouble onto the stage to be carried to the medical station.

He never refused anyone an autograph and was always very amiable. He gave generously to various charities and pre-recorded public announcements in favour of social improvement, against drinking and driving, the use of drugs, respect for the more fragile, the diverse, etc.

But his relationship with the press was the opposite. And when his wife, drummer Jenna Rogers, alias Miss XS, was found floating face down in the pool of their LA mansion with a bullet in her head, the media went to town, blaming him for her drug-induced death. I remembered the scandal. It went on for more than a year. The trial, his (masked) face splashed onto every paper, TV show and website. That poor girl! What a waste of a life! And poor, poor Piers! The man I knew could have never murdered anyone, let alone his wife.

During the trial, fans had worried about his excessive weight loss while the media hounded him 24/7. You couldn't change the channel or open a newspaper or navigate the internet without seeing his image plastered everywhere.

People spoke of nothing else for months and months on end and frankly, I personally had grown sick and tired of seeing that same made-up, angry face without ever seeing the person behind it. During the trial in LA, cameras had not been allowed in the courtroom. The fact that very few people actually knew what he looked like had almost dehumanised him.

Friends of his and Jenna's had testified how he had tried to wean his wife off the drugs, but she was in with a bad crowd, and drugs were part and parcel when it came to the rockstar lifestyle. She'd been in rehab several times but nothing had ever stuck.

When the trial had finally come to an end with his acquittal due to lack of evidence, his subsequent disappearance from the scene had sparked suicide rumours. To this day, people were still wondering whether he was still alive, or if he was wasting away in a trailer somewhere in the backwaters of Idaho.

That was pretty much the gist of his life. A life I had no idea belonged to Piers. If they only knew how resilient he was! He'd managed to pull himself out of that mess and start a new life away from the spotlight, surrounded by his people who genuinely adored him, not some projected persona.

Now everything fell into place: the huge Steinway, his aversion to bright, artificial lights, his stand-offish attitude toward any kind of attention, his desperation for privacy, the villagers' stony silence wherever he was concerned. Starry Cove protected him, and he protected Starry Cove in return. There wasn't a village problem he couldn't solve, working closely with the parish to make sure his people were never left wanting. This was the Piers I knew. Blade was just an act. A potboiler.

How could I have not known, not recognised him as my kindred spirit? We had both forgone a life that, in one way or another, had kicked us to the kerb. We had both divested ourselves from who we were, or thought we were. And now there was nowhere left to hide.

The next morning, I cautiously made my way down to the orangery where Piers was having breakfast and reading the paper. He was probably very happy to not be in it anymore. How everything made so much more sense now. But I had to tell him I knew. It would be wrong to let him go on thinking that I had no idea.

'Hey, good morning!' he said with a smile while pulling out a chair for me. 'Sorry about last night but the meeting went on forever! Are you hungry? Mrs Watts has made your favourite—'

'I have to tell you something, Piers,' I said as I sat down opposite him.

'I'm listening.'

'Mrs Nankivell came to see me yesterday.'

'Yes, I know, we had a nice chat.'

I swallowed. 'She... told me your secret. It just slipped out, I think. I hope it's okay. I won't tell anyone, of course. You can trust me.'

He looked at me, his eyes searching mine for any judgement or awe. When he found none, he smiled shyly. 'Ah, the old dear's been positively dying to tell someone. Well, I'm glad it was you, Kate.'

I smiled. 'So am I. You never know what those gossips can do!'

We laughed and he caressed my cheek.

'Seriously, I want you to know that your secret is safe with me. I know what it's like to be accused of something you didn't do, to have your home and your privacy invaded.'

He studied me in silence, then finally nodded. 'Okay. I appreciate it.'

'I know what it means to be under a spotlight now. It sucks.'

He laughed. 'You got that right. But it never used to be that way. Not in the beginning, at least. But I guess I need to reinforce the concept of secrecy with old Nan!'

'You know, I'm almost ashamed to admit it. Of all people, I *know* my celebrities. I should have known.'

'Well, my fellow villagers did a great job in protecting me.'

'So everyone in Starry Cove knows?'

'Pretty much. I grew up here. I spent a lot of time with my grandmother, my rock.'

'Ah, that's so nice. Is she… still with us?'

He raised an eyebrow. 'What are you talking about? Mrs Nankivell is my nana.'

I felt my jaw drop. 'Mrs Nankivell is your *grandmother*?'

'I thought you knew.'

'Knew? I knew absolutely nothing! Oh goodness, there go any investigative journalism ambitions *I* had!'

'She was instrumental in my career,' Piers said. 'Every decision, every big tour, I'd always call her on the phone and she'd give me the courage to go ahead, because she believed I had a gift. But with a proviso: that no gift is ever just that. You will pay for it dearly for as long as you have it. But even though I gave it up, I'm still here paying for it all. Every single award, every single show, every single penny.'

'But you are still famous. People want you back; do you not read the papers? Stop checking the stock markets and get on Instagram.'

He laughed and pulled me in for a kiss. A nice, slow one, full of gratitude and trust. And, well, a little something else.

I teased him by pulling away slightly. 'So does that make Robert your cousin?'

'Yep. Although he and I don't get along much. At all, really.'

'But why?'

Piers sighed. 'He never approved of my lifestyle. I think he resents that I wasn't here for Nan like he was. Says she missed me a lot. Instead of leaving Cornwall to follow my dreams, he wanted me to stay here.'

'Looks like he got his wish in the end.'

'Yeah, looks like it. I mean, I've seen the whole world and now I just want to stay here. Everyone is like family to me, and they've guarded my privacy so far.'

'Even still, I'm surprised the press hasn't managed to track you down,' I said.

He shook his head. 'Luckily, when we started out, we didn't use our real names. Yeah, we had stage names, but under that, we thought to protect ourselves with aliases. It's only thanks to that that I have total privacy. People think my real name is Kevin Sharpe. Good luck with that!'

'I'm sorry,' I said, 'to have just stumbled upon your life like this.'

'You were going to find out sooner or later. I'm just grateful that you're in it now.' He wrapped his arms around me and held me tight against his chest. 'No more secrets; no more lies. Because I think I might just more than like you, Kate!'

# 21

The next morning, Piers was up bright and early at the island preparing scrambled eggs on toast. It seemed to me that now that the cat had come out of the bag regarding his identity, he was more joyous, as if a huge weight had been lifted from his shoulders. He smiled more and spoke openly about the past, whereas before there was always a guarded silence.

Now that the floodgates had opened, it was lovely to get to know the real Piers and speak without fear of encroaching on any of his secrets. It was as if Piers had lost at least ten years off his age, and possibly the saddest ones, because he was full of enthusiasm. He suddenly wanted to go everywhere, see everyone and do everything.

'Morning,' he said with a sheepish grin.

'Morning. Is that coffee I smell?' I asked as I settled onto one of the stools at the island. I was allowed one or two cups a day.

He turned around to open a cupboard door and retrieved a huge, pale-blue mug into which he poured a copious amount of coffee. 'Drink up. I need you to be as lucid as ever today.'

'What's up?'

He waited for me to take my first sip.

'Mm, this is amazing.'

'Thank you. It's a special blend. Now try this.'

He turned off the gas hob and dished up some eggs onto a plate with a few slices of toast.

'You know, I like chef Piers,' I informed him as I began to eat.

'There's a lot more Pierses for you to meet,' he said with a wink as he leaned in to kiss me.

'Cheesy,' I remarked as I kissed him back.

'Don't kid yourself, you love it,' he murmured before he took my mouth again.

*I could do this all day.* I sighed in contentment for the first time in ages as he pulled back.

'Listen, do you enjoy your job?' he asked. 'You're not just here because of me?'

'I do. I wouldn't know what to do with myself otherwise. I do have a book in me somewhere, but I haven't sorted it out in my mind yet.'

'A book, huh? And you play the piano. Is there no end to your talents?'

I laughed. 'Look who's talking! Is there any instrument that you *can't* play?'

He thought about it. 'I've never played the Sousaphone before.'

'I can't even imagine what that is, but I'm going to have to look it up.'

'Don't bother. I just want you to know that I'm serious about us, Kate. And about your future.'

I hugged him and he held me tight. There would be time to iron out all the details later.

When I told the rest of the girls I knew who Piers really was, they hugged me.

'We're sorry we had to keep it from you. Even when you told us *your* real name, we just couldn't tell you. But Piers is a good bloke. He's not like they describe him. The press just likes to depict him that way. Don't believe everything you read.'

'Oh, I don't, trust me. Now I understand everything. No wonder he was always so cloak and dagger.'

'We all promised to protect his privacy. But with all the tourists coming down here lately, it's getting more and more difficult. He even tried moving to the cottage opposite yours when people started getting curious about who lived in the huge manor behind the old stone walls.'

It made sense why he had been so rude to me from the start; he assumed I was just another tourist passing through. Like me, he had been suspicious of every new face. His serenity depended upon it.

About a week later, as I was finishing off a report, Piers knocked on my office door.

'Kate, I'm going to need your help when you have a mo.'

'Of course, come in,' I said, saving my work on my laptop. 'What's up?'

'I would like you to help me organise an auction and sell some of my band stuff for a few charities.'

'Oh wow, that's an excellent idea!' He was finally opening up to the world again and he was all the happier for it. 'Have you got a lot of stuff to sell?'

He grinned. 'Come with me.'

So I followed him up the spiral staircase and down the back corridor to the secret rooms that were always kept locked. He pulled a key out of his pocket, turned it three times and stepped back for me to go in. On the threshold, I froze as my eyes swept across rows and rows of costumes and hats and accessories. The long walls were lined with endless racks of everything he had ever worn on stage. At the end of the long room were guitars, banjos, ukuleles, bass guitars, tambourines – any instrument you could think of.

I looked up at him. 'This is unbelievable!'

'There's more in the adjoining rooms. I've lost count of how many concerts we've done. Well, at least some good can come of it now.'

'So what are you saying? That you're not even considering returning to your music? Not even on a solo basis?'

'I can't. There is no way I am ever going to perform again.'

'Are you kidding me?' I said. 'You made millions of people happy with your music.'

He shook his head. 'I thought my life was over when I lost Jenna. I didn't even think I'd be able to come into this room again. But years later, here I am. Thanks to you, I feel happy again.'

I grinned. 'So do I. And I think you should let your softer side come out again. Write all those ballads that are inside you. I know the real you, Piers, and I love what I see.'

He tilted his head, searching my face. 'Yeah?' he whispered.

'Yeah,' I whispered back, studying my shoes as my stomach did a somersault.

He gently took my hands and bent down for a soft kiss. 'You're amazing,' he whispered. 'Let's go upstairs, shall we?'

I wanted to. God, I wanted to. Dr Chenoweth had told me it was safe. But did Piers really want to, with me looking like I looked?

'Piers, are you sure? I've got stretchmarks and this huge bump...'

'You are beautiful and nothing can change that, Kate,' he whispered. 'You decide how far we go; how does that sound?'

It sounded like heaven. I had never had that before.

I smiled shyly as I pulled him close to kiss him and let him lead me to his master bedroom for the very first time.

He was tender, he was kind. But he was also passionate and gave me everything I wanted. Everything I had always wanted and never been able to ask for. It was official. I was in love. Real love this time.

Piers pressed a button next to his bed and called Mrs Watts for some food. Then he called Justin with another button and told him the office was closed for today and that everyone was off duty until tomorrow.

'That was nice of you,' I said, snuggling up to him.

'Purely selfish gesture,' he said, wrapping his arms around me and pulling me up against him. 'I want you in this bed all day and I don't want any interruptions.'

'What will Justin and Mrs Watts think?' I asked.

He snorted. 'That it's about bloody time. And that I couldn't have chosen a sweeter girl.'

And so for the next few hours, we ate and talked and made love again until the sky turned black and it began to storm. Had I been in Tulip Cottage, the cracks of thunder would have sent Trixie and I diving under the bedcovers, but in the crook of Piers's arm, I felt safe.

While we lay in bed, exhausted, he rolled over to turn on the light and whispered, 'Kate. I need to say a few things to you.'

'Oh?'

'About the trial. You never asked me if I'm really guilty or not.'

I shook my head. 'Well, I never thought you were.' Which was true. The entire time the tragedy had been on the news, I never once thought he was to blame.

He ran a hand through his dark hair. 'I don't mean to be morose, but there are things you need to hear from me directly.'

I nodded. 'Okay.'

'It's about Jenna's death. You might know I found her in the pool in LA. She'd been shot. I called the police and before I knew it, drones were flying over my home.'

A huge boulder formed in my throat at the thought of the pain he must have gone through, finding her like that and not being able to grieve without cameras in his face. 'Oh my God, I'm so sorry…'

He shrugged. 'Over the years, Jenna and I had become completely different people. The fame had ruined our lives. Why the hell do people want to be famous anyway? Aren't there enough cautionary tales out there?' He ran a hand through his hair again, his eyes remembering. 'It's not a life: sleeping in a different bed every night, missing your own home, your family and friends. Not a moment to yourself, your mind always racing, never finding peace. Who the hell would want to be that confused and miserable all the time?' He sat up as it all came out. 'I just want to live in peace. Not be assailed every time I stick my nose out the door to get a pint of milk. I can't leave Starry Cove, even if I wanted to. I might be no one to these people, but they mean the world to me. They are, in effect, the confines of my new world. Because outside Starry Cove, I can't exist. I don't want to.'

'But are you not happy here?' I asked. 'With all your old friends?'

'Absolutely I am. But back then, my band were my best friends. Brothers in arms and all that. But we were so different. Everybody else was happy with the way things were going. They were having the time of their life. Partying. Drinking, smoking, drugs, waking up in a stranger's bed the next afternoon. I never did any of that.'

My eyes must have popped out of my head because he smiled, a hint of self-deprecation peeking through. 'You see? The rockstar stereotype. I never was that person. I *hate* partying. Always have and always will; I'd much rather go to bed early with a cup of tea and a good book. I mean, I just didn't fit the mould, you know? I was the boring one who worried more about sound checks and schedules and remembering the words. I felt a responsibility toward the others who were bent on going crazy every night. They wanted the rockstar life and I couldn't keep up with them. They were all enjoying it while I was suffering. And so was

Jenna, because she wanted me to live that rockstar life with her.

'People couldn't understand why I wasn't happy. In their eyes, I had everything you could want. But they didn't know that my parents died the day that I signed with my first label. I'd called my mum to tell her, but a policeman answered her phone and gave me the news. With her death in particular, I lost every last scrap of certainty. Nothing else mattered. But I was under contract and forced to go on tour or pay back money I didn't have. So I went. And sang while I was dying inside. There was nothing that could comfort me, or ease the pain in my chest. It wasn't just sadness or a sense of loss. I was physically ill with anxiety. I'd be gagging with panic attacks just as I was about to go onstage.

'Once, I even threw up as I was climbing onto the stage and grabbed a nearby beer to rinse my mouth out. And of course the press latched on to that, painting me as an alcoholic who couldn't even get on stage without a drink. They made out that I was always stoned, or high, or whatever else, when really I was so sick with grief that I could barely stand. It was so ironic. I had everything I thought I wanted and I didn't give a damn.'

'Oh, Piers…!' I whispered. Hearing him speak like this was breaking my heart. There was nothing I could say to soothe this deep sadness, so I settled to grabbing his hand and rubbing my thumb across the back of it.

He shook his head, obviously tormented by the memory. 'I hadn't expected fame so soon, and didn't have any time to adjust to it. And then the depression kicked in. I remember shooting an ad for a famous Italian designer and not being able to stand straight because I was so exhausted. It was my agent who managed to not get me fired.'

'I saw that ad,' I said. 'You were great. That song that you were singing, what was it?'

'"Designer Love",' Piers said. 'Originally, it was supposed to be "Designer Drugs" but I changed it. What's stronger than love? I'm telling you this so you understand that I'm a basic guy, Kate, trying to live as normal a life as possible.'

'Piers, I understand completely.'

'So when I say I can't go back to performing, this is what I mean. It would only bring back feelings that I've been trying to heal for years.' I nodded. 'I chose to isolate myself in this castle because I needed the protection and the privacy it afforded me. And now you need it too. But as soon as everything is sorted, I want to move to a nice, normal home. Would that interest you? A normal life?'

A normal life? 'I can't think of anything I want more,' I confessed.

'We'll get there, Kate. We'll get Will out of the picture once we've proven that he stole the files.'

'I hope so, Piers. For my baby's sake.'

'For your baby's sake, and ours. We'll be okay. I promise you that.'

# 22

By August, our Cornish summer was already dwindling while we chatted away and soaked up the last summer rays on our skin. The long evenings on the patio facing the back grounds had been growing unusually cold, our bare feet replaced by wool socks and mocktails turned into hot cocoa drinks. Such was the peril of the coastal life, I supposed.

Piers and I had grown closer than ever, sharing our most intimate thoughts and feelings: it was as if I knew him inside out. He insisted on taking care of me personally rather than calling on Justin or Mrs Watts for whatever was needed. We'd managed to get Trixie and Wolf in the same area, but so far, they were keeping to themselves. It seemed that they'd inherited their owners' trust issues. But we had got over all that. I trusted Piers with my life, which was a huge step for me, and he trusted me with his identity, which was a huge step for him in turn. All in all, we were doing splendidly.

On the night of August 10th, Piers drove us away from

the property in secrecy. It was all cloak and dagger and he refused to tell me where we were going.

'It's a surprise,' he said, grinning at me as he negotiated the sharp bends in the old country roads enclosed by the hedgerows.

It was a clear night, and the stars stood out like scattered diamonds on a black velvet cloth hovering just over our heads.

'It's so beautiful out here,' I murmured.

'You ain't seen nothin' yet,' he drawled as he came to the edge of a cliff and parked. At the push of a button, the soft top of his BMW slowly drew back and he lowered our seats down so we could look up at the sky.

'If I didn't know any better, I'd think you were trying to seduce me,' I giggled.

'Oh, I will, but first I wanted you to see this. Tonight is the night of Saint Lawrence. He was tortured on this very night, in 258 AD, as a shower of stars appeared in the sky. Onlookers said that those were his tears, and you're supposed to make a wish when you see one.'

And with that, he leaned over for a kiss. 'It's about time someone treated you the way you deserve, Kate.' Having said that, he produced a thermos and poured me a cup of hot cocoa. 'Be careful, it's steaming hot.'

'Okay, now you're just spoiling me rotten,' I gushed. I was not used to such kindness from a man. 'Thank you, Piers, this is just so lovely,' I whispered and took a tentative sip. 'Mmm…'

'Good, isn't it? I put in a dash of cinnamon.'

I smiled. 'You are amazing in everything you do.'

He grinned, putting his arm around me. 'Well, I *do* try…'

I gasped as a white ball of fire shot across the sky from far left to far right, taking its time and slowly dissolving at the edge of the horizon. 'Wow!'

He chuckled. 'It'll be like this all night. And for the next few days, as long as the skies stay clear.'

'I could stay here all night!' I exclaimed.

He kissed my forehead tenderly and whispered, 'We can stay as long as you want.'

I gasped again as another star, this one green, zapped from the north, disappearing into the sea. 'Look!' But before I even managed to say anything else, another one shot from south to north, passing right over our heads. And soon we fell quiet for several moments, squeezing the other's hand to signal another one instead of speaking, in fear of ruining the magical moment.

I lay back and sighed, content. How had this worked out so perfectly, despite everything? Piers was right. I did deserve happiness, and I intended to protect it for as long as possible.


August came and went, taking me by surprise. The air had cooled and the leaves were turning yellow, orange and red. One mid-September morning, as I passed the drawing room on my way to the orangery, I noticed Piers sitting by the window on the arm of a chaise longue, holding a guitar. I did a double take and slowed down. Piers with a guitar? Now that was something I never thought I'd see with my own eyes.

He sat on a stool, gently plucking away at his guitar. Single notes, really, not even chords or a riff yet. Any of his fans observing him would have never recognised him as Blade, the performer who used to tear up the stadium with his voice and electric guitar. I'd obviously caught him in the middle of a creative moment.

He looked up. 'Oh, hi, honey.'

'Hi. What's up?' I asked matter-of-factly as I leaned on the doorframe, and he beckoned me in. 'Are you sure? I don't want to interrupt you.'

'Of course I'm sure. I found this old thing under our bed while looking for my other shoe. Remind me to have a word with Mrs Watts,' he said with a grin. 'I have this melody in my mind but just can't seem to put it together. And words… My brain is exploding with words, too.'

I smiled back, thinking that Mrs Watts was a cunning woman indeed. 'Why that guitar in particular?'

'This one was my very first. It holds a lot of good memories for me. Probably the only one, as it is.'

As he said this, he stood up and went to the bureau where he started rifling through the bottom drawer. 'Where the hell are they? Ah, here we go.'

I leaned on the edge of the sofa opposite him as he produced a small packet and a pair of pliers. 'Let's re-string this baby,' he said, almost to himself. I watched as he set the old guitar on the coffee table and began to snap the strings in two with a dead clang, then lovingly replace all six of them like a mother with her baby. When he got to the fourth string, he lifted it so I could see.

'This is the G-string,' he said. 'Okay, terrible joke, I know, but we used to say it a lot when we were kids.'

I laughed, not because it was funny but because it was heartening to see the pure happiness on his face at the fond memories that must have been going through his mind.

'My father bought this guitar for me,' he said as he continued. 'And he taught me my first chords. Eddie ate dynamite. Goodbye Eddie!'

At the confused look on my face, he laughed. 'Oh, it's just a sentence to remember the names of the strings. E, A, D, G, B, E. Eat a dead grasshopper before everything. There's a million of them.' And with that, he plucked each and every string several times, twisting the pegs at the top of the neck until they pleased his trained ear. That was the thing with being a good musician. You didn't need an app to do the work for you.

'Cool. We have those for the piano too.' As if he didn't know. I'd seen the footage of him playing his ballads with a single spotlight on him and entire stadiums in hushed awe as his hands literally flew over the piano keys as skilfully as on the guitar. Some people just had the gift.

'So, Kate. Question for you. Why did you stop playing the piano?' he asked.

'Oh. I did it for years but I wasn't going anywhere and then I started working for Will. I didn't really have time for it after that.'

'Well, thankfully that's over. I'd like you to consider playing the piano again, if you like. Who knows, maybe we can do a duet one day.'

'Me?' I said. 'I'd rather listen to you, Piers. Can you play for me now?'

He smiled at me, then dropped his head and began to pluck away again. His face was like a changeling, now so far removed, more than ever, from the looks he wore on stage. I was becoming an expert on all the nuances of his expressions.

But there was no make-up that had been able to hide the lack of light in his eyes back then. Today, even if the skies outside the floor-to-ceiling window were grey, there was a light in them that probably hadn't been there in years.

'I don't know what this song is yet, but I've already got a title.' He looked down at his guitar, then back at me with a wry grin. '"Stripped". Which was basically what I've done a thousand times. But that's not the kind of stripped I mean this time. This time, it's more of an emotional stripping.'

'It really gives the idea of who Blade really was, under all the make-up,' I said.

He nodded. 'Exactly, bare and blunt. The Blade who is no longer, thank God.'

'What has brought you to… uh…?' I asked, fearing I'd break the spell if I made him think too deeply about what he was doing.

He shrugged. 'For years, I've been trying to forget everything. To suppress it down in the bottom of my heart. But it keeps on surfacing: the pain, the fear, the sense of guilt. Even if I didn't kill Jenna, I will always feel accountable for the fact that I couldn't save her. That our life, our relationship, our songs, the whole life we were building together just wasn't enough for her. That she needed an artificial paradise to be happy.'

'Piers, she had an addiction. It wasn't your fault, you have to know that.' *Just like it wasn't my fault that Will was abusive.*

'Yeah, that's what my therapist told me. She once said I should try and write a new song. Writing a new song is like starting a new life. It's a form of catharsis. God knows how many times I've tried, but I just don't think I can do it anymore.'

'But you'd like to…?'

He nodded. 'I think so. I'm in such a better place than I ever was, thanks to you.'

'Do you think you'll ever change your mind about playing publicly again?' I asked.

He shrugged. 'Probably not. I am more interested in living my life here, being part of a community instead of parading myself around for a bunch of strangers.'

In the past few weeks, he had, indeed, come out of his shell and integrated back into the community. He attended the village hall meetings, spoke out against drug abuse and donated more and more to his favourite charities, including one that housed pets as quickly and lovingly as possible. But he still had a long way to go.

'Maybe you just need to give yourself time, Piers.'

'Time? It's been years and I'm completely incapable of doing what I loved best. I did everything but write. I even became a bloody farmer just to get away from all the memories I can't bring myself to face. Maybe I'm incapable of fully healing.'

'Of course you're not. You just need to believe in yourself.'

'Believe in myself? I get stage fright at the mere thought of it. I can't ever go out there again, knowing that somebody somewhere still believes I'm guilty of murdering my wife.'

That shut me up quick.

'If I never appear in public again, I'll be happy. But I know I want to write songs. I want to write songs with all my heart, but fear just grips me and I can't move, I can barely breathe. I can't do it, Kate.'

'Then maybe you should write without thinking about performing it to other people,' I suggested.

'What do you mean?'

I thought about it for a minute. To write from the heart. That would be my dream.

'Just write for yourself,' I said. 'Forget about what it's going to sound like or what get-up you would have worn with the song, or even the fact that you're writing something completely different. This is a new you, Piers. You've turned the page and put it all behind you. What you've been through, all the hatred and all the uncertainty. You've come such a long way.'

He fixed his eyes on me as if I was speaking the gospel. In a way, everything I was saying was new to him, revealing a different world, another truth he wasn't aware of.

'I think I might have a job for you,' he said.

I chuckled. 'Another one?'

'This one is a one-off. I'm thinking of writing my autobiography. Showing the real me once and for all to dissipate the mist of Blade. And all the money will go to charity, even if it sells just one copy.'

'Are you saying that you want me to help you write it?'

He nodded. 'You're not the only one around here who can use Instagram. I found your page. You are brilliant, the way you portrayed other artists, showing their real side, but respectfully. Can you do the same for me?'

'Are you serious?'

'Of course. And I want to title it just like the song I'm working on: *Stripped*.'

'You've got yourself a deal!'

'Perfect! And now, enough talking about the past. Let's get out of here and get some fresh air, if you fancy it?'

'Sure,' I said, taking his outstretched hand.

We drove for about ten minutes before we reached Predannack Wollas, a National Trust site on one of Cornwall's most beautiful coasts.

'Did you know that if you visited a Cornish beach every day, it would take you more than ten *months* to see them all?' I cried out over the wind as I stood on the cliffs.

Piers, who was unpacking our picnic basket, laughed. 'How did you know that?'

'My dad told me when I was little. I wanted us to move down here, but we never did.'

'And look at you now, living the dream…'

I turned and grinned at him. 'I am! Thanks to you, too!'

'So am I,' he said, getting up to put his arms around my growing bump. 'You've turned my life around. I don't know what spell you've cast on me but I'm as bloody happy as I've ever been!'

It was true. Things were going well. Baby was fine, work was interesting and Piers was amazing. He spoiled me rotten, to the point that I realised that I'd never been treated like this by a bloke before. And he did it regularly, as if it was the most natural thing in the world. I had missed out on so much all those years I wasted with Will! But now I intended to give and get my rightful share of love and happiness.

One early October morning, I found Piers in the dining

room, barefoot and unwashed, his hair sticking out in every direction, his face as if he'd seen a ghost from his past.

'Piers, what is it? What's happened?'

He looked up at me, startled as if he hadn't seen or heard me come in. His eyes were bloodshot, and if I didn't know any better, I'd have said he was drunk or high. But I knew that look. It was grief.

'It's my buddy, Decker, from the band,' he sobbed. 'They found him dead last night. Overdose.'

I sank to my knees and took his hands. 'Oh, Piers, I'm so sorry…!'

And with that, I pulled him into my arms and held him tight, rocking him back and forth. As many times as I had done that with Will after a bad day at the office, this felt incredibly different. This was me comforting my love, who was mourning the death of an old, dear friend.

He swiped at his eyes as he tried to overcome the shudders that wracked his body. 'I don't know how many times I begged him to stop, that it was going to kill him. I couldn't save him, Kate. I can't save anyone.'

'Piers, there was nothing you could have done.'

He kept going as if I hadn't spoken. 'I tried, you know? God, how I tried, especially with Jenna. And yet, I'm here, alive, while they aren't. I don't deserve to be here…'

'Piers, stop talking like this now. You are a beautiful musician, and a wonderful human being. You deserve to be happy, and *alive*.'

But he went silent and closed his eyes, shutting me out. Of course, there was nothing I could say. So after a few moments I moved to get to my feet, to fetch him some water or a cup of tea, something that might help to soothe him. Without opening his eyes, his hand reached out and caught mine, tugging me back down toward him. I obeyed and he wrapped his arm around me, burying his nose in my hair.

'You are good, Kate,' he whispered. 'You're... I've never...'

'Shh,' I whispered, caressing the stubble on his face and he held me tighter.

'I'm so glad you're here. I don't know what I'd do without you in my life.'

'Me neither. You've given me hope,' I whispered in earnest. 'I never thought I could ever be happy again.'

And yet, here I was. I was deliriously happy. I kissed him tenderly, trying to infuse it with all the gratitude I couldn't hope to convey with mere words. After a few moments, he pulled back, breathless.

'I want to build a nursery and get some rooms for your own personal interests: a dressing room, a playroom, a reading room, whatever you need. Because I want to be this baby's father. I love you, Kate.'

Piers wanted to share his life with me and my baby. This generous, kind-hearted man wanted to build a family with me. 'Oh, *Piers...*' I croaked, and he took me in his arms again as my own tears threatened to spill. 'I love you, too.'

'You see the effect you have on me. You give me hope. I know that with you by my side, I'll be able to face anything life throws at me. And we have so many plans to make.'

And then the conversation turned to daily, run-of-the-mill things. I told him that I was still up to working because it gave me my sense of independence. It hadn't escaped my notice that Piers was filthy rich while I had absolutely nothing to my name. I was aware that love could end, and I needed to make sure I would be okay.

'What do you mean?' he asked.

'Well, I need to be independent in case something happens.'

'What's going to happen?'

'You and I… this… could end one day.'

His eyes widened. 'Is that what you think?'

'No, of course not,' I assured him. 'But I know from past experience that we never really know what the future holds. You might get tired of me one day and where will that leave me? I don't want to be left with nothing.'

Piers nodded. 'Okay, that makes sense. I totally support you being independent. But, honey, I want you to know that you don't have to be independent all the time. You and I are solid. Yes, we haven't known each other that long, but this is a growing together process, right?'

'Okay.'

'And please don't think these sad thoughts. Know that I will never tire of you. You, on the other hand, are dealing with a washed-out rockstar who has his moods. Are you sure you want to take him on?'

'You bet,' I said, wrapping my arms around his neck and kissing him.

'Sold,' he murmured, reaching for the hem of my skirt.

As the weeks rolled by and I got bigger and bigger, Piers and I became more and more solid. His kindness was endless and I knew I'd finally found the one for me. Someone who would always love me and cherish me. It was a heart-warming feeling knowing that, just like my Coastal Girls, I, too, had found my own little corner of paradise.

One late grey morning that promised a storm just before lunch, Piers came in as I was chasing up our shipments, his face livid. 'Kate. What the hell is this?'

And with that, he held up his mobile before my face. I jumped back, an uneasy, familiar feeling creeping into me. Nevertheless, I looked at the screen. Something had upset him deeply, and I needed to know what it was.

It was my old Instagram channel, *Where Are They Now?*

'Hi, this is Kate Miller, and you are watching my newest episode of *Where Are they Now?* But first, please like my channel so I can get more of these episodes to you. Thanks!'

It was an old segment, from the year before.

And then the screen was filled with images and footage of Piers as Blade, along with his band, Kyllyx Attica as captions filled the screen:

You guys are not going to believe this, but this week's segment is on the disgraced leader of Kyllyx Attica who disappeared in a cloud of infamy when his wife was found shot dead in the pool of their LA mansion. Believe it or not, we have finally found his hiding place: the tiny Cornish village of Starry Cove!

# 23

I gasped as images of the manor appeared. Every room, every corner of the garden! How had this *happened*? And then I saw myself, in the selfie videos I'd taken for Baby one day. I talked about my boss and my work and the manor and my life with him and all my other friends. And in one of the videos, I was horrified to see that Piers, unbeknownst to me, was actually in the background at the end of the enormous garden eating a sandwich. The image had been blown up and it was clearly him.

This is what Blade, AKA Kevin Sharpe, really looks like!

The captions rolled on as his music played in the background.

Let's just hope he doesn't watch my channel, hehe!

And then the captions stopped and my very own voice continued the commentary.

'This is the perfect place to come and hide if you don't want to be found! If you look closely... you'll just be able to glimpse the very reclusive specimen right... there! I can't zoom in anymore, I'm afraid, but I think he might be having his lunch. We all know that he likes his privacy and I've been hoping for him to make an appearance. Today is our lucky day! I just wanted you to know that from now on, I will share these gems with you...'

I could hear my blood pumping through my temples, and I felt like my heart was about to explode.

These were the videos that I'd made for Baby. How, how, how had this video got online?

Piers ran a hand through his dark hair. I could see the hurt in his eyes and his drawn face. He was silent, the muscles in his jaw twitching. When he spoke, his voice was very low, almost inaudible. 'All this time, I believed you. Your pretence of coming to Starry Cove as a single woman in difficulty was very clever, I have to say. You played on everyone's kindness by betraying them. The girls, the villagers. Even my nan. People like you, so hungry for their five minutes of fame, really have no shame.'

'Piers, no, you've got it all wrong. I didn't do this—'

'Please. To think I actually believed that you loved me. That you cared about anyone in this village. But now we know who you are. And if you so much as mention my name online again, I'll bury you so deep in lawsuits, you won't know what hit you. So my suggestion is that you leave now.'

'You can't really believe that I would do this, Piers!'

'I'll be sending you your severance package. Justin will drive you back to Tulip Cottage now.'

I clutched my chest and wiped my teary eyes. This could not be happening! My very worst nightmare!

'It's more than fair, and it will see you and your baby through a few years. I'm not a monster. But you and I are over. Goodbye, Kate.' I stared at him, numb, as he brushed past me.

Left with no other choice, I grabbed Trixie, holding her to my chest as she licked my tears. I climbed into the car where my bags had already been put in the back and I sat behind Justin who checked me in the mirror.

'I'm sorry, Miss Kate. Are you all right?'

I sniffed to clear my foggy eyes and nose and gave him my best smile. 'I am, Justin, thank you.' I kissed Trixie on the head. From now on, it was just her and me until my baby was born.

'Hang on, now, Miss, we're going to have quite the ride. And you might want to put on your sunglasses.'

'Sunglasses? But it's rain—oh!' I cried, scrambling to obey when the front gate opened and I caught sight of a maddened crowd of journalists and fans, all kept at bay by a cordon sanitaire of policemen and village folk.

The word was out. They had finally found Blade's hideaway. And were now making sure that there was not going to be any more hiding. Only, once again, the blame had wrongly been put on me.

'Hang on, Miss!' Justin called as he veered to the side and took off at unexpected speed, only to see that the crowd didn't end there. The entire road into the village was lined with fans waving little banners of the band's logo. An entire population now knew where Piers lived.

I hung on to keep from being tossed to the other end of the back seat.

'It's pure hell out here,' he said. 'Pardon my French, Miss…'

'You're bloody right it is, Justin,' I agreed as up ahead even more fans appeared. Some turned and began to run after us. 'Can you lose them, Justin?' I asked. I didn't want them following me to the cottage.

'Certainly, Miss. Hold on tight.'

My new life was in tatters, and there was nothing I could do to fix it. I'd have to start all over again someplace else, just like I knew I would. Re-endure all the fear, all the heartache and uncertainty. Only now, there was an extra burden on my heart. I had lost Piers's trust and his love. In my head, I began to write my apology letters to my nearest and dearest. Also, I had to let Tamsin know I was okay despite what had happened online. Even if I was nowhere near okay. So I called her.

She picked up immediately and I could hear Jake bawling in the background. I pictured her lifting him up and bouncing him on her hip. Such a familiar scene I'd witnessed a thousand times, and I wished now more than ever that I could see it again.

'Is this a bad time?' I asked.

'Sweetheart, are you joking? What on earth is going on? Are you okay?'

'Not at all,' I confessed. 'Did you see the video?'

'I saw it, yes. You never told me you were seeing a rockstar.'

'You know I didn't do it, right? The video, I mean.'

'Of course not. Just like you didn't steal any documents. This is Will's work again.' I sighed in relief. I knew she'd take my side. 'But you have to defend yourself. Make a statement.'

'Who would believe me? I must look like some kind of crazy celebrity stalker.'

Jake must have finally fallen asleep because she lowered her voice. 'Tell the police now, Kate!'

'No. They'd never believe me.'

'But why not? Will has to pay for all his crimes!' Tamsin insisted.

'I don't want anything to do with him anymore,' I whispered, choking back a sob.

'Okay, okay,' she said. 'I didn't mean to upset you.'

'I'm okay, I promise.'

'That's what you've been repeating to me for months. Is it even true?'

'It was. For quite a while. Piers thinks that I've betrayed his confidence and that I'm behind that stupid video.'

'How do you think Will did it?'

I sighed in complete exhaustion. 'It's my fault. I changed phones and numbers so he couldn't track me, but I kept my old account because there were a lot of family photos in there and I didn't have the heart to delete it. He must have hacked into it somehow.'

'Oh, Kate, I'm so sorry! Come home! I'll come with you to the police and we'll sort this mess out.'

'No,' I repeated. 'I just can't deal with it all right now.' And now, with Piers's money and influence no longer available, I didn't know who to turn to. Surely Lee wouldn't continue to work on my case after this, and I couldn't afford my own lawyer. I craned my neck as Tulip Cottage loomed ahead. 'I have to go now, Tams. I'll keep you posted.'

'Sweetie, take care. Call me.'

'I will. Give my love to Jake and Mike. Talk soon.'

Justin brought my stuff in for me and squeezed my shoulder, something he'd never done before. 'If you need me, Miss…'

'Thank you, Justin. I appreciate it.'

'Take care, Miss.'

'You, too.'

I watched him drive off, then turned into Tulip Cottage. It was like travelling through time to the day I'd arrived for the first time, when I was alone and afraid, wondering how I would manage. Back to square one. Alone. Again.

I dialled Emmie's number just to let everyone know what was up.

'Emmie…' I croaked.

'I know, it's all over the news. You can't come here; there are reporters everywhere!'

'Emmie, I was framed. Again. My ex hacked into my Google account and put together that segment.'

'What? Why?' she asked.

I sighed heavily, drained to a pulp. 'It's a long, long story…'

'We're coming to Tulip Cottage,' she said and hung up.

Emmie rounded up the rest of the cavalry, i.e. Nina, Nat, Faith and Rosie. It seemed that all they did was pick me up off the floor.

'I don't believe it!' Nina said as I poured the girls a cup of tea.

'Oh, believe it,' I replied as I reached for Rosie's mug. 'Starry Cove is on every news network. Actually, every news network is all over Starry Cove. There are vans and media trailers everywhere! Nina, I'm so sorry. You must be worried about your own privacy!'

Nina nodded. 'It's okay, Kate. It's not your fault.'

'But how did this even happen?' Rosie asked.

'I'd made some videos of myself around Rosestones for my baby one day,' I explained. 'But I forgot that my Google account is connected to my cloud, so Will hacked into it and figured it out. Easy-peasy. I'm just lucky he doesn't know which cottage I live in yet. But he'll find me, and it won't be long before the police come knocking on my door. I only hope the villagers won't feed me to him after what happened to Piers. Not only do they think I'm a thief; they also think I've betrayed Piers's and everyone else's confidence.'

'Nonsense. People here know who you are,' Faith said as she reached for the sugar bowl. 'This Will has to face the consequences of what he's done He's ruined your reputation, not to mention blown Piers's cover.'

I shook my head as Trixie jumped up on my lap. My little friend had been worried about me, judging by the way she never let me out of her sight. I caressed her soft fur. 'Guys, I don't know what to say or do. All I know is that if he finds out where I live, he'll come down here himself, drag me back to London and sue me for full custody of my baby.'

'That's not happening,' Nat said.

'I don't see how anyone can stop him…' I whispered, defeated. In the space of an hour, I had lost my job, Piers and the respect of everyone in the village. And as far as the girls were concerned, I was grateful that they hadn't even doubted me when I told them what had happened. They had immediately switched into Mama Bear mode and huddled around me, trying to find a solution. 'Plus, Piers is probably going to sue the pants off me,' I added.

'Oh, he will not!' Nina assured me.

'I wouldn't be surprised,' I answered. 'He made me sign a waiver that I wouldn't be taking any video or audio of him, nor reveal any information whatsoever on him. As if I would! I know only too well what it means to go into hiding for your own sanity. But he doesn't believe me.'

'He will, Kate. He just needs time to sit back and realise that it couldn't have been you. That Will simply hacked your computer.'

'It seems to me that your ex has lost control of reality if he thinks he can get away with this. First the accusations of theft and blackmail, and now this?' Nat said. 'He seems delusional.'

'Oh, he's more than that. He's dangerous. In any case, I can't stay now. I have to leave. I'm like a sitting duck here, waiting for him to find me...'

'Leave? And go where?' Faith said.

'Anywhere but here.'

'But you'd be alone,' Rosie whispered, her blue eyes huge and moist. 'At least you have us here!'

I found myself wiping my own eyes. 'I know, and I'm going to really, really miss you guys...'

'Then stay, Kate,' Nina urged. 'We'll figure it out. We'll vouch for you to the police. And we'll talk some sense into Piers. The poor sod is so used to being hounded down like a fox that he doesn't recognise a good thing when it happens to him.'

'Oh, no, we're over. You should've seen his face. He hates me now.'

'Oh, please,' Emmie chortled. 'You can tell all the way from Squally Isle that you two are in love.'

I wrapped my cold hands around my hot mug. 'Not anymore. It's all gone to pot...'

'Kate,' Faith said, putting her warm hand over mine. 'If we know Piers at all, he'll come to his senses. And as far as the police are concerned, all we have to do is explain everything. That you ran for your baby's safety. You have to stay. Your new life is here, in Starry Cove.'

I was tempted, of course. In the space of a few months, I had come to love these women deeply. Not only for their kindness and generosity toward me, but for the fact that, from each one, I'd learnt a lesson on how to become the person I wanted to be. Thanks to them, I also knew what kind of mother I wanted to be. I took the best from each one: Nina's assertiveness, Rosie's sweetness, Emmie's kind spirit, Faith's sixth sense in knowing what I was going through and Nat's practical approach to problems. And so much more.

They were such rounded personalities who had been through so much personal trauma due to being with the wrong man. But they'd found and supported one another unconditionally. And to know that they were doing the same for me, the new kid in the neighbourhood, literally speaking, was tremendously touching. It was like living in a fairy tale.

But real life was another story altogether, and lately, I'd been reading too many romance novels where everything fell into place in the end, where girl and boy met and fell in love and were happy until they dropped dead, preferably at a ripe old age with litters of grandchildren visiting on the weekends. I was worried that that kind of love wouldn't be on the cards for me.

I nodded. 'I do want to stay and be with you all. I couldn't ask for anything better for myself and my baby's future.'

'Then it's settled,' Rosie said, beaming. 'You stay.' As I began to protest, she held her hand up to stop me. 'No buts! We'll figure this whole thing out – together.'

Nina got to her feet. 'Well, first things first, I'm calling on that hothead to knock some sense into him.'

I looked up at her. 'Would you give him a message?'

'What do you want me to tell him, sweetheart?'

I bit my lip. 'Would you please tell him that it had to be Will? That I would never do anything to hurt anyone, let alone… him?'

'Of course.' Nina smiled as a chorus of 'Aws' and arms encircled me.

'And, when you're ready, we'll notify the police so you can tell them your version,' Nat said.

Between the threat of Piers suing me and Will and the police on my tracks, I was in between a rock and a hard place. So much for my new Cornish life in Starry Cove.

'I'm grateful to all you girls. Everyone here has shown me nothing but kindness, from dear Mrs Nankivell to you, to all the shop owners to… Piers. And I've repaid you with—' I stopped, the remorse stifling me. '—lies. I'm so, so sorry, but I had no choice. I didn't know who to trust, and every day that went by, it became more and more difficult to confess.'

'You poor, poor thing!' Rosie cooed. 'I'm so sorry! What you must have been through!'

I shrugged. 'Yes, but that doesn't justify the lying…'

'You did what you had to do until you felt safe.'

'We all know that once you've told one fib, it has a snowball effect and just gets more and more difficult to talk about. But it doesn't matter now. We're all here for you, aren't we?'

'Of course,' chimed the choir of Coastal Girls, my dear, dear friends.

'Now all we need to do is sort you out and get you back on your feet again,' said Rosie.

'I'm sorry. All I seem to do is attract problems…'

'Nonsense,' she said. 'You should have seen the state I was in before I found the courage to quit my old job. I was an absolute mess, letting my boss treat me like crap. But I have to thank her, funnily enough.'

'Why?'

'Because she convinced me into coming down here, during the Christmas hols to boot. I was supposed to investigate The Old Bell Inn and eventually sack the manager, who I ended up marrying!'

'Mitchell?'

'Exactly! So you see, not everything happens for the worst. And Cornwall gave me the shove I needed to make my life better. It's doing the same for you, too.'

'How,' I asked, and I couldn't help the exasperation that crept into my voice, 'is any of this a good thing?'

Rosie took my hands in hers. 'It is an excellent thing because just when you think things can't be any worse, they get better. Wait and see.'

'I wish I had your faith in life.'

'Trust us, we've all been there.'

'I hate seeing you like this,' Emmie said, pushing my now long fringe out of my eyes. The kindness of this gesture undid me completely. There were still good people around.

# 24

As October turned to November and the press and Piers's fans gradually dwindled to a few die hards, my exile from Rosestones Manor was taking its toll on me. Piers never answered my calls, as I'd expected, but still I tried.

Nina, on the other hand, had finally managed to get in touch with him. As it turned out, because of the invasion by the press and his fans, he'd fled Rosestones to an undisclosed location. He did not want to be contacted, especially by me. There was no hope of us even remaining friends. So I decided that it was time to cut my losses once and for all. 'I'm ready to talk to the police, now.'

'Good,' Nina said. 'We'll come with you.'

I nodded, whispering a resigned 'Thank you.'

'I've absolutely ruined my life, haven't I?' I wondered aloud as Nina drove us down to the police station in Truro. One of the girls leaned forward to squeeze my arm in support, but said nothing.

Surprisingly, it didn't take long to make a statement. I told them what had happened, from the very beginning. I wrote out my statement, after which each and every one of the girls vouched for me by signing a document. They made a call to the Metropolitan Police. And then it was over. The epic showdown I'd been envisioning never materialised, and I felt silly for thinking it would have happened any other way than this.

When I got home, the girls offered to stay and keep me company, but I needed to be alone. I know I should have been relieved about not being hauled off to prison but the possibility of Will entering my baby's life terrified me more than anything. The custody battle would be another thing entirely. And on top of that, I'd lost Piers, the lovely relationship that we had been developing, day by day, hour by hour, smile by smile. Piers and I were so similar, although worlds apart, of course. But we understood each other deeply. I had told him things about myself that I had told no one else, not even my Coastal Girls. And yet, it hadn't taken him much to forget any of that and believe the worst of me.

Not that I had had many to begin with, but even my requests for piano lessons had been cancelled by my students' parents. I was officially a pariah. So much for the Starry Cove protective shield. At least I was still transcribing for Nina, which allowed me to keep my head above water for now. It sounded silly but the sound of her voice kept me company while I worked. And she made me laugh as she often made self-deprecating comments to herself about a sentence she'd just dictated, stopping herself to say, 'Ugh, that sounds like shit! What power lines have *I* been swinging from?'

A light tap at my window made me turn my head. An early winter robin, very similar to the one at Rosestones, stood on the sill, its wings spread out as it leaned in, cocking its eye at me as if to check on me. The silly thought that it could have been my robin, Cherry, filled me with joy. She knew me and I knew her. We were friends, and she'd come to see me when I had disappeared from Rosestones.

'Hello,' I whispered, not wanting to frighten it away. 'Have you come to see me? Are you hungry?' I cooed as I reached out to the uneaten sandwich on the side table. 'Let's get some food in you, then…'

It pecked at a few crumbs that fell to the windowsill and grabbed a hold of a bit of crust before it flew away. I hoped it would be back tomorrow.

Yawning, I went back downstairs, found the remote, and settled in for an evening of total, abject misery.

The next day, I got a visit at Tulip Cottage from Robert, who was waiting for me in the front garden.

'News travels fast here, huh?' I said sheepishly.

He shrugged, raising his medical bag. 'I came to give you your monthly check-up.'

'You didn't have to bother,' I answered as he followed me into the sitting room. 'I'm fine.'

'I don't believe that for a second, Kate,' he said and I involuntarily baulked with shame. Every time someone called me Kate for the first time, I was reminded of how I'd deceived every single person in Starry Cove.

I shrugged, dying inside. 'Of course I am. I know I'm not the one who betrayed Piers's confidence.'

'Who do you think did?' he asked.

I sighed a long, drawn out sigh. 'My ex. And because of him, Piers never wants to see me again.'

'But he loves you, Kate.'

I turned to the sadness in his voice. Had I underestimated his affection for me?

'How would you know that?' I asked. 'From what he told me, you two don't talk.'

He ran a hand through his hair, as if resigned, and it dawned on me that I may have hurt him without even knowing. That when he was warning me away from Piers, it was because he had feelings for me himself. This quiet, wholesome man had never indicated to me that he had any interest in me beyond the realms of his profession, so I had no real reason to think otherwise. And yet, there was something there, just under the surface. Words unspoken. Fleeting looks. A willingness to linger. At this point, I'd never know.

'People say they'd never seen him so happy. You managed in a few months what everyone in the village has been trying to do for years. You brought him out of his shell. Don't let him go back in.'

'I—I can't. Nina said he doesn't want to be contacted. He doesn't believe me.'

'He will. Just tell him you love him.'

If only it was that easy.


The next evening was the school recital. They were doing the musical *Frozen* and Nina's eldest, Chloe, was playing Princess Elsa. I didn't want to go, but I had helped Chloe practise her part and I knew I couldn't miss it.

I took my seat next to Nina and Jack in the front row and looked around the auditorium that was packed with proud parents, wayward little siblings and nervous teachers.

I leaned over Nina and touched Jack's arm. 'Jack... I wanted to tell you I'm really, really sorry. I never meant to endanger anyone's privacy, let alone Nina's.'

Nina stared at me and then turned to glance at Jack, who sighed, shrugging his shoulders. 'I'd do anything to protect her. But I know it's not your fault, Kate. Let's just enjoy the evening. We all need to relax.'

Nina made a mock-impressed face at me and hugged me. 'It's okay, Kate. We'll all be okay.'

For a man of few words, Jack was a gem. I believed him when he said he wasn't angry at me, but the sword was hanging above our heads, waiting to strike.

One of the teachers, Miss Andrews, whom I recognised from Chloe's rehearsal, leaned in between Nina and me. 'Uhm, we have a problem.'

Nina looked up. 'Is it Chloe? She was a bit anxious on the way in.'

'No, Chloe's great. It's our piano teacher. She's stuck on the A30. She's not going to make it in time. But Chloe tells me that you have been helping her with her songs, Kate?'

I shrank back.

'Is there any way you could stand in?'

Panic rose into my stomach. 'But... I only know her songs. The other ones, I have no idea!'

At that, Miss Andrews shoved a sheaf of music sheets under my nose. 'You have ten minutes, maybe fifteen.'

I looked at her in horror, then at Nina's beseeching eyes. I owed it to her family big time. Perhaps tonight, I could begin to start making it up to them, in this, the smallest of ways.

Small to them, perhaps, but for me? I was terrified of playing in public. I cowered inwardly. How the hell did I always manage to get myself into these pickles? If I'd kept myself to myself, I wouldn't have to have done anything at all, thus exposing myself. *Come on, it's not like you're a concert pianist in incognito*, I told myself. *Get a grip and help the kid out, for Christ's sake.*

I got to my already shaky legs. If I couldn't manage to play it right, I'd have to just play the chords or improvise. A recipe for disaster if I'd ever heard one. I only hoped Chloe and the kids could manage. And that Jack and Nina would forgive me if I let them down again.

'I'll give it a go, but please don't blame the kids if my playing leads them astray.'

Miss Andrews looked like she was going to wilt with relief.

'Kate, thank you, you are a true star!' Nina and Miss Andrews hissed in unison.

'Yeah, well, don't thank me yet,' I said, glancing at the music sheets while making my way backstage in sheer horror. There was an electronic keyboard. I plugged in my earphones and went through the first few pieces while keeping an eye on the clock. Five minutes already? But it wasn't as bad as I'd thought. It was rather repetitive as musical songs often were, thank God. And it turned out that reading sheet music was just like riding a bike. Even if I couldn't practise all of them, I should have been able to muddle through well enough, *Always living on the edge and hanging on a prayer, Kate.*

I was still playing when Chloe passed me by, squeezed my arm, mouthed me a silent *thank you* and winked at me. That little girl had gumption! I had come tonight to support and encourage her, not the other way around, poor girl! I flashed her a smile in return.

Sweating buckets now, I put the finishing touches on my numbers just as the curtains came up and the ice harvesters and Kristoff appeared on stage. *Here we go. For Chloe and all the kids.*

To my surprise and utter relief, it was an absolute success with standing ovations galore, particularly for Chloe. I'd never seen such happy kids and such proud parents and it filled me with joy. One day, God willing, I'd be clapping my hands off and crying at my own little girl's recital.

The success of the musical gave me the confidence to get out there and help people when they asked for it rather than shying away and putting myself down. So when Faith told me her crew was busy on another property and would I help with staging a home, I jumped at the chance.

It was a beautiful coastal home high above the cliffs. A bloke called Dieter helped us unload all the stuff and after she briefed me on what the owner wanted, we got to work.

It was a very modern home, with lots of glass that made the most of the incredible views. I wondered about the lives of whoever was going to live here: whether they were happy or, if, just like Piers, money couldn't buy their genuine happiness. I sincerely hoped they were.

When we were done, Faith disappeared into the kitchen

to turn the kettle on and I sat back, exhausted, but satisfied. The cottage was so beautiful. Faith had done an amazing job. She had put in beautiful objects, but also things that made you feel at home. I would have done anything for my home to look this beautiful. Maybe one day.

Faith returned with two steaming cups of tea and some biscuits and sat down on the settee next to me. We drank in companionable silence.

'You know, Kate, there was a time when I dreamed of having a home of my own. *Any* home,' she finally said. 'I wanted it to be full of beautiful objects, but mostly, things that made me feel comfortable and settled. So when I was young, in one of our foster homes, I sewed myself a cushion that I could stick my arms through and hug. It was the shape of a house.'

'Aw...' I said. I could really relate to that. We had had different lives but Faith and I were very similar. Probably more similar than anyone else I'd met here, if I really thought about it.

'I got lucky to be surrounded by people who make me feel at home. Kate, you're in the right place here.'

'I think so,' I agreed.


'Hmm, this was a great idea,' I said to Rosie as we sipped mocktails at Books On The Barge, keeping an eye on the shop for Emmie. She was right to be proud of this place.

'Lucky us, getting paid in cakes and booze!'

'I think I'm going to be sick,' I said, pushing away the last bite of my second slice of chocolate cake. 'It turns out you actually can get enough of this stuff...'

Felicity began to whine in her cot, and I reached out to rock her. 'I can't believe that in a couple of weeks, I'll have my own little bundle of joy.' And at the thought of that, I burst into tears. 'I'm sorry, Rosie. What a wet blanket I am. I'll bet you're happy we met…'

'Why do you put yourself down so much, Kate?' she asked, taking my hand. 'You are such a lovely girl. So you've had a bit of a shit life so far. But I am proof, and so are the others, that people love you. You will come out of this, and it's not going to be a man that saves you. Because we can save ourselves nowadays, you know?'

'I know,' I whispered. I would be fine on my own. But I wanted to be with Piers.

It was then that I decided I couldn't stand it anymore. Piers had to speak to me eventually, didn't he? It might as well have been now. And if he hadn't returned home from wherever he was hiding, I had nothing left to lose. So when Emmie returned, I trudged up the hill, noticing how much more difficult it had become in the space of only a few weeks. Not that Justin ever left me to walk it, but the difference was noticeable. So was the change in my figure. Now I was starting to really waddle.

When I got to the gates, I stood for a minute to catch my breath, surveying the famous grounds that had once been private and untapped by the screaming throng of fans. There were still a few stragglers hanging around, but the majority of the fans and paparazzi had gotten bored when it became clear that Piers had fled the manor. Even still, it had been a few weeks before the village had returned to its previous tranquillity. Despite all that had happened over the last few months, it felt like only yesterday that I had come here for the very first time, when Patsy had sent me away, and Piers had apologised and fired her. I wondered how long it would take him to hire someone else in my place.

Blowing out a last heavy breath, I pressed the intercom.

'Yes?' It was Justin's voice.

'Hello Justin, it's Kate Miller. I realise that this is unexpected,' *hell if it was*, 'but could I please speak to Piers?'

'Miss Kate!' he chimed. 'I'll be out d'rectly!'

Meaning I couldn't go in, of course. How quick was the descent of the humiliated!

The gate opened and he scurried out toward me, turning to check behind him every now and then. 'It's so good to see you, Miss!'

'And you, Justin!'

'I'm afraid Mr Henshaw isn't, er, in at the moment,' he said regretfully.

'Oh. Okay. Thank you, Justin. Sorry for wasting your time. Please tell him I stopped by when he gets back.'

'No worries. How are you, Miss?'

*Bloody miserable without your boss*, I wanted to cry. 'I'm doing well, thank you.'

'I'm glad to hear that. You look well, if I may say?'

'Thank you. Justin… how is he?'

'Not too well, Miss. I think he misses you terribly, but he won't speak about it.'

'Could you please tell him I miss—? Never mind. Thank you. It was good to see you.'

'And you, Miss. Will you be needing a ride back?'

'Oh, no, thank you.'

A loud sound made us jump and when he turned and

pressed a button behind him, I realised it was the gate intercom. Piers? Had he changed his mind? Did he finally want to talk to me?

Justin huffed and glanced at me before speaking into the intercom. 'Yes, Miss Patsy?'

'Justin, who are you talking to out there?' came a screech.

He swallowed in what I could only guess was fear. 'A friend, Miss Patsy. I'll be there d'rectly.'

'Is that what's her face, the pregnant one?'

'It's Miss Miller,' he informed her, rolling his eyes at me apologetically. 'I'm so sorry, Miss. This is highly inappropriate.'

'Will you tell her,' she continued, well aware that I could hear her, 'that I am back, and that Piers doesn't want to see her ever again? I swear, she's the worst thing that ever happened to him.'

Well that was rich, coming from her! I couldn't quite believe it – to turf me out like I meant nothing was one thing, but to replace me with Patsy? A look of horror took over Justin's face, and he pressed a button to silence the intercom.

'Are you sure I can't drive you back home?'

I shook my head. 'No, thank you, I'll best be off...'

I turned and headed for the main path. No crying. Especially in my condition. I had to get over myself once and for all. But more importantly, I had to get over Piers.


When, huffing and puffing I got to the bottom of the hill, someone called my name. I whirled around to see Robert.

'Oh! Hi!' I cried.

'You all right? You look... what's wrong?'

'It's probably just the exercise,' I said, swiping at a tear. 'I'm not used to it anymore.'

'You're crying. Did you just hear about Patsy's return? Don't read anything into it; I'm sure he was in desperate need of help with the company after you left.'

'How does everyone know about Patsy but me?' I croaked.

Robert took my arm. 'Kate, you're too upset to be alone. Come back to my practice and keep me company for a while. I know the old dears in the waiting room will be thrilled to see you.'

A million things had happened since I'd helped Robert out at the clinic; it was almost a lifetime ago. I had been under the impression that he wasn't all that happy with me lately; his short sentences and lack of eye contact told me that he didn't approve of any of my actions and he was right. And yet, he was still courteous and considerate. That was the mark of a true gentleman.

'Really, I'm okay...'

'No, you're not. Remember you have the responsibility of a baby. If you're unhappy, she's unhappy.'

I knew he had my best interest at heart. Unlike Mr Rockstar up the road. 'Okay, then,' I said miserably. 'Thank you.'

'Come then,' he said, offering me his arm, which I appreciated as I was feeling rather ragged. A combination of the steep hill and the huge disappointment at the top. Well, who needed him? I was going to fly solo from now on. My main priorities were staying hidden from Will and giving birth to my baby. End of.

We walked in silence into the village, greeting people here

and there. What respect he commanded, Dr Armitage. He was a good man, despite our initial misunderstanding. He had a kind heart. I wondered if it was true that he was dating Dr Kelly Kernow, the local vet. They were well suited to each other.

'Are you sleeping well?' Robert asked as I climbed onto the examination table at the clinic. 'Any more nightmares?'

I snapped out of my thoughts and looked up into Robert's inquisitive face. 'Erm, less than before. I'm okay, actually.'

'Do you get tired around the house?'

'I'm always tired. Sleepy.'

Except for when I was at Piers's. How could I sleep when I wanted to spend as much time with him as I could? It was literally impossible. And now?

'I'm not going to prescribe you anything beyond folic acid. I want you to eat as many colours as you can. Don't forget your fibre. And cut down on the cakes.'

'Well that's not going to be much fun,' I sighed.

'Nonsense,' he said. 'Life is full of great stuff outside of baked goods.'

I shrugged. 'If you say so, Doc.'

But I had to know what was really going on. So when I got home with a clean bill of health, I typed a WhatsApp message to our Coastal Girls group:

Went up to Rosestones but never got past the door because of Patsy. She says that I ruined Piers's life.

To which each and every one of the girls answered:

Emmie: She's just trying to rile you!
Nat: Piers would never say that!
Nina: WTF? Never!
Rosie: Why is she always so mean?
Faith: She's just jealous!

If they seemed pretty confident that it wasn't true, why couldn't I be the same? Amongst us all, I had been the one to win Piers's heart. I should be the one who had the most faith in him and not believe a single word of it all. But they hadn't seen the look on Piers's face when he sent me packing. They hadn't seen his entire future crumbling in the bat of an eye.

That night, the girls came over with bags of comfort food and we draped ourselves around the furniture and on huge pillows on the floor to watch a boxset of *Friends*.

'Patsy just wants to pretend that Piers is in love with her, you know,' Nat said. 'She's always had a thing for him, and I don't think she can take no for an answer. She's just like Phoebe here, completely out of touch with reality.'

'That's not true,' Rosie defended. 'Phoebe can be more down to earth than the other two. She's the street-wise one.'

'True,' Nina agreed. 'She's the grittiest and the gutsiest.'

'I wish I was gritty and gutsy,' I mumbled.

'Oh, honey, you so are!' Emmie assured me.

'Absolutely!' Faith chimed in. 'The way you changed your life around, just like that? Patsy could never do that.'

'She's doing it now, isn't she, if she's back with Piers...'

'She's *not*,' Faith said. 'She just... thinks she is. It'll only be temporary until he can get someone else in, I'm sure of it.'

'Just like I said before,' Nat said. 'She's just like Phoebe.'

'Phoebe's not out of touch with reality,' Rosie said, putting her glass down. 'Did I already say that, by any chance?'

'Round and round we go,' Nina sighed as she poured the girls some more wine while I reached for my mug of hot chocolate.

'Do you want me to give Justin a ring and find out what's really going on?' Nina offered.

I shook my head. 'No, thanks, I don't want to look too needy...'

'So what can we do?' Emmie asked.

'Nothing,' I croaked as they all looked around at each other in silence.

'Here,' Rosie said helplessly, passing me a packet of Reese's Pieces.

# 25

As November melted into December and the first heavy snows came, I used the weather as an excuse to hunker down in Tulip Cottage with Trixie constantly by my side, bless her sweet little soul. Really I was hiding away, dreading every sound that was unfamiliar whilst the girls brought me groceries and news on the happenings of the village. The final few stragglers hanging on for Piers had finally disappeared.

The girls tried to get me out of the house several times, regaling me with tales of the Christmas lights all around the village. Christmas: I'd been looking forward to it all year. I had envisaged myself all settled in and happy by the time Christmas had come around. I had even bought a tiny Christmas tree for Baby because I didn't want her to come into this world in a house that lacked festive cheer. I wanted only good things for her. But I was struggling with the cheer part. It just wasn't in me. Losing Piers had taken the joy out of my life.

My mobile rang, showing Faith's number.

'Hey, Kate,' she said. 'Fancy a tour of the vintage markets in Little Kettering to cheer you up? I have to go for a client's house I'm doing up.'

I debated. It was cold outside and I was miserable. All I wanted was to wallow away here on my own. But then I thought, *Do it for Baby.*

'Is that up the coast?' I asked.

'It's the next village down, where the Old Bell Inn is.'

'Is your client a vintage lover, then?'

'Yes. She's got great taste. Understated but not monochromatic, as so many people tend toward.'

'What's life without a bit of colour?' I agreed.

'So you'll come out? It's cold but it's sunny at least.'

'I'll come out, Faith. Thank you.'

'Yay! Be there in ten!'

And she was.

'Look at you, all pretty!' she chimed, stepping in to hug me as soon as the door opened.

'You're the pretty one. You look lovely. You always do,' was all I could say.

She took my arm. 'Off we go, then! We'd normally walk it, but I'm picking up stuff today – and I don't want to make you trek all that way in your condition!'

'I really appreciate that.'

'So how are you feeling?' she asked as we drove down Meadow Lane across the bridge that was drowned in fairy lights for the season. My, Starry Cove really had pulled out all the stops! I had never seen it at Christmas, and I regretted never visiting during the winter. It was truly a winter wonderland.

I shrugged. 'I guess I've got good days and less good days.'

She nodded. 'Yeah, tell me about it. Luckily, the good ones become more and more with time.'

'Yeah?' I asked, grateful for her positivity.

'Absolutely! And we're all here to pick you up on the less good days, no matter the reason for them.'

It was comforting to have someone who, for better or worse, had your back. Will had never had my back. If anything, he would be the first to attack me. And as far as Piers was concerned, the entire infrastructure of our love had completely collapsed in an instant.

As we neared what seemed like the gates to an open market, we parked off to the side and Faith put her arm through mine in a natural, amicable gesture that filled me with warmth.

'Just look at this,' she sighed happily. 'This is one of the many reasons I live here. There is a joy for life that I haven't found anywhere else, you know?'

I could see it on her face, a joy that she had embraced whole-heartedly. Body and soul. Yes, it was partially because of her love for Henry, and his for her, but there was obviously more to it. Faith had endeavoured to be happy. She had desperately sought happiness, and when she'd caught it by the tail, she hadn't ever let it go. I wanted to be like her. I wanted to be happy.

'Thank you for thinking of me today,' I said through a tight throat.

'Of course, Kate! Come on, let's get stuck into the local wares,' she said. 'I can just feel we'll unearth a few gems today!'

And so we began to weave our way through stalls that were brightly lit with Christmas lights, while Christmas carols rang out over the vast flurry of sellers and buyers.

'Actually, this is nice,' I offered, admiring a beautiful wool rug. It was huge, with several shades of blues and greens that called to mind the sea and sky.

'Hey, you're right!' Faith agreed, running her hands over it. 'This is pure wool too. It kind of looks like that place where the sea meets the sky.'

'That's just what I was thinking.'

'Sold!' she said, calling the stall keeper over to haggle.

Faith clicked on her keys to open the car boot so that it could be loaded by two burly men whom she seemed to know very well. 'Give my love to Alf, will you?' she called over her shoulder as she linked her arm through mine again and we continued on our way.

'Now, curtains,' she said. 'For their living room. Which ones?'

'You're the designer,' I pointed out before I spotted a beautiful set of thick cream-coloured linen curtains with faint blue stripes.

She noticed them too and her eyes widened. 'Now these are gorgeous!' she whistled, then waved the stall owner over. 'They'll match the rug perfectly. Please, Angie, have you got any more of these?' she asked.

The petite woman with a very long neck nodded. 'Just two more, I'm afraid,' she replied. 'The other one got lost.'

'I'll take all three, then,' Faith said, bobbing from side to side with glee. 'They're going to love these! Have you got a bed quilt, and some throws? Anything blue or green?'

The woman nodded and beckoned her to a pile of patchwork quilts and Faith went straight for the prettiest one. It had a flowery border with blue, patchwork tulips and a purple and green clump of irises in the centre. That alone would have made the bedroom gorgeous, but then she added a maple bench for the foot of the bed and two side tables complete with linen-covered lamps.

'I need a beautiful kitchen table and a grass rug and weaved chairs!' she called, beside herself with joy, half to herself and half to the owner.

It was quite heart-warming to see someone so enthusiastic about the simple things in life. Will wouldn't have been caught dead in a vintage market. His furniture was all exclusively stuff imported from Italy. Well, my own home was going to be the farthest possible from the house we shared. Mine was going to be, if nothing else, full of love for Baby. It probably wouldn't be very fancy, but it would be ours. For now, I was happy to be safe and warm. The rest would come in time.

I fingered a linen tablecloth. It had an exquisite texture and had crocheted edgings to make a border. Other than that, it was very simple but stunning.

'Ooh, that's nice!' Faith said. 'They'd love this.'

'Sold!' I laughed.

There were many more objects to follow, such as cushions for bay windows, frames, armchairs, mirrors, garden pots, a Welsh dresser, tablecloths, lamp shades, glass vases, copper vases, ceramic vases, seagrass rugs, alpaca throws, etc. Of course it wouldn't all fit in Faith's car, but it became clear that she had relationships with all the sellers here: some of the pieces she would come back to collect another time, and some of the sellers were more than happy to deliver to her.

And then I found it. A delightful, tiny Delft ceramic soap dish, no bigger than the palm of my hand. It was perfect for my bathroom. 'How much is this, please?' I asked the stallkeeper.

'Eight quid,' was the answer. Eight quid was two days' worth of groceries for me. Piers had paid me well, and his severance package had been very generous, but I was still scrimping and saving as I geared for Baby. Pretty soon, I'd have to start buying her things. Which reminded me.

'Faith? Do you know of any second-hand shop for baby stuff? I need to get cracking.'

'Sure!' she said. 'I know a great place! How about I take you tomorrow? I have to get this stuff back to my client now or I'll never hear the end of it.'

'Of course, that's great. Thanks so much. If there's ever anything I can do in return for you, just let me know.' I turned my back on her to pay for the soap dish; a little Christmas present to myself.

At that moment, her phone rang. 'Hello, Nina? Yeah, she's still here with me. Hang on. Kate, Nina wants to know if you'll do an emergency transcription by tonight. She says it's only about a couple of hours. Are you up for it? She'll pay you double.'

In truth, I was exhausted. All I wanted was to get home and kick my boots off. But if Nina needed me, I was there for her. 'Of course. Tell her I'll go now.'

'Nina? I'll drive her to you now on the way to my client. See you soon, love you, bye!' To me, she said, 'You are a gem. I can see you're tired. Do you want me to call her back and say you can't tonight? She'll understand.'

'No, that's okay, it sounded pretty urgent.'

She smiled at me and hugged me. 'Come on, then, I'll drive you up there.'

Nina and Jack's farmhouse was festooned with all things Christmas inside and out. They had worked very hard with Chloe and Ben to get the house ready in time for Christmas. In the front garden lights were fashioned into the shapes of a sleigh, reindeer and Santa, while all the windows were ablaze with candles.

She met us at the door, full of apologies as she let us into the hall dominated by a huge Christmas tree. 'Kate, I'm so sorry to do this to you; are you okay with it? I can always tell them to sling their hook until tomorrow.' There she went, always so protective.

'It's fine,' I assured her, my eyes searching for a chair.

'I'd love to stay, but my client is waiting for me,' Faith said, giving me a hug. 'See you guys soon!' And with that, she dashed back to her car to deliver her purchases.

Nina put her arm around me and a mug of hot cocoa into my freezing hands. 'I'm so sorry to bother you, but Ben is having trouble with his homework and my PA is AWOL. It seems we're depending on you so much lately. I'll make it up to you, I promise!'

'Don't be silly, it's the least I can do after everything you've done for me,' I said as I plonked my bag down, suddenly remembering I had my soap dish in there. I pulled it out to check it. It had broken into three.

'Oh…!' I moaned.

'Oh, it was so pretty! Jack,' Nina called. 'Get the glue, quick.'

Jack padded into the kitchen in his bare socks, lightly touching my shoulder with a 'Hey,' just to remind me that we were okay.

'This is an easy fix,' he said, disappearing and coming

back with a small bottle. He sat on the island and went to work as Nina and I went into her office. 'I really appreciate you doing this,' she said. 'Like I said, I'll pay you double time…'

'Nina, if anyone owes anyone, it's me. So please. It's on the house.'

'We'll see about that!' she exclaimed. 'Can I get you a slice of Jack's apple crumble before I see to Ben?'

'I'd love one,' I answered, setting myself up for work. I opened a new Word document on her laptop and pushed Play on her Dictaphone. Just a couple of hours more and I'd be home in my PJs.

When I was done, Nina was so happy with my willingness to work that she asked if I wanted a full time job; her PA was becoming increasingly unreliable. Would I accept it? Of course, and thank you very, very much! I promised I wouldn't disappoint her.

When I was done, Jack drove me home. Because the roads were icy, he drove slowly, which gave us time to chat.

'You okay then, after all that internet stuff?' he said, casting me a glance.

'I am, and very grateful to all of you for forgiving me,' I said coyly.

'Kate, any one of us would have done what you did,' he assured me. 'You have nothing to apologise for.'

'What is it about this place?' I asked him. 'What makes everyone so nice?'

He laughed. 'Trust me, we can be pretty unforgiving at times, as you've found with old Hardhead up the hill.'

*Piers.* It hurt to even think about him. 'Well, he's right.'

'Nonsense. He'll come round and forgive you. Just give him time.'

I didn't want him to just forgive me. I wanted him to love me.

'I don't know, Jack. It's pretty much over, it seems,' I said as he pulled up before Tulip Cottage. 'Well, thanks for the ride. See you guys soon?'

'Sure,' he said, helping me down to the ground. He was such a gent. 'Night, Kate!'

'Night, Jack, and thank you!'

Knackered but at the same time elated, I walked to the front door. It felt good to reciprocate people's kindnesses. And it made me see how sad my own little cottage was, all dark and lonely. Except…?

I stopped in my tracks.

'What's wrong?' Jack called from his Jeep.

'There were no lights on when I left…'

Jack came to the door with me, sensing my hesitation.

I put my key into the lock but the door was unlocked. I stiffened. Someone had broken in. Oh dear God! Had Will found me? Was he hiding inside, or was he sitting on the settee waiting for me with a glass of wine in his hand, as cool and deadly as the last time I saw him?

Jack put his hand on the door as I took a deep breath to calm my pounding heart. He pushed the door open wide and I let out a scream.

# 26

'Surprise!' came a chorus of voices and I was so startled and ready to flee, I actually jumped before I realised what was going on.

Jack patted me on the back and made a hasty retreat as Faith appeared, all smiles as she beckoned me back in. 'Don't tell me we scared you!' she said, then called back to the occupants of the cottage: 'I told you it wasn't a good idea to let ourselves in!'

Rosie appeared at the door as I approached, shaking and near tears. Now that had been a very, very close call. I exhaled to steady my nerves as they led me in.

There, in my tiny little, unrecognisable living room, the Coastal Girls had gathered and worked their magic.

I gawped at them, then looked around again, speechless. The place looked like one of those coastal, beach-themed cottages you see in the magazines all decked out for Christmas. And as my eyes wandered over the room, I began to recognise each and every item I had helped Faith choose for her client.

'Robert has a spare set of keys. We wanted to surprise you. I hope you're not mad?' she asked, but all I could do was stare.

The first thing I noticed was the sea-sky rug both Faith and I had liked lying in the middle of my living room.

My hand shot to my mouth. 'What—Oh! Is that…?'

'Yes!' Faith cried out, taking my elbows. 'Do you like it? Please say you like it!'

'All this…?' I croaked. 'All these beautiful things… for *me*?'

'Yes! It's our gift to you!' Nina asked.

'How… how did you even beat me here?' I cried.

'Ah, I know my shortcuts!' Nina replied with a grin. 'But with the slippery roads, I only just got here. I really, really wanted to be here to see your face!'

I covered my mouth as my eyes burned with unshed tears. I nodded and swiped at my face as everything became blurry. 'But, but…' I faltered as the words melted away in my tight throat. And then I got it. Faith had taken me around on purpose to see what I liked. 'There was no vintage-loving client?' I asked her.

She rolled her eyes. 'Well, yes, there is, but you come first!'

Rosie clapped her hands and let out a soft squeal. 'Oh, your face! Are you happy? Come and look around; there's so much more to see. Come, come!'

'But… but…' I repeated as they dragged me into the kitchen where there were six white oak chairs around a round table, covered with a floral tablecloth.

'We know you like floral patterns,' Rosie said. 'So do I, so that was my department!'

They led me to sit on a sofa I'd admired and began to

laugh and chat as I simply stared at them and around the room again, shaking my head and uttering a thousand thank yous.

'Oh my God, how can I accept all this kindness? I'm so grateful, and so embarrassed...'

'You don't mind, then?' Rosie asked, visibly relieved. 'We have no idea what boundaries are sometimes, you know?'

And then I spotted the cream linen curtains with the thin, blue stripes. And the coffee table. And the end tables. It was almost too much to take in at once.

'Wait until you see upstairs!' Nina said with a grin and I was swept up the rickety staircase. I wiped my eyes and saw that the brass bed was adorned by the patchwork quilt with the tulips I'd so loved.

'Oh my word!' I croaked as Nat pulled me into the second bedroom where I stopped dead in my tracks. There was a cream armchair and a crib with a changing table and a cot, a pram, a bassinet, a sling to carry her around in, a rocking chair, a chest of drawers and a closet to put her things in. And the windows were adorned with beautiful linen.

I looked up at the kind, happy faces of the women that had gone to so much trouble for me.

'You,' I said, wagging my finger at Nina, 'pretending there was a work emergency!'

Nina laughed. 'It was the only way to keep you away from the cottage long enough! I knew you wouldn't say no if I asked you for help.'

I continued to stare at them as tears continued to well in my eyes and I couldn't see anymore. They all closed around me and reached out to kiss me and hug me, and I was in a cloud of affection and generosity that I had never in my life experienced before.

'I can't thank you enough, but how can I accept all your generosity?' I whispered. I was never ever going to be able to pay them back for all this. Not in a million years.

'This is not generosity, Kate,' Emmie said, wrapping her arms around me and giving me a big hug. 'This is friends being friends. We wanted to do this for you. Anything you need, sweetie, we're here for you.'

'Oh…' I pushed down a sob. 'Thank you. Thank you so, so much! And thank you from Baby!'

They laughed and practically swept me back down the stairs where there was a huge cake on the sideboard that I had managed to miss in my shock.

'We all have something else for you,' Emmie informed me as she produced a gift bag. 'These are all mementos of our own breakthroughs which we want to give to you now.'

'What? But you've already given me so much. Your friendship alone—'

'Hush, Kate. You are a kindred spirit. We want you to have these gifts as a sign that things will get better for you. So here's mine.' And with that, she handed me a pretty box with a ribbon atop. 'Open it.'

When I removed the lid, I found a first edition of *Jane Eyre*.

'Like it? It was the first book I bought when I opened Books On The Barge. Because I felt that we had so much in common. When I bought it, I knew I was going to be okay.'

'But Emmie, it's much too meaningful for you; I can't accept this.'

She put her hand on mine. 'It's important that you do,

Kate. It's for good luck and courage. It's a sign that you can and you will be happier very soon.'

'Oh my gosh. Thank you. I'll treasure it forever.'

'And this,' Rosie said, handing me a gorgeous turquoise fruit vase, 'is the first vase I ever made in Cornwall. The first vase I made without bawling. The others were all black and crooked, but when I made this one, I smiled the whole time. I knew I was going to be okay. And so are you.'

'Rosie, it's beautiful. You're sure you want me to have it?' I ventured, looking back and forth between her and the vase. No one had ever given me anything so precious before.

'Of course!' she said. 'We have all been where you are now, and I can only tell you that you'll be okay.'

'My turn,' said Faith as she pulled out a large object wrapped in tissue paper. 'This is what I made when I was a teenager in and out of foster families with my sister, Hope,' she said. 'Open it.'

I slowly unwrapped a gorgeous, oversized cushion with a colourful cottage printed on it, with two arm-sized holes in the sides.

'Oh, my God, this is a Home Hug!'

'Yes.'

'Faith,' I croaked. 'It's so heart-warming, thank you…'

'Me now.' Nina grinned, handing me a pretty gift bag. Inside, there was a book. 'This is a special edition of the first book I wrote. I had never been poorer or lonelier. But I knew I'd had a story in me.' It was gorgeous, with a dark-blue cover full of stars shining in relief. The title was *Written in the Stars*. 'It was the moment my luck turned because it eventually became a movie and changed my family's life. Now I want to give it to you, Kate.'

'How can I accept something so important?'

She shrugged. 'It's all about believing that things will get better. They will. You just have to be patient and hang in there.'

'Thank you, Nina. I love it. I love all of this. You have been so, so kind to me…'

'Wait, don't forget me,' Nat said, leaning over to heft a bag containing a large, white frame. 'This is the first article I wrote after I quit my old job. It's about girl power and I wrote it the moment I knew I shouldn't be afraid to really speak my mind. No woman should ever be afraid of anything, Kate, am I right?' she asked.

I nodded in silence as my eyes blurred again. No woman should ever be afraid.

'Oh, Kate,' Emmie cooed. 'Don't cry. We've overwhelmed you; we're so sorry…'

I shook my head and dashed my knuckles over my eyes. 'No, I'm the one who's sorry. I don't deserve any of this, or any of you.'

'Stop it. Of course you do,' Nina said, taking my hand.

'I don't,' I insisted, sniffling and blowing my nose.

'Hush,' Nina said as she leaned in and in a moment, I was enveloped in a group hug, arms around me, hands holding mine, kisses on my cheeks and soft words of love and encouragement buzzing around my head. 'We've all been there. We've all been afraid. We've all been hopeless, with children to raise and not a hope in sight. But with a little bit of luck and some friends, we made it. And so will you, sweetie. You've got to believe it.'

I dried my eyes again and nodded. 'I want to. I really want to.'

Emmie patted my arm. 'You were so, so brave to do what you did, Kate.'

I snorted. 'Brave? I ran.'

'You did what was right for you and your baby. No one can blame you.'

'Please, don't… What ugliness I brought into your beautiful little village!' I moaned in anguish.

'You have brought so much joy to our lives. You're one of us, now. And if some other woman ends up in Starry Cove looking for an escape, we know you'd do the same things for her as we've done for you.'

'I think at one time or another, we were all on the brink of despair,' Nat said. 'We've all been there, and without a shred of hope. But look at us now!'

'That's for sure! Were you ever so poor you ate your leftover breakfast toast for lunch and felt it was a gourmet meal?' Nina countered with a snicker. 'Because I have. I had three jobs at one point and I could never make ends meet. The ATM practically froze every time I went near it. You, my dear Nat, had a huge house.'

'That I hated because it was miserable and friendless. I pined after Lavender Cottage for years. Just a simple home where I could be happy.'

'And I got kicked out of the home I'd renovated and built for my old partner,' Faith added. 'Never love a rockstar with a gorgeous mansion. Oops, sorry. But trust me, Piers is nothing like Gabe.'

Rosie and Emmie looked at each other and snorted. 'Guess we're the lucky ones,' Rosie said. 'I had an airing cupboard for a home back in London and I couldn't even afford that.'

'And I had a real shithole of a place with damp stains that the landlord refused to sort out and a cold, cold fiancé that hardly knew I existed,' Emmie said.

'But you were about to marry into a very rich family,' Rosie pointed out. 'So as far as being between a rock and a hard place, I win!'

'You make it sound like a competition,' I mused.

'Aw, Kate, things are better here in Cornwall. It's like a magic spell or something. The minute you get here, your luck starts to turn.'

'If you need an expert on a broken heart, I can help you,' Faith said. 'And he was a rockstar, too, like I said. He was – well, still is – a piece of work. Not as bad as he used to be, though. He said he was nothing without me, that he adored me, but he always treated me otherwise.'

I nodded. I knew that women like myself were aplenty, unfortunately. To think that a man like Will, or Gabe, could actually treat us the way they did. That they actually thought it was okay to do so made my blood boil.

'I know,' I whispered. 'There are so many forms of abuse. Physical, psychological...'

'And lying. He cheated on me. He got someone else pregnant. He left me. So I moved out of our home. But then he wanted me back, like I was his plaything. Luckily, I got myself out of it.'

'That must have been hard,' I said.

She nodded. 'More than hard. It was soul-destroying. But, you know, you get through it. My friends were there for me. You don't have to heal on your own, Kate.' She reached out and put her hand over mine. 'You're here now. Among friends who've been there. Let us help you the way we were helped.'

'Thank you. I am grateful. I guess it just takes a long time to heal.'

'Then you take your time. Just remember that as long as you have your health, you're home free. That's what Henry always says, anyway.'

'How did you meet Henry, then?'

She smiled to herself. 'The funniest story. Well, not at the time. Actually, it was dead embarrassing. I was floating in our pool. In the raw...'

'Noooo!' I giggled.

'Oh yeah,' she said with a huge grin. 'He had the keys and let himself in with an elderly couple to see the house. As you can imagine, our relationship didn't start off on the right foot.'

'Oh, my! How did you become close, then?'

Faith shrugged, her face soft with the memory. 'I stopped trying to be miserable and gave in to happiness.'

Give in to happiness. Could I do that? Find happiness? It wasn't for the want of trying, but lately, everything I did just seemed to lead to more unhappiness.

I thought that coming down here and disappearing would make things easier. Living a simple life. And yet, the moment I met Piers, things became complicated in a completely different way.

'And as far as Piers goes,' Nat said, reading my mind, 'he'll change his mind. He would never do anything to hurt you. Even if he believed that you brought the press here.'

'Which I didn't. Why would I do something to jeopardise him? And me, for that matter? I came here to hide, so I know all too well how important anonymity is.'

'Of course, we believe you,' Faith said, rubbing my

shoulder. 'And deep down, Piers must know that you didn't do it.'

'You guys… thank you for believing in me. Thank you for all your support. I only wish I'd met you years ago. You're all so sweet!'

Nina smirked. 'Not so sweet when one of us gets hurt!'

At about midnight, they decided to leave en masse. It had been a lovely evening where food was eaten, wine was downed (except for me, of course) and friendships were strengthened.

'See you tomorrow at Faith's, but don't forget you're at ours on Christmas Day,' Nina said as she put her coat on. 'And don't forget your overnight bag; you're sleeping over!'

'Okay,' I laughed. Driving back through the snow would not have been a good idea anyway.

'All right, everyone, see you soon!' we all chimed in unison, and the feeling of belonging filled my heart with joy. I had made the right decision to return to Starry Cove: it had brought me friends who were the salt of the earth.

Once they were gone, I looked around the cottage. It was so *me*, with a touch of all the girls, too. It was absolutely perfect!

# 27

The next morning was the twenty-third of December. The girls and I were all invited to Faith and Henry's home above St Ives for Christmas Eve, so I'd already packed all my presents, written all my cards and made a Christmas pudding the size of a wheel. Once I finished my breakfast, I'd go out and get a few more bits for Baby.

As Trixie and I were sitting having my delicious breakfast of toasted bread with jam and butter and a decaf tea, the doorbell rang. I wondered whether it was Mrs Nan, since she'd said she'd come to see me again. But when I peered through the peephole, I got a surprise and I flung the door open.

'Noah!'

'Hi… Kate,' he said, trying my name on for the first time while shoving a huge bunch of flowers under my nose. He was telling me he was okay with it all.

'Oh, they're beautiful! Come on in. Can I get you a cup of coffee, and not any of this decaf rubbish?' I offered as he stepped into the living room, whistling.

'Gosh, this place has changed, hasn't it?'

I stepped into the kitchen and turned the kettle on, smiling. "My girlfriends surprised me.'

'Wow,' he said as he sat down. 'So how are you? I wanted to come earlier but I figured you were a bit overwhelmed,' he said as I poured his coffee, waddling over to him.

I eased myself into my armchair. 'I'm okay. I could be better, but we can't have everything.'

'I heard about you and Piers. I'm sorry. I want you to be happy, Kate.'

I smiled at him as I sipped my tea. 'Thanks, but I'm a big girl.'

'If you ever need me, for anything – babysitting, a leaking tap, dinner – I'm here for you.'

That last one was said with a wink, and I rolled my eyes, but I couldn't help smiling at him. I put down my cup. 'That's very sweet of you, thank you.'

Noah was such a fine bloke. There was nothing he couldn't do. He was a skilled builder, a loyal friend and a good shoulder to cry on. But I was done crying.

He drained his mug and got up. 'Well, cheers for the tea, but I gotta go. I only stopped by to say hey. Remember what I said, though. I'm here for you.' I reached up to hug him and he patted my back. 'Take care of yourself,' he said, giving me a kiss on the cheek.

'Come by often, whenever you feel like it. I mean it. I'll always have time for you.'

'I will,' he agreed as he backed away from me toward the door. 'I will. Merry Christmas, Kate.'

'Merry Christmas, Noah.'

When he closed the door behind him, I felt an unexpected

sadness. I had gotten used to having company all the time.

I must have dozed off, because when I opened my eyes it was getting dark outside. I had planned to run a few errands. I looked at the time. If I hurried, I'd just about make it to Jago's Bend Or Bump bazaar before he closed for Christmas.

'Hey...' Jago said, kissing me on both cheeks after I'd squeezed my huge frame through the door. 'I was about to close up. What are you doing here on this beastly night?'

'Oh, I just needed some more stuff for Baby.'

'I got you covered,' he said as he took my elbow and guided me to the back where I'd never been before. 'This is where I keep the *good* stuff!'

'You sly dog,' I laughed as my hands caressed a beautiful vintage maple rocking chair.

'It's Edwardian,' he said. 'At least that's what Faith says.'

'It's just gorgeous. How much?'

'For you, thirty quid.'

'Are you kidding me?' I said, reaching for the price tag. 'It says two hundred here.'

'Ah, but those are DFL prices,' he explained to me with a wink.

'But I am a DFL,' I protested with a laugh.

'Not anymore, you're not.'

'Jago, what am I going to do with all of you guys?'

He chuckled. 'It's been re-upholstered recently with a brand-new pattern that Faith chose. You like?'

I caressed the durable yet delicate material, smiling at the Beatrix Potter theme. 'I *love*,' I sighed. 'Go on, then.'

'Okay, then. I'll deliver it to you ASAP,' he said.

I pointed at him. 'Before the baby is born?'

He laughed. 'Before the baby is born, I promise!'

'You got yourself a deal, my friend!'

'Do you want me to drive you home?' he offered as he opened the door and we looked out into the dark night. 'It's absolutely filthy out there.'

'I'm okay, I've got my car.'

'You sure? Emmie would have my head if anything happened to you.'

'Nothing's going to happen to me, Jago,' I assured him. Not with this precious cargo inside me. I'd drive at a snail's pace just to keep her safe.

'All right, then. But drive carefully,' he said.

'I will. See you tomorrow night.'

'Right!'

Jago was right. It was a filthy night, with snow beating down against the windshield faster than the wipers could get rid of it. The road was very slippery but I went slowly.

Shivering, I burst through the front door and rushed to start a fire in the hearth. Immediately, the flames began to lick at the logs I had placed; I watched the flames as I pulled the throw over me and I settled myself onto the settee for the evening. It was almost Christmas. My due date. Not much longer to go. I couldn't wait to look into my daughter's eyes.

I must have dozed off, because when I woke up on the settee, it was completely dark. The fire had died and the room was chilly. I reached for the poker and blew the fire back into life, getting soot all over my hands.

*Time for dinner, I guess.* Not that I was hungry. I checked my phone. There were a few messages from the girls and one from Robert asking me how I was doing. I texted them all back and then I had absolutely nothing to do except for fix myself a light supper and look forward to a quiet, boring evening in front of the telly.

I perused through the cupboards and in the end opted for baked beans on toast. Simple, reasonably nutritious and perfect for a lazy evening. Ah. Can't forget dessert. There was a bit of Jack's amazing apple crumble left. Just enough for two servings. I dished myself one and was about to put the plate back into the fridge but then thought, *Who am I kidding?* and scooped it all onto a dessert plate. Might as well make the most of eating for two while I still could.

And that's when I noticed something on the outside of the windowsill. It was a box. I drew the throw over my head and opened the door to retrieve it. It was made of sturdy cardboard but light enough to carry without too much effort. Probably one of Nan's cakes or a hoard of peanut butter by Robert. It certainly wasn't love letters from Piers; I knew that much.

I carried it to the coffee table and opened it. A chill ran up my spine as my knees began to buckle under me. It contained case file folders marked *CONFIDENTIAL* in red block letters. I recognised them immediately as the ones Will had stolen and stashed under his bed. He was here in Starry Cove! He had found me!

And then, over the howling wind, I heard a loud banging on the window behind me.

# 28

I whirled in surprise to see Will's silhouette in the dark window, and my entire body froze. He was outside, in my front garden, with only a pane of glass separating us. He couldn't come in. He couldn't touch me. And yet, I couldn't move out of sheer fear. I couldn't even find the courage to scream as my legs buckled under me.

Even in the dark, I saw his eyes glistening like a snake's. 'Have you missed me?' he called through the pane.

I don't know how but I managed to shake my head. I tried to summon the strength to get up and crawl to my mobile to call the police. Instead, my eyes filled with silent tears of horror as I prayed that he would not be so stupid as to break in. I prayed that Trixie would stay asleep in my bedroom, well-hidden under the covers.

'Thanks for your directions to Starry Cove. You couldn't have been clearer.' He laughed. 'I figured I'd let you get settled and comfortable before I came. That way it's much better revenge, don't you think? Aw, look at you, so disappointed! You thought you were out of the woods, didn't you?'

'What do you want?' I called out, summoning courage from the deepest part of me, where my indignation and my anger had been suppressed by fear.

'Isn't it obvious? I want you and our baby. Now go upstairs and pack. It has to look like you planned to leave.'

I opened and closed my mouth in horror as silent tears slid down my cheeks. No. I would not let fear dominate me. Not when I needed answers that would set me free. I had to protect my baby.

'Why did you blame me for the blackmail?' I called, surprising him.

He shrugged. 'It was the easiest way to get rid of you. You were always so clingy.'

Of course, now that he had Sophie, he had someone else to order around. 'But then why did you hack my account? Why did you leak Piers's information? Why do all this to get me to come back?'

Will frowned, pushing his face closer to the glass. 'Who?'

'Piers…'

'I don't know what you're talking about, but if you mean the rockstar, then I did it because I knew he'd fire you in a heartbeat if he thought it was your fault. Then you'd have no choice but to come back,' he explained lucidly as my mind raced for a plan.

If only I'd asked Jago to deliver the furniture tonight, I might have stood a chance until he came. But I was on my own and I had literally no weapons to defend myself with.

'Did you think I'd never find you? Come on, let's go.'

'No. I know it was you who blackmailed those people. I saw their personal files hidden under your bed,' I said. 'I also saw that your new girlfriend has moved in.'

Will frowned, realising that I wasn't bluffing. I had really been to his house, really seen its new contents.

'I saw them the same morning that Mr Wise discovered they were gone,' I assured him.

'Whatever,' he said, rallying. 'Yes, I stole the files and blackmailed my clients. I needed the money. But I'll just tell the police *you* hid them there for revenge after I dumped you. Who are they going to believe: a junior partner at a prestigious law firm, or some crazy woman who disappeared off the face of the Earth to Cornwall to stalk some has-been rockstar? By the way, you can keep the copies.' He grinned, immensely pleased with himself.

'You got all that, Jago?' came Piers's voice from behind Will, and we both jumped.

'Yep,' came a familiar voice as Jago stepped out from the shadows, his mobile still pointed at Will. 'Brought your chair, by the way,' he said with a grin, but I could tell that he was livid at the scene before him. He must have seen Will when he arrived and called Piers.

'The police are on their way,' Piers said, moving in on Will. 'Which is lucky for you. So I suggest you wait for them, seeing as we've got your car surrounded.'

'Piers!' I cried as I unlocked the front door for him. 'What are you doing here! They told me you'd gone away!'

'Not too far, though,' he whispered. 'I'm here, now, and so is the cavalry.'

I wanted to throw myself into his arms, to cover him with kisses. He'd come back for me!

Relieved, I stepped out into the wind and spotted the silhouettes of Jack, Henry, Mitchell and Shane as well. They had all rallied to help me! Real chivalry wasn't dead.

Will eyed the men, sizing them up. Too many to take all in one go, even if he fancied himself a warrior. 'I want a paternity test. Now,' he demanded.

Piers shrugged. 'I'd be more worried about seeing the sun through bars.'

A moment later, two police cars arrived, sirens blazing; the high-pitched wailing was almost unbearable as it filled my tiny living room. In one move, police agents spilled out and readily handcuffed Will.

'I'll be back!' he spat over his shoulder as they carted him off. 'I'll be back with my army of lawyers! You'll never see that kid again if I have anything to do with it!'

Panic took over my mind and body. I could hardly breathe at the thought of my baby being taken from me.

'No, no, no,' I pleaded as Piers finally took me into his arms.

'Kate, calm down, please.' He gently took hold of my chin and looked into my eyes. 'There is nothing he can do to you or to your baby. They're going to put him away and even when he comes out, no court in the world would allow him joint custody, let alone full custody. It's over. You and the baby are safe.'

'But you don't understand!' I cried. 'He's powerful! He gets everything he wants!'

He pulled me to his chest. 'Not this time. I will protect you from him. The whole of Starry Cove will protect you. You're one of us now.'

The DS came up to me, her kind eyes searching. 'Are you okay for me to ask you a few questions?' she said.

'I'd already spoken to the police, but I'll tell you everything I know,' I replied.

And I did. I told her everything about me right from the beginning. That I was from London and that I'd been wrongly accused by my ex for stealing documents and blackmailing his famous clients at Wise & Templemann. About finding the documents under his bed while looking for a bag to run away. I told her how afraid I was that Will could get custody of my baby. And I told her about the girls who had vouched for me and signed a document to that effect. And that he'd made a false appeal online making me look like a dangerous psychopath.

'Had the police contacted you directly? Telephoned you?' she asked me.

I shook my head. 'No, but my boss sent me a text telling me to confess and return documents I never had. Will had them the entire time. I think your colleagues made a call to the police in London?'

'I'll look into that, but if they haven't been in touch, then they're not looking for you.'

'So they're not going to arrest me?'

'No.'

'I'm free to go?'

'Well, we know where you live in case something rears its ugly head, but I think that's unlikely. If the Met police had said anything about looking for you, then my guys would have been in touch already. Like I said, I'll follow up and see where the case is at. You just try to relax.'

And then she did the strangest thing. She patted my hand. 'You'll be okay. You have plenty of good people on your side. Starting with this one,' she said, grinning at Piers before she left us.

'So you believe I'm innocent? That I didn't sell you out?' I finally asked Piers.

He hung his head. 'Forgive me, Kate. I'm so used to people only wanting one thing from me that it blinded me to the truth. You're infinitely kind, Kate. The girls kept telling me what I already knew, how you would never do such a thing. I mean, if you had posted the video, surely you would have mentioned my real name? Even though I knew, deep down, that you hadn't done it, I had already shut my feelings down completely. And I was so embarrassed of how I'd treated you.' He swallowed and wiped his eyes, trying to regain control. He cleared his throat. 'But when Jago called me to tell me that there was a man lurking in your front garden, I knew I had to come. I'm so sorry. I should have known you couldn't do anything like that to me. Can you forgive me?'

'Oh, Piers, of course I forgive you! Who told him about Tulip Cottage? It was Patsy, wasn't it?'

He nodded. 'She saw his appeal on the internet and contacted him.'

'She wanted to get rid of me so she could get back with you.'

'Yes, she was convinced she had a chance with me. But honey, Patsy was never more than an employee, I swear. I only love you.'

I hugged him as I began to bawl uncontrollably. 'I love you so much, Piers! Please promise me, whatever happens to me, that you will not let him take my baby! Please don't leave her with him!'

'You and your baby will have nothing to worry about, Kate. I promise you. Okay?'

I wiped my tears but new ones kept coming.

He held me to his chest. 'Now go pack your bags. You're staying with me at Rosestones. I have new and improved security and a cartload of ways to make you forgive me. Unless you want me to start here?' he whispered, now nuzzling my neck.

'Hey, hey, not in front of the lads!' Jago called and they all came to clap Piers on the back and gently kiss me on the cheek.

'Thanks, my friends,' Piers said. 'I can take it from here.'

'Well, I should bloody well hope so!' Mitchell laughed. 'Rosie is not going to believe any of this.'

And one by one, they stepped out the door to give us some privacy. Piers promised the police we'd go to the station in the morning to give a deposition, which was just as well. I could hardly think straight.

'Honey, it's okay,' he whispered to me, his hands holding my face. 'I'm here now, and I'm never leaving you again. I'm so sorry for what I put you through.'

I hugged him with all my strength, which, in my case, wasn't much. The stress of all that had happened that night was making me physically weak, as if I'd been swimming for hours. Come to think of it, I'd been feeling like this for days. Could it be a bug? Tomorrow, I'd call Robert and let him know. After all, I was incredibly close to my due date.

And that's when a wave of pain rippled through my stomach. *Oh!*

'Piers, get your car...'

'What? Don't you want to pack before we go back to Rosestones?'

I gripped my lower belly as another wave began to swell. 'Hurry!'

His face whitened as it finally dawned on him. 'Oh my God, is it time?'

A splash at our feet was my answer.

'Holy shit!' was all he could say in response.

# 29

Scarlett was born in the early hours of Christmas Eve, with hardly any fuss at all.

As I held her in my arms, I could barely see her beautiful features as tears of happiness glazed my eyes. This was the best thing I'd ever done in my entire life and I was going to dedicate every living moment to making sure she was the happiest little girl who ever lived.

Piers had been with me throughout the labour and was now enveloping us both in his strong arms as if he never wanted to let go. I watched as he kissed her little fists, his eyes finally swinging to mine.

'What a little miracle,' he whispered as he took my mouth with his. 'Are you feeling okay? That would've absolutely destroyed me. Where do women get the strength?'

'I think we're born with it,' I giggled softly, not wanting to wake Scarlett. Just like in the Christmas carol 'Silent Night', all was calm, the festive din of the ward having wound down to a cosy, Christmas hush, and the faintest of Christmas carols whispered from the nurses' radio station in the distance. The overhead lights had been turned off in favour of the Christmas fairy lights above each door. It was a blissful, exhausted moment for many new mothers down the corridor. Tomorrow morning I would go and congratulate them and welcome their little miracles into the world, too.

A faint knock on the door made us look up. There, in an excited but hushed bundle were Emmie, Faith, Nat, Nina and Rosie, bearing flowers and balloons and all manner of gifts.

'Hi,' Nina whispered. 'Congratulations!'

'Thank you,' Piers and I said in unison and glanced at each other with an ear-to-ear grin which was not lost on my Coastal Girls.

'Come in, come in,' I beckoned them.

'We're not crowding you?' Nat asked, but pushed forward anyway.

'Oh, please. Scarlett, meet your beautiful, kind, crazy Coastal Aunts.'

One by one, they tiptoed in, delivering me gentle kisses on my cheeks and forehead, as hushed exclamations of joy filled the room.

'Oh my God, she is perfect,' said Rosie as she swiped at her red cheeks, pretty much followed by the rest of them.

I looked at the faces of my friends. 'Thank you. From the bottom of my heart. I couldn't have done any of this without you guys. I wouldn't even be here if it hadn't been for your friendship. I owe you all more than I can say.'

'Nah,' Faith said. 'You'd have managed just the same. You're a fighter, you are.'

I smiled at her. Then took a closer look. I don't know

what it was, but something about her. A new light in her eyes. A light that I knew very well. 'Faith?' I whispered.

'What?' she said, looking all innocent, but I knew her by now. And she knew me, too. She grinned and nodded.

'You're pregnant, you sneak!' Nina hissed. 'Now I see it. I *thought* you were acting differently!'

'I didn't want to steal Kate's moment,' she whispered, beaming now that the cat was out of the bag.

'Steal?' I repeated. 'Come here, you, and give me a hug.'

She complied and the girls piled on top of her. 'How far along are you?' Nina asked.

'Only two months,' she breathed, bursting with joy.

'They'll grow up together and be the best of friends,' I promised her. 'And all you ladies are not going to be getting rid of me any time soon.'

'You promise?' Emmie asked in a squeak of a voice.

'I promise. It will always be all of us together, no matter what.'

'Okay, now I'm going to cry,' Nina said. 'Rosie, pass me one of your tissues, will you?'

'No more crying,' I said. 'From now on, just pure joy. For all of us.'

Piers watched in silence, a huge grin splitting his beautiful mouth. 'Amen to all that,' he said.

'You guys get some rest,' Nat said. 'Tomorrow night, we'll be back.'

'I won't be here tomorrow night,' I said. 'I'm going home.'

'With me,' Piers informed them and they clapped him on the back.

'What the hell took you so long?' Nina said. 'Good lad!'

*

The next day, Piers brought me back to Rosestones. To my surprise, it was festooned with *Welcome Baby Scarlett and Kate!* signs everywhere, alongside Christmas decorations galore.

'I know how much you were looking forward to Christmas,' he said as we settled down on one of the sofas in the drawing room. 'I didn't want you to miss out.'

'Oh, Piers, thank you so, so much for everything you have done for me. And Scarlett.'

'This is only the beginning, I hope. Kate,' he breathed, 'will you marry me?'

I gasped. 'What?'

'Will you marry me?' he repeated.

I gawped at him, unable to speak.

He ran a hand through his hair. '*Bollocks*. I knew I'd screw this up. I have a ring but I left it in the car. I wanted to do it in a romantic way, during a romantic dinner with romantic candles and romantic—'

'Piers,' I whispered. 'This is *very* romantic,' I assured him.

'It is?'

'Absolutely.'

'Oh, Kate, I don't want to live another day away from you. I was a real arse and if you can ever forgive me, I'm asking you to give me the chance to make you happy.'

'I'm already happy,' I assured him.

'So it's a yes?' His eyes searched my face.

'Yes, of course, yes!' He picked me up in his arms and spun me round, kissing me hard on the mouth as he lowered me back to the ground. And then I yawned in pure exhaustion. 'I'm sorry…'

'It's okay, honey. Go to sleep now. I'll watch over you both.'

I nodded, my eyes heavy. 'Okay, Piers,' I whispered.

'We'll make loads and loads of plans. And when the baby is old enough, we'll travel the world.'

'But I thought you said you were sick and tired of travelling…'

'Not with you, I won't be! We'll teach Scarlett all about the different cultures and all sorts of things. It'll be an enchanted life for her. For us. I love you guys more than I can ever explain,' he whispered hoarsely and I caressed his wet cheek.

'No more tears, remember?' I whispered back, my eyes closing.

He kissed me. 'Yes. From now on, it will be only joy.'

Absolute bliss. With Scarlett in my arms and Piers's arms around us, it already was. In Starry Cove, I had finally found everything I had always wanted. Friends who were like family, a man who loved me, a home. And I had given life to a little Cornish girl. What more could one ask for?

# Epilogue

## Six months later

The following summer, our first together as a family, Piers and I were married on the grounds of Rosestones. It was a simple wedding, more like a summer fete, with bunting and games and music. The entire village was there: Emmie, Nina, Nat, Rosie and Faith (plus huge bump) and their families; Laura, Nan, Justin, Mrs Watts, Piers's staff and even Noah, who'd shown up with a huge bouquet of flowers, a bright smile, and that girlfriend from Australia he'd mentioned.

'I'm really happy for you, darl,' he said, kissing my cheek and caressing Scarlett's little fist.

There were also Ralph and everyone from The Rolling Scones, my piano students and everyone who'd ever been kind to us.

Even Wolf and Trixie had managed to become friends. Apparently, neither of us girls were immune to the charm of the alpha males of Rosestones. As I watched, they panted away happily while dividing and conquering the guests who seemed to be the most inclined to part with their food.

Robert brought Kelly Kernow, his vet girlfriend. They were such a lovely couple. His ex-wife had finally resigned herself to the life she'd chosen without him and had to watch him be happy again with someone infinitely kinder.

'Close your eyes,' Piers murmured as he lifted Scarlett from my arms. 'I've got a surprise for you.'

'There's more?' I asked and then I heard a squeal. A very familiar squeal. I opened my eyes to see Tamsin rushing toward me, arms outstretched.

'Oh my God!' I cried as I threw my arms around her. 'You tricked me! You said you couldn't make it!'

'Surprise!' she cried back. 'You look amazing, Kate! I'm so happy for you! And oh my God, look at how Scarlett's grown!'

'It's been three months since you last saw her, of course she's grown. Which reminds me. I want you to come visit more often, missy.'

'I don't think so,' she said.

'What?' I said. 'Why ever not?'

'We're moving down here to Starry Cove!' she squeaked. 'I wanted to surprise you, but we've just bought a cottage and Faith is doing it up for us!'

And that was when I saw her husband Mike, with a full head of hair, fit as a fiddle, and little Jake on his shoulders. I stared at him, my heart welling with even more joy, if possible. 'Mike!'

'Regression!' he cried, wrapping me in his arms as Jake hugged my head.

'Oh my God, I'm so, so happy!' I sang over and over again. 'We'll all be so happy here!'

And then I began to bawl with happiness for my friends,

who had been through so much and had come out the other end stronger than ever before.

'Kate, stop it,' Tamsin said, though she was wiping away her own tears. 'You're going to ruin your make-up.'

The girls circled us and raised their glasses. 'To old and new Coastal Friends!' Nina toasted, followed by everyone's loud cheers.

'Hear, hear!'


As for Piers, he no longer felt the need to hide away behind the walls of Rosestones as he wanted to lead a life as normal as possible, particularly for Scarlett, whom he was in the process of adopting.

So we'd moved out of Rosestones and bought Tulip Cottage, which we knocked through to the empty one next door. Noah did the work, of course. He'd assembled a small team and was doing well. As far as Rosestones was concerned, we decided to let it out for weddings and other important events.

But there was more, the best part: Piers and Robert had agreed to meet in private and had emerged red-eyed, their arms around each other like long-lost brothers meeting after years apart. It was a sight to see, which Nan nodded at with approval.

'Only you could bring those two back together,' she said, caressing my cheek. 'Thank you, Kate, for entering our lives and making them much, much better.'

'Thank you for accepting me, and agreeing to rent out the cottage to me. I wouldn't be here if you hadn't!' I replied, and we hugged.

And Will Compton? By his own confession recorded by Jago, he was finally charged with the theft of a little over two million pounds. We wouldn't be seeing him for a very long time.

*And* we were working on Piers's autobiography, *Stripped*. It was all true and authentic: about his stage fright, the effect his parents' death had had on him and how different he was from Blade. Even the photos included in the book showed the real Piers. Just him, for the world to see, with no make-up and no crazy outfits. Just jeans and shirts, in the garden with a shovel, with Trixie and Wolf.

There were pictures of him crouching over his song books, cooking, working in the grounds, all things he does now. And, just as a nod to his past career, a final black and white picture of the back of him with his guitar, facing the bright lights of a stadium so brightly lit, you couldn't see anything else. Just like our future.

# Acknowledgements

HELLO AGAIN, my lovely readers, you loyal lot, you! Thank you again and again for buying and reviewing my books! This means so much to me! As we work on our wips, authors never truly know how our work will be received, so I'm always grateful when it goes well!

Of course, no book is only the work of one person, so I'd like to thank my amazing agent Lorella Belli who always has my back, my wonderful editor Aubrie Artiano, and publisher Head of Zeus/ Bloomsbury who have come up with yet another gorgeous cover!

And of course, my beloved, DH Nick, who continues to provide my writing nest with hot water bottles, warm blankies, endless cuppas and cakes! I love you and I couldn't have done any of this without you!

# About the Author

NANCY BARONE grew up in Canada, but at the age of 12 her family moved to Italy. Catapulted into a world where her only contact with the English language was her old Judy Blume books, Nancy became an avid reader and a die-hard romantic. Nancy stayed in Italy and, despite being surrounded by handsome Italian men, she married an even more handsome Brit. They now live in Sicily where she teaches English. Nancy is a member of the RNA and a keen supporter of the Women's Fiction Festival at Matera where she meets up once a year with writing friends from all over the globe.

**Thanks for reading!**

Want to receive exclusive author content, news on the latest Aria books and updates on offers and giveaways?

Follow us on X @AriaFiction and on Facebook and Instagram @HeadofZeus, and join our mailing list.